SPAT THE DUMMY

# Spat
## the Dummy

A NOVEL

*Ed Macdonald*

ANVIL PRESS VANCOUVER | 2010

Anvil Press Publishers Inc.
P.O. Box 3008, Main Post Office
Vancouver, B.C. V6B 3X5  canada
www.anvilpress.com

Library and Archives Canada Cataloguing in Publication

[TO COME]


Printed and bound in Canada
Cover design by Black Eye Design
Interior design by HeimatHouse

Represented in Canada by the Literary Press Group
Distributed by the University of Toronto Press

[FUNDER LOGOS HERE]

The publisher gratefully acknowledges the financial assistance of the Canada Council for the Arts, the Book Publishing Industry Development Program (BPIDP), and the Province of British Columbia through the B.C. Arts Council and the Book Publishing Tax Credit.

Dedication

# { 1 }

Brace yourself.

In the creepy church basement, I heard someone behind me reminding a friend that, *We're only as sick as our secrets.* I scoffed and sneered at the floor. Somewhere, though, in a dark corner of my mind, I chose to keep that cliché as my first intentional belief. Since that evening I knew that I would cut loose, eventually, and tell all of my secrets for the cure.

It's hard to know where to start because it's all clumped together. Peeling through it is like reading a wet newspaper; also, odd bits want to be up front. For instance, I used to have this daydream:

We're in a bar; me and that little prick folk singer whose name doesn't matter. He's trying to start something, so I warn him, *I'll mash your fucking skull into a fucking pulp, you ass-eatin' fuck.* But he won't quit the smirk and the jabs. *Get the fuck out of my sight*, I say, but he won't stop. Barking. Breathing heavily through his nose, bull head tilted down, daring me. Finally, he calls me *Dummy* and my eager right hook lands with a satisfying crack. A left uppercut rattles some teeth. Finally, we're on the cement and I'm stomping on his all but hollow head with my big boot. He plays guitar, so I crush the fingers on both of his hands with my heel. It's my gift to the world—a little less folk music.

The finger mash always sent me back to reality. That

daydream always brought a warm surge of mock power with a little tail of remorse for balance. In all, it took about five seconds to play out, but it was free speed that I felt was good for the heart.

I had imagined that scene hundreds of times with small revisions here and there, different settings and combat styles. I kicked him to death for something he did, years ago, at some party. I don't remember what, exactly, but he's a little prick and his songs sound like commercial jingles performed by an elf with a fake Irish accent. Mind you, if I ever saw him again, I'd probably say hello.

In the stupid real world, I would never hit anyone unless I had to. They'd have to start it and hit me pretty hard to get a reaction. Not many of us can just turn and walk away when things get physical. I can. But I'm built, as they say, like a brick shithouse. I retain exactly eight point six percent body fat. You'll never know, so I'm also, six feet, two inches tall. People say I look like an Irish Antonio Banderas. I'm not really Irish, obviously. I'm Canadian, though I was born in Quebec.

Of course, I have never, until now, told anyone about the action-packed scenarios that I had so often used to get a little rush. Violence has to be repressed and I'm hyper aware of what's expected, because I'm always trying to pass as regular and unaware. People suspect that I'm not as soon as they see me, but they can't lock you up on suspicion. At least not yet. Admittedly, it's all going that way.

I don't know why I have the kind of rage that inspires visions like the adjustment of that loathsome singer. I just do. It has always been in here with me, waiting. I can't say why. Obviously, I have normal, monotonous hours, too. I see most things for what they are, I think. I see beauty in imperfection and potential in the vast Nothing. I had a friend with a hook for a hand, who told me, *Spat, you're a slightly more iconoclastic version of Satan.*

*But I'm real,* I told him. *And that bitch was just made up to scare idiots.*

In groups, the norms always hate me. Always have. I don't know why. I give change to panhandlers and I drink fair trade coffee. I do these things because I am not, as that old nun used to say, evil.

In his assessment of me, the first shrink who took a look in said that my development had been stalled by lingering adolescent behaviours that had severely narrowed the perimeters of my existence. He was exactly right, so I told him that he was dead wrong and rolled my eyes. I shook my head as I sauntered out of his office. *Don't quit your day job, Sigmund.* It was true that I had not changed much since my retarded jog through puberty.

Everyone said that I was the spit out of his mouth so my father called me Spat. I liked it because it rhymed with brat and because no one else had it. I forget my real name.

I aspired to be like him and I was glad to be a dead ringer. He couldn't read to me, so he taught me to box, to cook a roast, to hot wire a car, to stare down a dog. He taught me a canon of bad jokes, countless true stories.

I was thirteen before I realized that Poppy was hated by most of the people unfortunate enough to have had to contend with him. Through the years, he had been a bag man, a card shark, a loan shark, a pool shark—any kind of shark he had to be. He made it to grade four in school. They kicked him out for assorted hilarious crimes. He peed in things like pencil sharpeners and desk drawers. He would nearly shit his pants trying to fart during morning prayers. No one expected him to amount to anything and, as far as any of those people could see, he didn't.

His real education, as he reminded me daily, was *in the gutter.* He had been knifed, shot twice, arrested three times. The longest sentence he served was a year. I was sixteen at the time, so I stayed on my own. Poppy's brother, Hank, would check up on me and take me to the prison on visiting day.

When he was young, it seemed that a life of good fortune was assured for Poppy. He had shaken hands with Johnny Cash.

He had kissed Brigitte Bardot on his twenty-first birthday. He was handsome and strong, but like all things that live fast and are prone to fight, he aged quickly.

Poppy loved me, but had nothing but distrust for everyone else. I have a secret about him, but I have to work up to it. It's big. There was a night, about ten years ago, when I tried to make myself pass out so I would stop thinking about it. I got drunk and banged my head on a wall a few times, then held my breath until the lights went out. I don't recommend it.

+    +    +

When we lived in Willis, Ontario, my idiot wife and I met this couple called Rob and Linda. They were from Montreal, too. We did everything with Rob and Linda. Rob and Linda, Rob and Linda. He worked for the construction company that was re-building the East Bridge. He was my age, the same make and model. Linda was a busty, blinking toad of a woman trapped under a heap of stripy blond hair. She looked as though she had never removed her make-up and had been painting over it for years. She hardly ever tried to make small talk with me, so I didn't mind her. Rob and I both hated the town and the dicks who populated it, so that's what we had to talk about. We always joked about how Rob had better finish that bridge so we could get the fuck out of there.

We made it back to Montreal three months after Rob and Linda and found a place in the Mile End. They were just four blocks away in a flat twice the size of ours. Linda and the former Mrs. Ryan shopped and guzzled wine together. Her name isn't important so let's call my ex by the old pet name that I gave to her on our second anniversary—Hitler. She was relieved to have Linda for a friend because Linda had morbid depression which made her more of a listener than a talker. Also, Linda drank so much that Hitler looked like a teetotaler by comparison. Comparison was their pastime. One would name something, and then they'd declare whether or not they liked it. Then they'd say *Really?* Or *Me too!* Depending on their like or dislike for whateverthefuck. If you listened to it for more than a minute, you'd lose bowel control. Rob and I used each other as the excuse for not coming home on time or for an escape from the subtle tortures of our domestication.

It happens to most couples. The illusion is harder and harder to maintain once the novelty has run out. Then it's only a situation or, as it was in our case, a predicament. Hitler and I could never depend on each other for anything because we didn't trust each other. Neither of us wanted to give in and be the one to end it, though. Rob and Linda split because she drank all the time.

By telling this secret I'm betraying a good guy, but, like I say, for health reasons, I can't carry any more privileged information. I don't think it matters, though, because he never reads.

One night, me and Hitler played poker with Rob and Linda over at their place. Early in the evening, Linda got a call from her sister in Laval who was going into labour. After an inane discussion, that we all knew would result in their leaving, Linda and the Fuhrer drove off to get away from us men and to watch Linda's sister push another kid into the world. Rob and I sat outside and drank beer, talked about nothing. We listened to the Pixies, thankful for something to fill the dead air between us.

Drunk and feeling a bit natural, my buddy Rob told me that he enjoyed an occasional tube steak. He asked me if I was shocked and I said no, quickly, so as to not seem as shocked as I was. I smiled and nodded as he rolled a joint and told me about how, since college, he liked polishing the odd knob. He didn't want me to get him wrong: he loved pussy. He and Linda still had a great sex life, blah, blah, blah. I barely heard the words he was saying. All I could think of was how everybody says gay guys give good head because they know what another guy would like and actually enjoy doing it. I had never even experimented as a kid, let alone gotten a hummer from a man.

I had long since given up on oral satisfaction after getting married to the great dick hater. A blow-job from her was like being mauled by a wet cheese grater.

Rob and I probably should have gone inside, but I was really into it as soon as I had convinced myself that things wouldn't be too weird afterwards. I was also as high as ten bass players. I knelt on their picnic table, whipped it out, as they say, and he engulfed it. Besides the profound physical sensation of being entirely swallowed for the first time ever, it was exciting—like starting sex all over again. What would the neighbours think if they happened to see? It was all illicit and new and modern.

I imagine every man holds his cock in high esteem, but I think about mine literally thousands of times a day. I have celebrated it in every conceivable way. In my twenties, it was photographed more than Madonna and certainly displayed more range on screen. Even now, he's always raring to go. No matter what the hour of the day, it's always noon in my pants. It's a wonderful cock.

When it was over, Rob was afraid that I would find it awkward to be around him. Frankly, I had to fight the urge to kiss him. I decided then and there that Rob was the only man on Earth who I liked. I assured him that there was nothing at all unusual about him blowing me and that I would never, ever reciprocate. Finally, we had a real common interest besides our stupid friendship which, like the majority of them, was never anything more than a hollow distraction from the misery of the Dark Ages.

Hitler suspected something, I think, because I looked, as she said, "pleased with myself". Were she not the source of all evil, she would have used my weekly mic check from Rob as grounds for the divorce instead of citing mental cruelty. I'm not cruel. Or mental. I keep all of my cruelties safely tucked away in the old head jar. I'm just a bit vocal sometimes.

Just as she and I separated, Rob and Linda's divorce became final. They were always a step ahead. Rob wanted to hang at my place and get baked all the time. He'd become a vegetarian.

He read books by people pretending to be enlightened. He started depending on me which was horrifying.

I waited for him to take a vacation and then I moved to my place on Duluth. I left my share of the rent for two months, so that there would be no beef between us. I would see him once in a long while, scuffing through the Plateau. I always pretended not to notice him waving at me. I suppose that's a small cruelty. Fine, I'm cruel.

+     +     +

Most of the brain cells are in tight little knots that the tiniest of child rug makers could never untie. Some of them are long and smooth. Snaking through the grey matter, they wait for your guard to fall and then they pierce the membrane between Real and Imaginary. I have many of these cells. I'm trying to learn to be honest and calm and normal, but the weird cells prevent it.

+     +     +

Everything turned to shit that winter when I had stopped into a bar on the Main called Gilda's. I just wanted to get warm. They had a cinq à sept, a happy hour, and they didn't play crap music like every other place in the neighbourhood. I quickly became a regular, giving up my seat at Debris. The bartenders at Gilda's seemed cool with pretty much anything and they'd leave you alone unless you felt like talking.

One night, I was doing shots, wondering why I kept staring at the dwarf television perched above the dartboard. A woman of about seventy sat next to me and lit a cigarette with a candle. We chatted about whateverthefuck. Now and again, I would catch her studying my face, intently. She said she had seen me around so I pretended to have seen her, too. She had the crazy vibe, but she was funny, so I didn't mind her. When I asked her name, she blanched. She sipped her rum and subtly adjusted her wig by pushing her finger tips into the front of it. She looked me in the eye, finally, and said, *My name is Polly Beene*. I thought she was being funny, answering with the name of some ancient cartoon character, but she watched, closely, for my response. I could tell that she had regretted saying her name, but was still curious to see my reaction. She said, *You don't remember me*. I had a chill. I asked if I should know her. She shook her head no and tried, clumsily, to change the subject. Eyes down, arthritic hands patting the bar, she mumbled something about a draft in her apartment. Again, I asked if we had met before. She looked at me, warily, and I could have guessed.

*If you're Spat, I was a friend of your parents.*

I realized that I was holding my breath. If she had said that she had known him and not both of them, then I would have assumed that she was some old slam of Poppy's. Because she said "parents", it meant that she was from the time before my mother left. Seeing my face, she began a long apology. As much as I tried, I couldn't respond. I was embarrassed, but I wasn't sure why.

I couldn't imagine Polly Beene as a young woman because all of her gestures, even the words she used, were ancient. Rum, cigarettes and, least of all, time had not treated her kindly. She had worked hard for the lines in her face. Cigarette smoke coming out of her seemed wet like fog. I always glanced away on the sickening exhale.

The next time I saw her there, she was in a chatty mood and told great stories about dancing with the old man at Le Repaire. She had not been, it turned out, a friend of my mother's. She was one of many women who Poppy saw regularly. Over and over, she told me how she loved him. Maybe a small part of me wanted to ask her if she had ever met my mother, but I didn't want to get into it.

Sometimes, you meet people and you know that you should keep a healthy distance in case everything goes sour. I knew there was a good chance that Polly might know the big secret. I knew that she could say the wrong thing at any moment and open the lid that I had been holding on to from the inside, but I wanted to hear about Poppy. The more I heard her voice, I could almost place it in a party heard through my bedroom wall. My feet didn't go anywhere near the end of the bed. Back then, on those exciting nights, I kept my eyes wide as though that could help me to hear. As the din grew, I always struggled to stay awake, resenting my place outside of real life. Every time Polly named another character from the past or told a familiar story, the more images I would see of those days: the kitchen cupboards, fingers making roads in the dust on an end table, my father's chair, a thin lightning bolt crack in the plaster behind it.

*Finn was a beautiful dancer, too. Your father needed a lot of room when he got up to dance.* She laughed, happy to remember it. *The women kept him in their sights the whole time he was up. And he was generous, too. He always made me feel like I mattered.*

*Me too*, I said.

*I still miss him.*

*Me, too.*

+    +    +

In school, I was keenly aware of the differences between me and them. They had normal parents with normal lives, I thought. They had family dinners and wore sweaters. I listened to Motorhead and smoked weed. Conspicuously, I wore the same clothes every day and I didn't talk to anybody. No one talked to me unless it was to try and start something. My reputation was a communal work of fiction. I slept in a car, they said. I had a knife in my sock, of all places. My father was in the mob. I walked the halls like a prisoner, sneering at the smug fuckers who always had something to giggle about as I passed.

The day I turned thirteen, everybody started calling me Dummy. That nun said it when I answered, *Thou shalt not Dance* as the Fifth Commandment. *No, you big dummy*, she said, choking on her male voice. A wave of nausea moved through me. The word felt, as it was intended to feel, like a pronouncement. It stuck, immediately. It was Big Dummy for a long time, then, when they discovered my name, it became Spat the Dummy. About a year to the day of that christening, a little prick from NDG blissfully announced that he knew for certain that I had what we still called VD. So then I was each individual venereal disease with my new designation attached. Syphilis Dummy. The Clap Dummy. Genital Warts Dummy.

My eyes had been blackened so many times in fist fights over the D word that, once, I had to be kept home for a month. It was to heal a retina, but it was also a reprieve during which they would decide what was to be done with me. Because of my invisible wound, I wasn't allowed to jump around or cry. I wore an eye-patch, which I loved. Poppy gave me puzzles and a Bar Six every day. We watched "Midday Matinee" and "All in the Family." Of course, he knew I wanted out, but there was no other school that would have me. Quitting was not an option. It was the only unbreakable rule in our house. I had to go every day. Every desolate, crushing day.

I used to get a calendar from the bakery down the street and, gouging an X into each numbered square with a ballpoint pen, I counted down the days to every break in the school year.

The name Spat the Dummy followed me right to the end of high school. I didn't go to the graduation ceremony. Poppy took me to Sex Palace, instead, where I got a blow-job from a girl named Comet who wore blue lipstick and smelled like the square blade of bubble gum that came with hockey cards. It was the first time me and Poppy ever got drunk together. He got the DJ to announce that I had just graduated. People sent drinks to the table; all the girls came by to make a fuss. He was proud of me, so nothing else mattered. We laughed like old friends would and blew a wad of cash on shots and strippers. I was a free man, but more than that, I had instantly become what I had always wanted to be: Poppy's best buddy.

One of the things he had instilled in me during my single

digit ages was to have respect for people nearing the triple digits. So, a month or so after meeting her, I had begun walking Polly to her place after drinking at Gilda's. One day, the bartender told me that she hadn't been around, so I went to a depanneur, got beer and smokes and a *National Geographic* for her. When I arrived at her place, she was excited to have some company. She told me she hadn't been out for a week and it was obvious, as she said the words, that she was just realizing how long it had been. The air was thick with used breath and cooking. Sour smoke. I asked if she had been sick. She said no. It was clear that she was a little shaken by something and was working hard to conceal it.

We had a few drinks and I twisted one up. I had to blow it out the window so as to not taint the aroma of her tobacco. Of course, I steered the conversation to my father and their nights together. Her stories never went anywhere, but I loved hearing any detail of Poppy's life from when he was living it well. I liked the small camaraderie that grew out of our combined effort to bring him closer in time.

There were framed pictures all over to testify to Polly's lost beauty; wishful mirrors crowding the middle of the walls. I could see why he spent time with her back then. Each of the photographs was from the same period. She was probably in her twenties, but looked a bit older as they all did then. Young people still imitated adults in those days. Things hadn't yet turned the other way around.

Just before everything changed on that day and my life began its swift metamorphosis into shit, Polly Beene told me this story at her tiny kitchen table:

*We went to The Black Orchid Room one night to see The Beau-marks. Everybody was there. Everybody we knew. It was way too crowded and we didn't have a chance of getting a seat. Your father goes to talk to a guy behind the bar and two minutes later, we had the best table in the whole place.*

*So we're watching the show and having a ball and Finn asks me to dance. We get up and we're all over the floor. I accidentally bump this woman behind me and she said something to me like ... like ... Watch out, Bitch! Well, Finn heard that and he trips the guy she's dancing with to get back at her, only the woman trips, too. She falls over the guy and her tits come right out of her dress!*

She started laughing and it was hard not to join in, even though it didn't strike me as being all that funny. Polly couldn't stop cackling. Her eyes were locked on me, her face was red and she was tilted in her chair. It made me uncomfortable, the way she kept looking at me. Finally, I gave up smiling. Though she still seemed to be breathlessly laughing, something in her eyes had changed. She began to shiver a little. Fat tears left shiny, crooked trails on her cheeks. One pulled itself from the middle of her chin. Though the corners of her mouth were still pulled back in a taut grin, her expression had become one of horror. She spoke, but through her sobs the words were clipped and barely audible.

*What?*

She repeated the sentence. I couldn't understand it, but I was shaken by how she dreaded what she was saying.

*I can't understand you, Polly ... What's the matter?*

Then, in her eyes, I could see it all. Polly knew the big secret. It had always been there every time we spoke, but, like me, she had pushed it deep into the dimmest part of her memory. She gripped the table with both hands, letting her lit cigarette roll toward me. She began to lose her breath. I tossed the smoke into the ashtray and put my hands over hers.

*Calm down. Take a deep breath.*

Again, she locked her eyes on mine and began to cough. Years of deferred sadness descended on her.

*Breathe, Polly.*

She gulped a breath as though she were drowning in the air. She held it for a second and pulled in another. She put her arm up, hiding her face.

*I'm sorry. I'm so sorry, Spat.*

I went to the sink, ran the water and quickly pinched a lipstick smear from the rim of a cup. As I filled it, she downed her drink and let the empty glass hit the table with a crack.

*I'm sorry*, she said. Then our friendship ended: *I was there when he did it.*

I felt a jolt through my body, head to feet. I saw stars popping in and out of my periphery. I thought the words *I have to go* but I said, *I think I should take you to the hospital.* She didn't respond. Hand shaking, she poured a splash of rum into her glass and swallowed it.

*Polly. Let me take you to the hospital. Just in case.*

Her shivering intensified.

*Polly.*

She threw me a look and seemed surprised to see me.

*Finn?*

*It's Spat, Polly.*

*Spat*, she repeated, as though she were learning the word. Confused and heartbroken, she studied my face.

*Spat.*

*That's right.*

Her expression became graver. She looked away.

*I can't talk to you anymore, Spat.*

*What?*

*I can't see you or talk to you about your father anymore. It's just too hard when I remember that night.*

I knew that I should have turned and walked out, but I couldn't move. I wanted her to say what it was that she couldn't forget. As much as I dreaded it becoming more real, I wanted it to be out in the open. For the first time, I might have wanted to finally relinquish my grueling denial.

*Go. You have to go.*

*I'm sorry*, I said, without knowing why.

*Go! Go away, Finn!*

I walked south through the Plateau, unable to lose the burning sting of change all over me. People could see it, I think. Everyone got out of the way. I dug a joint from my coat pocket and lit it. I knew that it would be impossible to go back to the way I had been. She was a living witness, so there was no denying anything anymore. *I was there*, she said, *when he did it*. Like something born unwillingly in a dangerous place, I was, from that moment on, wide awake. All of the torment I had owed for years of evasion was pulsing from the center of my chest. Old dread. Old panic. I coughed up a grey cloud and clenched my jaw, swiping a tear from my hard face.

At the base of a tilted street sign, there was a mangled, long abandoned bicycle. No doubt pounded by sidewalk plows and bleached by a couple of vicious years, its remaining wheel was nearly folded. I considered the chain and the rusted lock that still protected its dead charge. I put the joint in the corner of my mouth and began tugging on the chain. My foot against the base of the pole, I nearly pulled my arms out of their sockets trying to break it. The links were chunks of ice in my hands, but I couldn't stop or even consider why I was doing it. To my amazement, the lock broke and I was thrown upward, onto my heels. I let go of the chain and it crumpled at my feet with a few soft clinks. I kicked it to the curb and spit out the roach that was burning my lower lip. I plunged my hands into my pockets and continued walking.

Me and Hitler went to a play once because her cousin had the lead. In it, the guy said to the other guy, "*Why do you want to talk about everything? Why do you want to drag it all down?*" I played that moment on loop until I got to my place. I wasn't sure why, but I was anxious to shave and get cleaned up. When I think of it now, I was getting ready for life in the place where things can only be as they are.

*Keep swimming.* That's what Poppy always said. The sharks have to or else they drown. The same feeling that smothered me when he died began pressing from all directions. The brightness of things and seeing how alien I was in this world became too much to endure. I did push-ups to burn off some of the frantic energy, but my arms were too rigid and facing the floor was too frightening. I changed clothes and sat on the couch. I realized that I had come to a decision. I was afraid to think the words, but the resolution had already been made.

# { 2 }

My Uncle Hank's house is in Outremont, a twenty minute walk from my place. We rarely saw each other. There was no rift between us. We weren't close because we reminded each other of Poppy, but not in any nostalgic way. For years, I had never understood why my image of my father changed around Hank. Whenever he and I met, Finn's ghost loomed over us; eavesdropping and pulling the dust of the past into the light.

I walked north on Parc to Bernard, sneering at the stupid fucks driving their shitboxes to nowhere, spewing their rot into the air. I didn't rehearse my questions for my uncle because I didn't want to chicken out and end up sitting in Café Republic, flirting with the college girls who work there. One was a would-be model who wouldn't cross the street to talk to me if I was barfing up million dollar bills. She made small talk with me once, though, so she is now a possibility, however remote.

Hank smiled through a painful wince as he stood aside to let me in. Why he hadn't given up that cavernous house was beyond me. It was enough space for a family of eight, occupied by a man who would have been content to live on a shelf in a shed.

*Still no car*, he said, chuckling.

*No*, I said. *I haven't given in yet.*

It was the safest topic for us. We would simply repeat the same shit whenever we met so that we wouldn't have to say anything. He was always amused by my hatred of cars. As far as I can see, nothing good ever rolled off of an assembly line and burning fossil fuel is dumber than bingo. Everyone can see that the machines are very slowly rising to very slowly kill us; not with their renegade digital minds, as all of the science fiction of yore had promised, but with their sweat. Everyone smells it coming, but it's not cool to speak up. In the so-called free world, we are all secretly suicidal; perverted by the profound hypocrisy which we have willingly, if not greedily, inherited. It's all part of our charm.

*I was surprised to hear from you, Spat. What brings you over?*

*I need some information*, I told him. It was clear that this made him uncomfortable, but most anything did.

*You want a drink?*

*No, thanks*, I said. Now he knew it was serious. He sat and muted the TV, waiting. He was still a big man, big in the forearms and shoulders from years in construction. His face was ruddy, but not so much from drinking. Blood pressure, probably.

*I thought maybe you were looking for work*, he said. *I don't know anybody anymore.* It occurred to me that he was trying to change the subject before it had even been raised.

*It's not that. I was wondering if you knew where my mother is.*

It became increasingly awkward, the longer he went without responding. He started to speak but the words lodged in his throat; he didn't appear to be breathing. He blinked several times as though to make sure that he was where he seemed to be. Finally, he said with the smallest voice, *Your mother?*

*You know where she is? If she's alive?*

*She's alive.*

He got up and went to the kitchen. I assumed he had gone to get an address or a pen and paper to write down her numbers. I waited. Alone, I noticed, here and there, the clues of Hank's private chaos: a broken saucer gathering dust next to the couch, ancient issues of the Gazette stacked to be a table for an overloaded ashtray, a row of plants, so long dead that they were turning black. Throughout my childhood, he had never been without a camera, but there wasn't a single picture to be seen. I remembered over-hearing Poppy telling a story about Hank being distraught about something and turning on the two front burners of the stove. He waited for them to become red and then pressed his hands onto each one. I vaguely remember seeing him with both of his massive hands bandaged when I was little. He was trying to sip hot coffee with them and that struck me as funny. Hank wasn't crazy; he just didn't have the good sense to foster indifference.

When I was about five, Hank picked me up from school in his boat of a Chevy. He was afraid of something, but I couldn't have guessed what it might have been. I squinted up at the car deodorizer which was a picture of a naked woman with a beach ball, framed in red. I wondered if she and my uncle were friends. Hank had never picked me up before and I asked him why I couldn't walk home. He said that we were going for a drive. There would be ice cream. I don't remember either of us saying much of anything after that. We drove in circles. I asked him where we were going but he didn't answer. After a while, he parked near the mountain. He gripped the top of the wheel and put his head on his hands. I had never seen a man cry before that moment. It was scary. I told him that I wanted to go home. He seemed deaf. He just stared straight ahead for a long time. Eventually, he took me home. No ice cream. For years, I had no idea what that was about.

I considered how formal his full name sounded, how it seemed wrong for him. I wondered how old he was. I imagined, as I waited, that I emitted some kind of lunatic waves that were too much for James Henry Ryan. That was why he was hiding in the kitchen. I was beginning to regret even mentioning my mother.

Finally, I called his name. *Hank?* There was no response and I wondered if he had fled through the back door. I went to the kitchen where I found him in front of the stove. I checked, with a glance, to make sure that it was off. Hank was staring at the floor. Again, he spoke in a shrunken version of his normal voice, almost whispering.

*I'm sorry, Spat.*

*Sorry about what?*

*I always wanted to tell you. Every time I thought of her, I always thought of you, going around not knowing.*

He folded his arms and hugged himself. I realized that he was afraid of me, afraid of my reaction to what he had to say. I told him it was all right to tell me anything. Then the fucking water works started and I just wanted to slap the shit out of him.

*What's the matter, Hank? ... Do you know where she is or not?*

*I have an address, but it's not in Canada, Spat.*

*Well, where does she live?*

*Australia.*

I almost laughed. I don't know why. I suppose it was the most unexpected answer. In a few seconds, I imagined the place and seeing her there—some old stranger who was, at the same time, the most familiar person. I could not remember her face and there weren't any pictures of her in our house. I only knew the version of her that had been formed, years earlier, by a child's persuasive imagination. There was no question that I would be going there. I had never been out the country before, except for the honeymoon with Hitler in New York and another trip a few years later for her cousin's Vegas wedding. The cousin and the gibbon she married were rich assholes who flew everybody in to see how much money they had spent on shit so tacky, even I could tell. We got drunk and danced until they asked us to stop.

*I always wanted to tell you.*

*It's all right, Hank. I could have asked before now ... Don't cry, man.*

*Your father wouldn't let me tell you.*

*What?*

His loyalty to Poppy was maintained by what he saw as a debt. Finn took care of Hank when they were little. Their mother was a drunk; their father was gone most of the time. No one knew where. I've never seen a picture of them, either. If Hank did not feel obliged, there would have been no love in him for his dead brother. *I know why*, I thought.

*Well, when he died, why didn't you tell me then?*

*I didn't know how much you remembered of her. I was afraid to tell you.*

*Why?*

He shrugged and admitted, reluctantly, *In case you got mad.*

From my look, he took an unintentional step backwards. He wanted to explain. *Well, I thought*, he said, *if you're anything like him ... Well, I just didn't know what you would do.*

I had to freeze and diffuse the rage before I spoke.

*What?*

*I didn't know how you would—*

*You couldn't tell me over the phone?*

He backed up a little more and finally turned away.

*Hank*, I swear, *you can tell me anything ... Poppy's dead ... And you have no reason to be afraid. You're the only family I have left.*

*That you know of.*

*Yeah.*

*I'm so sorry, Spat.*

Before I could tell him to stop apologizing, the question was out. It was as though the words had lined themselves up without my noticing and had been waiting for their chance. *Do I have a brother?*

Hank turned to face me. His demeanor became that of a star witness in court and he eyed me, intently. Suddenly, he seemed resigned to spill everything.

*Do you remember him at all, Spat?*

I remembered the baby, the intruder. I recalled the screaming of the one whose arrival brought the end of our little family. But I adapted. I adapted to losing her to him. Though I could not fill it, I accepted the empty space she had left. Poppy never talked about her. The one time I asked about my mother, I must have been twelve because I didn't have the name Dummy yet. Without saying the words, he made it clear that the subject was off-limits. He didn't want to hit me, so he left for the day. I didn't ask about her again. As time went on, I would always feel guilty for wondering about the woman who had deserted us. Out of my fearsome loyalty to Poppy, that's what she had become—a deserter. Of course, I knew that she had been driven away. I knew it, but in childhood denial is often a necessity for survival.

*No. I don't remember him*, I said.

He knew I was lying. I didn't want to dig it all up at once, though. I decided to just get the address from him and go, but now he wanted to talk.

*His name is Mick.*

Now, it seemed as though I had to ask something specific.

*Are you in touch with them?*

He considered me, briefly. *Yes.*

*You've always been?*

We talk a few times a year. Ann calls with ... an update.

All at once, I had to get out of there. I couldn't look at him. I told myself that it was because our conversation seemed disloyal to Poppy, but I knew that Hank had been there when it all ended. Another witness. For a second, I heard the hiss of the rain on that night, the loud music coming through the walls. I turned and headed for the door. I told Hank to call me and to leave a message with the address and a phone number. He was telling me to wait, but then stopped himself. I left the door open and when I stepped outside he closed it, promptly, behind me.

I woke up to being on Laurier, walking east. I doubted the reality of going to meet the foreign half of the family. I decided that my interest in them would pass. I stopped at the SAQ for a bottle of gin and then headed up Parc, toward the mountain.

On the icy gravel road that winds its way up to the lookout,

I drank the warm gin in tight sips. I scuffed and muttered to myself, sneered at the occasional jogger. What sort of lunatic goes running in that kind of weather? Ice crystallizing in their lungs, they would be coughing up blood, I thought, by the time they stopped. My hands were cold. I cursed Hank and the weight of the past.

When I got to the top of the mountain, I knew that I would find the chalet closed; its huge wooden rafter squirrels standing guard in the dark. I finished the gin and threw the bottle, listening to it lightly clinking in the naked trees before smashing, sweetly, on a rock. Safely drunk, I turned and started downward.

# { 3 }

When the ringing started, I was in a jungle where most everything was still. There were panthers in the trees, watching me, but I knew that they weren't a serious threat. I turned in a circle, watching for movements in the thick, sweating underbrush. Shards of sunlight pierced the mist at the top of the canopy where unseen birds were calling to each other. I heard muffled voices but couldn't discern the direction. The words could have been reversed or otherwise mangled, but the tone was that of casual small talk. I meant to say hello, but a deafening bird call burst from my throat, instead. It rattled my skull so severely that splashes of toxic fluid escaped my neck and soaked the brain. This gave me a surge of nausea. I immediately thought that there's nothing beautiful about a bird call to the one who's making it. This observation seemed significant for some reason. I was exhausted by the effort but I dropped my jaw to call again. There was no answer. I recognized the ringing as the phone, but I stayed, listening, in the imagined jungle. A cat fell from above and landed at my feet. It looked up at me, its eyes widening. Its body was wrinkled with anxious, ready muscles. I was pulled back to the waking world, but kept my eyes shut, hoping that the ringing would stop. The ear-stabbing tone sounded after my recorded voice.

*Spat! Pick-up, if you're there ...* She whispered, *Fuck ... I have to talk to you. And it's not about the divorce or anything like that. It's important.* Before the machine's robot voice could finish saying *End of message,* I knew I would not be phoning her. Even when we were married, I probably wouldn't have returned that call. *Important* to her always meant money.

I tried to get back to sleep, but my head was cleaved from the gin. I got up to take a piss and caught a look at myself in the black mirror at the end of the hall. I looked like an elongated version of Poppy, stuck in a perpetual night. I didn't let myself get soft like a lot of guys my age, but my face was grey, older. Forty, for fuck sake. The problem child at forty; I embarrassed myself.

As I pissed, I realized that I would most likely spend the rest of my life alone. Women who were still game wanted me for a one-off. Then they wanted to be friends; the kind who never see or speak to each other. With me, they didn't even pretend to be after something long term. That was fine because I preferred sex to everything else and anything more felt like an intrusion. They always liked that I was so eager to please. I could always make them laugh, too, until they drifted away; looking for someone bland and predictable who was willing to sit on the nest and wear a tie. If I were a man whore, I'd be stinking rich. I'd probably have a little more self-respect, too. Maybe even some respect from other people. Never should have gotten married. No one should. It's not natural. It's perverse.

I was so high at my wedding, I would occasionally tune out and then return, wondering what the next part in the hilarious, slow-motion slam dance might be. It was hard to not laugh at the priest's sing-song delivery of the marriage rules—laws to which he, being a bride of Christ, would never be subjected. It was impossible to take any of it seriously.

My blushing bride was blushing because she was mortified. She knew they were all sneering at her beaded back, thinking that our merger would last a year, maybe two. *She's just collecting some merchandise and her man looks drunk.* In fact, she had just realized what kind of contract she was about to sign. We went through the church bullshit for her mother, that dripping venom sac who refused to look me in the eye or utter my "crude" name. Her father certainly didn't want to be at our wedding and her sisters looked like sideshow prostitutes, all gooned-up as bridesmaids. They quietly snickered, identically, throughout the idiotic play.

The Virgil family was sad and smug and deluded. Even their maid could make you feel as though you were raised by jackals. They had a maid. Eating with them was like going to a sort of autopsy luncheon during which any expression of enjoyment would have been considered to be in bad taste. They got twenty dollar pies from the bakery. My betrothed didn't have much time for their drivel, either, but didn't want to get cut from the will. She was adopted and anyone who met her at a family gathering was alerted to this fact, immediately. Not surprisingly, she always felt the need to separate herself from them. We visited her people only when we were summoned and that was rare. *Just play along*, she'd say, whenever we found ourselves in their territory. That's always the worst advice in any situation. Pricks and cowards play along.

Her family's generalized dread had left them isolated, confined by the comfort for which her crusty old fuck of a father had struggled his entire coffee-spooned life. Constance, Hitler's mother, looked like an old man who was always angry about being in drag. Besides being hoisted, by marriage, from beneath her daughter's class, she believed, too, that I was simple. Sometimes I'd play it up for badness. *Constance. Are these trees Cristamthamuns?* If she could have killed ten people and gotten away with it, I would have been nine of them. She was always reading one of those books about ancient and mysterious prophets and soothsayers. She didn't like that I didn't believe in heaven or hell or purgatory or limbo or souls or ghosts or angels or second sense or goblins. The contempt I was feeling for the latest resurgence of boil-in-bag spirituality, was equal, in intensity, to the gnawing malaise I got from eating shellfish. The mass, it seemed to me, was an all but transparent prelude to mass murder. I suppose for some, that's the attraction.

The ex used astrology for religion. She was always in a snit about Saturn arriving to or leaving some imaginary house in the sky. I would ask her how, exactly, the planets and their movements could affect her life. How could millions of people born within the same period of time share the same traits and fate? *This is the sort of thing that cave people would have gone in for*, I'd say. *Shut-up*, she'd say like a surly teen, and then avoid my blasphemy by stomping to another room to work on her chart. I'd sometimes offer to get her some goat entrails so that she could determine whether or not she should cut her hair or pay the phone bill. *You have no soul*, she'd say, as though that were the worst accusation anyone could hurl at an enemy.

Belief is still the most hazardous escape from reality; the uber-drug. If I could have been on that one, I would have been admired for being high all of the time. I might have been a prophet of some sort instead of a spook-less meat contraption.

Feeling the full weight of my hangover, I went back to bed and hoped that sleep would let me in again. It used to be comforting, the hangover; the self-inflicted sickness that could put me down, however briefly, and dull the serrated blade of my inexplicable rage. I shut my eyes and tried to pretend my way back to the jungle, but the ringing returned. The machine intervened.

*Spat, I know you're home.*

How did she know? Did Mars tell her? Was Venus spying on me, feeding her information?

*Pick-up ... Spat ... You know I won't stop calling.*

I didn't try to guess as to what she might have been after. In my head, she was being relocated to a black corner where the darkness would slowly erode her from existence. I had gotten rid of every picture, every present, anything from our time together that she hadn't already taken with her. The machine blasted its startling beep and the synthetic voice said *End of message*. I gave up on the jungle, opened my eyes and tilted my head back to see up the window's dress. Snow was creeping earthward, behind the thin curtains, quietly burying the city. It was that time of the winter that feels eternal. Getting out of bed seemed all the more offensive, now.

I opened and closed my fists. They were still sore from my battle with the chain. I wondered why Hank hadn't phoned. I speculated that he had been in touch with my phantom mother. She might have told him, I thought, to keep her whereabouts under wraps. Anything was possible. It occurred to me that she may not want to be reminded of her past. Maybe she had created a whole new history for herself. If she were willing to go all the way to the other side of the world to escape her situation, it was likely that she had long ago relegated me to some dark corner.

The ringing started again. I had to resist the urge to grab the phone and smash it into dust. I could hear her crying and resented it.

*Spat ... I have to talk to you ... Pick up the fucking phone!*

When we were married, she would only cry if she knew that she was in the wrong. Such an adolescent attempt at manipulation always looks funny on an adult. Sometimes the harder she'd cry, the louder I'd laugh.

*You are so fucking cruel!*

I picked the Gazette out of the snow and cursed the cold fingers reaching up to grab my nuts. I slammed the door shut and walked, quickly, back into the warmth. I spread the paper out on the kitchen table and skimmed the Help Wanted ads. I have never been the candidate described in any of them. I have no degree in anything. I have no career goals and my French is laughable. I am not even a self-starter. I had plenty of the settlement from the hospital left, but that money had to last until ... something. I had this idea that, eventually, something new would come along and everything would simply fall into place for me. I would suddenly know what to do and where to go and who to be. It was a notion that bordered on astrological stupidity, but I had developed the habit of hoping for it. Also, spending any significant amount of that money always put me right back in the waiting room; standing up for the shit-eating doctor fuck, who simultaneously covered his ass while telling me that an "error" had been made in regard to my father's meds. Looking at me, the will to break the news drained out of him. My fists were clenched, my teeth were about to bleed from the pressure of my bite. My breathing was slow and steady, my eyes fixed on his. For a while, I vaguely wondered if maybe he or some nurse had recognized Poppy as the man who, years before, had beaten up or robbed their dad. Maybe that accident was really a revenge killing. Either way, it was an event that gave Poppy what he had always wanted—money to leave behind for me.

While the coffee gurgled its way into the pot, I rolled a joint and listened to Tricky. His cover of "Black Steel" is my song. I saw him on the street, one day, but I was too shy to say anything. I'm probably his oldest fan.

I had been getting exceptional weed from an elderly hippy on Villeneuve. Smoking the ganga is the most sensible way to get adequately baked without ending up with a shotgun in your back and Doberman piss on your new acid wash jeans. I don't do serious shit. Meth dealers should be decapitated. Meth dealers, fundamentalists of any breed and the oily politicos— kill them all. Fucking leeches.

The ringing.

*Spat ... There's something we have to talk about and it's important. You can pick up the phone or I can come over there. Take your pick.* She waited. When it became clear that I wouldn't be answering her plea, she gave up the reasonable voice and went back to her normal growl. *You fucking asshole. I hope you're dead.*

That delighted me. I laughed to myself and then cackled so loudly, it was astounding. It couldn't stop until whatever was inside found its way out. I dropped the scissors and the bud and covered my face with my hands. When it subsided, I was amazed by a desire to rush to the phone and beg her for forgiveness. For only a second, I wanted to plead with her to take me back. *I'm lost and I'm scared and I wish I were anyone else*. The thought of that made me laugh again. I don't know why her hatred had struck me as being so funny and I did not expect that my laughter would leave such a large space for the gloom. There was a black wing placed across my shoulder, but I decided the weed would take care of that. I wanted a drink, but it was too early. I never drank before noon. That was a rule.

When she arrived, banging on my door like a cop, I was in the shower. I was sure that she would give up as soon as her cold knuckles were sore enough. In the meantime, I sang to myself. She didn't quit, though. I stepped out of the shower and listened to the relentless pounding. I chuckled, dried my hair with the only towel. I put it around my waist and went to the front windows to make sure that it was her out there. She looked frazzled. She had spotted the slight movement in the blind and stopped banging. She spoke in a normal voice, *Let me in, Spat.*

If I had not let her in, she would have felt that her presence had some impact on me and I couldn't allow that. I pulled the door open and tried not to react to the cold.

*Hey, Patty,* I said, because that's her real name. Hitler suits her better, but it's Patricia. She was named after her father's sister who disappeared on a trip to London.

*Why didn't you answer the phone?*

*Because I knew it was you.*

*Look, Spat ... There's something I have to tell you.*

I smirked in an attempt to hide my sudden unease. *What?*

She came in and sat on the couch. She pulled her jacket around her as though she had felt a chill. *I'm pregnant.*

I wanted to throw-up.

*Holy shit.*

The day that the divorce had been finalized, I had gone to her place for one last brawl that ended in a farewell fuck and a promise to never see each other again. I wanted to ask why she had gone off the pill. I wanted to suggest that it was some sort a scam. If we couldn't fight, I didn't know how to talk to her.

*There's more,* she said, and I knew I wouldn't like this part.

*I'm not sure if it's yours.* As stunned as I was, I almost felt sorry for her. I wasn't sure why, but I wanted to console her and tell her that it didn't matter.

*You skanky fucking whore.*

*Oh, go to Hell, you big prick.*

*Who was it?*

*None of your business ... A guy I met at the school.*

I tried to think of a way of finding out who he was. I needed, at least, to get a look at him.

*So what do you want?*

*I don't want anything. I just thought you should know.*

*If it's mine ... I want visitation rights.*

I couldn't think of the word "custody". Of course, in reality, the idea of being someone's father scared the shit out of me. In that moment, I only wanted some sort of revenge. And what if she were lying? What was she really up to?

*You never wanted kids before,* she said, timidly, as though she were afraid of me. That was another one of her ploys—playing fearful. The idea was that I would soften up and she could get away with whatever she was trying to pull. It was the moral victory she was always interested in. I didn't give a fuck about looking moral, certainly not in front of her.

For a while, we said nothing. I clutched the side of the towel and studied her face. She didn't look pregnant. She didn't have any sort of glow or extra weight. When would it become obvious?

*So ... What, are me and this other ... contestant supposed to have blood tests or—*

That made her mad. She stood up and approached me, threateningly. *Never mind, you selfish piece of shit.* She nudged me with her cold elbow as she made her way to the door.

Watching her leave, I clenched my fists and hoped that she wouldn't turn to see my fear, my aching sadness. When the door shut, I didn't move for a long time. Dry, I let the towel fall to the floor. I put my chin on my chest and for the first time in years, I sobbed like a baby. Though it made no sense, I couldn't help thinking that I had done something wrong. I wanted *to hate her, but failed to muster it. I loved her again, in some new way that I that couldn't articulate. I thought it was brave of her to carry a baby that could have been fathered by someone as fucked-up as me. To stop the sobbing, I called up rage against the other man. I saw myself kicking his faceless head in with my steel toed boots. I'll fucking kill him,* I said, as though someone were watching. *He's fucking dead.*

# { 4 }

The sidewalk teetered under my feet. There were dirty silver patches of ice here and there, scuffed by many hapless heels. It was cold, but I was full of gin and didn't care. I stepped into a phone booth and rolled a joint on the top of the black box. I smoked it there in the upright glass casket, filling the space, erasing the outside with a cloud. *This box of Heaven*, I thought, *is mine*. I let the roach fall and disappear into the below. I sang "Aftermath" to myself. I hoped that some prick would bang on the door, wanting to use the phone. No one did.

Warm and buoyant, I walked up Clark toward Saint Joseph, pretending to not know where I was going. I stopped, in the middle of the street, to take a piss. A car blared at me and finally crept around. I turned and sprayed the passenger door with steamy poison and laughed. *Get out and walk, fucking chicken shit!* As I put my cock away, I yelled, *Lazy fucks! I hope your balls fall off!* This struck me as the funniest thing I had ever heard. I bent over, folded my arms and laughed for a long time. Spit dripped from my smile as another car horn blared at me to move.

*Fuck you!*

+ + +

I knew where I was by the smell of that revolting incense

that she used to cover the stench of her attempts at cooking. I didn't want to open my eyes and be right. I didn't want to open my eyes and let the light into my head. I was lying on my side. My elbows nearly met my knees. I was fetal, clenched as tightly as a seed. The upholstery imprinted my face with its weave. I could hear her moving around in the kitchen. I wished that I had died in my sleep. Tried, but couldn't remember arriving there.

*Spat?*

I pretended to be asleep. She knew better.

*There's coffee. Get up.*

I winced. There was an unfamiliar chemical taste in my mouth. Toxic sweat made my shirt stick to me. I still had my boots on. I took that as a bad sign.

*Spat?*

*All right*, I barely said. I opened my eyes and immediately shut them again. I tried to remember the night before, but there was a fistful of pages missing near the end. I vaguely remembered an argument with her, but none of the words. I took a deep breath and sat up. Once again, I opened my eyes, but slowly this time. I was startled to see her sitting across from me. Her expression was that of a scientist studying an old test subject; intellectually present, emotionally absent.

*I'm sorry*, I said.

*I don't care.* It was a mere statement of fact. If she actually did care, she would have tagged that phrase with *you fucking asshole* or something like it. I wanted to leave, but I also wanted to know what had brought me to her lair. I sat up, gingerly, wincing at the heavy pulse in my brain.

*I'm sorry*, I repeated.

*So?*

I nodded, assessing the situation.

*When did I get here?*

*You were outside screaming at me so I had to let you in. That was at about three this morning, thanks.*

I was about to apologize again, but realized that remorse was no longer an acceptable currency. I sighed and wiped my face with my hands. I remembered being in the phone booth cloud and imagined, for a moment, being lowered into an upright grave.

*What's going to happen, Spat?*

*What?*

*If this is your baby, what's going to happen?*

*I don't know what you're talking about.*

*I can't have you around when it's born. I can't take care of two babies.*

I stood up, looked around for my coat. All of my blood rushed to my feet. I thought I might pass out. Still, I managed to say, *How do you know you can take care of one baby?* I knew that would do it.

*Listen, you fucking bag of shit,* she said, standing. *I don't want you coming around here. Whether it's yours or not, it has nothing to do with you.*

*If it's mine, it's mine,* I said. *Where's my coat?*

*You didn't have one. Now get the fuck out.*

That was a bit disconcerting. I tried to remember losing it, but nothing came to mind. Realizing that I would have to phone a cab and wait there for it or else freeze on the walk to the metro, I tried to make a provisional peace with her.

*Will you phone a cab for me?*

She sighed and folded her arms.

*You're such a disgusting mess ... It breaks my heart.*

It broke her heart? I knew that must have been hormones talking; heart-softening pregnancy hormones that would replace her spiked armor plates with feathers and make her less likely to eat the future infant. I tried to think of the most responsible sounding lie.

*I'm trying to get straightened* out, I said. Then, before I knew it, I added, *I'm going to Australia to meet my mother.*

That was a genuine surprise for both of us. *Good for you,* she said, as though I had just told her I was going to quit smoking. *I think it's about time.* She leaned back and watched me as you would some hatching reptile.

*Me too*, I said, wondering why she was so unfazed.

*Was this Hank's idea?*

I felt a tingling on the back of my neck, the tentacles of conspiracy.

*What do you mean?*

*He told me she lived there. I knew she didn't drown, like you said.*

*So ... you knew all about her.*

She shrugged, shook her head. *Just what he told me. He showed me her picture, once.*

*So ... did you and Hank talk about this a lot?*

*Not really. He told me your mother lives in Australia with your brother. That's all. I never mentioned it because I figured you'd throw a big spaz.*

I went to the door, too anxious to think of a parting shot. She was saying something, but it didn't connect. I walked out into the piercing cold and began to run. My shirt was nothing in the icy wind. My jaw began to tremble. I stopped and scanned the street for a cab. Seeing none, I ran as fast as I could to the metro.

The relief of being on the relatively warm subway platform was almost enough to quell my anger, but not quite. I hated that fucking bitch and her kid and Hank. I hated my mother and my asshole brother, whoever they were. World, go fuck yourself.

I stepped onto the train and sat in a seat near the door, opposite a sleeping student. The thin white wires from his headphones disappeared under his parka. I imagined pulling him up to his feet, cracking his nose with my forehead and taking that coat. Instead, I dropped my head and counted quickly, silently, to avoid thinking. At four hundred and thirty-six, I arrived at the Mont-Royal stop. I braced myself for the cold as I climbed the sixty-one stairs next to the escalator. With each step, with each number, I could not help but see moments in my head of me and Patty together: Parties, birthdays, beaches, and her body when there was still mystery there, rooms in which we'd lived, fleeting happiness. The closer I came to the top, the colder the air. I pulled my arms into my chest and sneered at the few people who noticed my state.

At the top of the stairs, I remembered this secret: When we were on our honeymoon, I woke-up early on the second day and went out for a walk around the block. I had never been to New York before and I was high from the buzzing potential all around me. I was in Mid-town, walking west on Fifty-third street. There was a tiny, cluttered porn shop wedged between two massive buildings. The Middle-Eastern man behind the counter barely glanced up from his book as I entered. I pretended to be searching for something specific, looking at the backs of video cases. As I made my way past a wall of giant dildos, I noticed a small island of blue and red booths in the back. The exaggerated audio coming from one of them was making me chuckle until I noticed a pair of legs in the corner. She was no more than eighteen, tilting her head and dropping her bottom lip to indicate that she was more than available. She was transmitting the welcomed signal that she had no boundaries whatsoever. She approached, pausing to give me time to look away and call it off. I watched her, knowing the future and knowing how unforgivable it would be.

Her face was long, her skin the colour of caramel. Her leather accessories were, in fact, brightly coloured plastic. Her glossy skirt was short enough so as to not be a hindrance. She smiled at me while cautiously reaching low. The many bangles on her wrist clinked as she rubbed my crotch. I asked how much and she listed the prices the way a telemarketer spouts the over-recited script. When I paid her, she backed me into a tiny booth, opened my pants and giggled at my hardness. She rolled a condom over my better half and I fucked her against the wall. She played it up, moaning and panting, making it clear that the owner would not object to our spur-of-the-moment romance. Her breath smelled like beer. When it was over, she patted my ass and cooed in my ear. *Baby, that was amazing.* It was a sophisticated touch to show that she was a pro. I pulled my pants up, closed my belt. A wave of heat passed through me.

*So long, Baby*, she said.

*Yeah*, I managed before striding directly to the exit. When I looked back, she seemed younger. She was fifteen or sixteen, maybe, but I immediately assured myself that she couldn't have been that young. There must have been some regulations regarding a minimum age requirement for the whores working the jerk-off booths in the porn shops of Manhattan. There must have been. Dazed, I went into a deli and ordered a coffee. I went to the men's room and washed my cock in the sink. My heart was pounding with that old, familiar excitement that, only hours before, I had publicly sworn to never feel again. At the same time, I had never hated myself with such intensity. The cold edge of the sink made my scrotum retreat. The water was too hot. *Fuck, Fuck, Fuck, Fuck,* I whispered.

That was the event that kept me in my marriage for ten years. Guilt, as I had learned in Catholic school, built the greatest of bonds. It was the glue that fastened us to our fearful faux morality.

I returned to the room and my sleeping wife and almost puked with shame. I showered until I could face her. I had to forget what I had done if I were going to make it work. Because marriage is unnatural, it has to be made to work. I understood. I knew that what had happened on my walk had to be left behind or she would eventually see it. Naked, still wet here and there, I ran and jumped into the warm bed where she was just waking up. Hoping that I was not infected with anything, I planted my face between her legs where it would spend much of the next year. I owed her. She had no complaints, but she was a bit surprised by my renewed zeal. She chalked it up to love, I suppose. There were numerous moments like that one when I would envy her naiveté.

By the time I had made it back to my place, I was quaking so much that I had trouble walking. I ran a hot bath and sat, shivering, on the side of the tub until there was enough water.

I undressed quickly, denim corners and buttons scraping white lines into my pink skin. I sank into the painful and then perfect heat, staring at the violent splashing below the faucet. The phone rang. The machine recited my curt out-going message: *I'm not home!*

*Spat?* It was Hank's voice. *I have some information for you.*

*Choke on it and die*, I muttered to myself.

He began listing numbers and directions, so I slid under the water where his voice couldn't reach me. The pressure on my ears was comforting. Finally, I felt muscles relax and the quaking stopped. I puckered my lips to reach the rippling surface and pulled in a breath of air. I settled into my liquid shroud, content for the first time in days. My headache and nausea seemed like little more than details in my miserable story. I wanted to sleep under the warm water, stay there for good.

Out of nothing, I began to imagine the mysterious baby growing in Patty. Gradually, I felt the serious discomfort of new love. I wondered if the baby could hear my thoughts while I was, as it was, submerged and warm. I imagined inhaling the water and sent, instinctively, I suppose, a message into the field: *No matter what, I'll protect you.*

+    +    +

Bathed and fed, I rolled three joints and smoked one. I wanted out of my place, so I pulled a jacket on over a couple of sweaters and walked to the Main. I tried to think of alternatives on the way, but I ended up in front of Gilda's.

The bartenders nodded and grinned at me when I came in. The Clash boomed from new speakers and that made me happy. "Daddy was a bank robber, but he never hurt nobody ..." I sat at the bar and spun an empty ash tray.

*What'll ya have, my friend?*

*Gimmie a couple of shots of gin with a bit of ice*, I said. There wasn't anyone there I knew. It occurred to me that I used to know more people. Some people. I had a best friend, years ago, in my ludicrous twenties. I wondered where he was and smirked at the phrase "best friend". After forty, people are less inclined to sustain the foundation of bullshit on which friendships are built. People have kids or habits or startling revelations that leave them insular. Anyway, enthusiasm for other people wanes when we recognize that speck in the distance as Old Age approaching with Death taking up the rear. Days that were infinite grains of sand on the beach become pennies counted. I preferred being alone. Most of the time.

He placed the glass in front of me and said, *Cheers*. I drank it down and then slid the glass back and forth between my hands. "Train in Vain" started and I sang along to myself. "*Oh, Baby, stand by your man ...*" The bartender returned, smirking.

*That was fast.*

*I'm a growing boy,* I told him.

*You want another one?*

*Why not?*

He brought the bottle and filled the same glass with a couple of shots. He knew I didn't give a fuck about decorum. Not like a real customer.

*That's too bad about your friend,* he offered, in his serious voice.

*What friend?*

*That lady you used to talk to here.*

*Polly,* I said.

*Yeah. She was a nice lady.* I felt dread falling through me. *Yeah,* I said, pretending to know what he was talking about. *It's a shame.* I remembered that playing along is always the dumbest move, but it was too late to go back.

*I think that's the worst way to go,* he said. *Fire.*

I tried not to react. The muscles in my legs hardened.

*Mind you,* he added, *it was the smoke that got her. At least she didn't have to burn up.*

I nodded, but I couldn't speak.

This is a secret and it's pathetic: I wasn't sad about Polly. I felt sorry for myself. Somehow, now that she was gone, Poppy was even further away than before. I downed the second double, paid up and left. I walked by her place to see if there was evidence. The kitchen window was boarded up. Soot, like the lingering shadow of flames, blackened the bricks above it. I tried to stop it, but couldn't help seeing her struggling to get to the door as the black cloud swallowed her. I lit a joint and walked north on Saint Dominique. Out of nowhere, I hated that bartender for telling me the news, for knowing it before me. I decided that I would never go back to Gilda's. *Fuck them.* I dug into my front pocket for my keys. I held them, tightly, in my cold hand and gouged a thin line into the parked cars as I passed. Though this usually brought some momentary joy, for the first time, it felt juvenile and futile. Why bother when the cars had long since won the battle for supremacy? Scratching their candy coloured shells did nothing to clean the air, nothing to take the tiny seeds of death from our blood. Carbon monoxide, Nitrogen monoxide, Nitrogen dioxide, Formaldehyde, Sulfur dioxide, Benzene and Polycyclic hydrocarbons flow from them every hour of every day, so that lazy pricks can feel sexy and free. The last car I keyed let out a digital wail as though it had felt the injury. It screamed for its man to come and protect it as I fled, running.

# { 5 }

At the Wyre internet café, I found far too many pages on Australia. I discovered that this jaunt to the southern hemisphere would cost me at least three thousand dollars. Of course, this meant using some of the settlement money. I dreaded touching it, even investing it. The bank leeches had a million ways to gradually separate me from my unlucky fortune, but I didn't fall for any of their scams. Patty was always trying to get me to buy stocks with it, but I never did. She just wanted to exert some control over it since she knew that she'd never have it, even after the inevitable divorce. I had decreed that the compensation paid for the accidental termination of my father was to be left alone unless we absolutely needed it. The settlement was a hundred and twenty thousand dollars. I got soaked by the lawyer, but that hardly mattered. I didn't care about getting rich; I just wanted the hospital to pay. It wasn't nearly enough. Real payment would have been the hands of the person who had administered the medication. Those incompetent hands in a glass box would have been a sign that the hospital fucks understood what they had done.

Admittedly, over the years, I had chipped away at the death money now and again. It paid the rent during long spells when no one would hire me. It paid for weed when I couldn't. It was the layer of cushion between my ass and the world's boot. It seemed fitting, somehow, that it would now take me to meet my mother.

She had become less of a phantom and more of a real person. I wasn't sure what I wanted to get out of our reunion. I knew there wouldn't be any great celebration. I only wanted a clearer picture of my past, of myself. I wanted to see this brother she'd chosen over me. I wanted her to see what a fuck-up I had become and for her to shoulder some of the blame. All of it, maybe. I wasn't sure, though, if meeting her would be worth stepping out of the narrow hallway of my existence. My denial had shored up the one-sided walls around me for so long that the notion of letting go of it was beginning to seem reckless. Reality was waiting out there, ready to pounce.

I did a search for a local travel agency that specialized in trips to Australia. I took down the address and walked toward it. On the way, I looked at coats in store windows. I stopped and bought one from a French guy with a lisp. He was so unusually friendly, I felt normal and welcomed there. With my sweaters and jacket in a bag, I wore my new coat. I was thankful to be warm and felt somewhat invisible again.

+   +   +

When I came to the travel agency, there was a display in the window that made not going to Hawaii seem like a crime against humanity. I imagined the beaches in Australia and thought I was getting a bargain: a chat with my mother and a tan to boot.

I was surprised to see Linda behind a desk, clicking away on a keyboard. She stood-up when she saw me, smiled broadly.

*Spat!*

Hey, Linda.

As she hugged me, I assumed that I would get a good deal.

*How are you?*

I shrugged. *I'm all right.* She looked different.

*You look great*, I told her. Her drabness was gone, she was happy. She looked younger than she had when she was married to Rob and no longer reminded me of a rodeo clown with a hormone deficiency.

*What brings you here?*
*I'm going to Australia.*
*Oh! To see your mother?*

I kept my smile on and tried not to react. I silently wished Patty dead, but then quickly took it back.

*Yeah, I'm going to see ... Mom. She called. Wants me to visit, so—*

*That's great!*

Fucking Patty always had to tell everyone everything about us. Well, everything about me. Full disclosure to anyone who happened by was her way of staying, in her miniature mind, on the righteous high ground. I was perpetually in rubber boots with bread bag socks, slopping around in the stinking bog of my filthy nature.

*Australia is beautiful*, she said, seriously. *Everybody says.* I sat on the plastic chair in front of her cluttered desk and tried to seem as casual and care-free as possible. She typed as she smiled at me, only glancing at her screen.

*I haven't seen you in ages. What are up to?*

*Oh ...* I couldn't think of anything to say. *Just family stuff. How about you?*

*Well*, she said, *I've been sober for a year as of two and a half weeks ago.*

*Oh? I didn't realize you had...You know...that big a problem.*

Rather than saying, *You've got to be fucking kidding*, she only grinned at me and pressed her lips together. *I feel like I'm alive for the first time in years. No, the first time ever*, she said, getting softly choked-up.

I wanted to leave. I hated when people pretended that quitting a bad habit induced some epiphany that the rest of us were supposed to envy. I hated the arrogance that so often sizzles under mandatory humility. Like when you have to eat dinner with a priest and you mention the subject of blow-jobs and everyone shakes their head and stares at the table and the priest calls you "vulgar". Linda looked at me with veiled pity. I realized that I probably reeked of dope. *Fuck!*

*How are you, Spat?*

When people ask twice, it's because you look like shit, but probably can't see it. It creeps up, like everything else.

*I'm doing great, Linda. Going down under.* I thought of a bad joke, but decided against it. She didn't look so much like the giggler that she'd used to be.

*I think that's absolutely fantastic. Is your Dad going with you, or ...* She trailed off, holding the last note for a second with her eyebrows lifted. I stared for a moment, wondering how much brain damage she had inflicted upon herself. How could she not remember that detail? Maybe the subject of Poppy came up so much that it created, at least in drunk observers, the illusion of his being alive.

*No. He's staying here,* I said. She smiled.

*Is there a Lady friend going with you or—?*

Lady friend? What the fuck was that supposed to mean? Lady Friend is a term people use when chatting politely with a middle-aged, unfuckable man with a face like a Bonobo and slacks. Linda had become a version of Respectability that she had most likely gleaned from reruns of some old TV show. It had that kind of falseness and vapidness.

*No. Flying solo,* I said, brightening so as to endure the rest of our meeting.

*I find that hard to believe,* she said and gave me your grandmother's coquettish smile as she tapped the Enter key.

*I have a few great deals for Australia.*

She began a litany of dates, regulations and seemingly random numbers. None of it made sense. I was set to tell her what I wanted, but there was never an opening to say it. Finally, I just started agreeing with whatever she suggested. Buying anything always made me feel like I was being robbed, but paying for that trip made me sure of it. When it became clear that I would be spending a day in the air to get there, I started to change my mind. At least on a boat there would be a chance to wander around, twist one up and get a bit baked. On a plane, there was nothing but sitting and waiting; repressing the urge to go ape shit and trash the place.

Wanting our meeting to end, I handed her my rarely used plastic. Minutes later, everything was arranged. Linda smiled at me and tilted her head as the itinerary printed. *She looks retarded*, I thought.

*I can't believe how great you look, Linda.*

*Thanks, Spat. Listen ...* She dropped her volume and leaned forward, slightly. *If you ever want to talk about your drinking ...*

*What?* I flinched. She looked as though a week's worth of gas had suddenly thundered out of her.

*Nothing. Never mind. You have a great trip.*

She stood, so I stood. She embraced me. She held on for a few seconds longer than normal. I stuck my ass out, pulling my crotch away, as even the slightest pressure or vaginal proximity could cause it to swell. I almost told her to get off of me when she finally let go. She smiled at me with an insightful sadness that pissed me off the way an SUV would.

*Well. Thanks for everything.*

*You take care, Spat. Don't forget to apply for your visa.*

*I won't.* I turned and muttered, *Ya fuckin' weirdo.*

Back on the street, I was a bit giddy. I felt as though I had just gotten away with something. To celebrate, I stopped in at Debris for a quick one.

+ + +

Stumbling out of Debris, into the cold evening, I felt the pockets of my new coat to make sure that my tickets were still there. Happy, or something like it, I grinned at the sleet that was starting and made my way home. There was no beginning or middle to my fall. The end was all of it: knees first then face to the sidewalk. I stayed as still as I could. Nothing felt broken, but everything hurt. My nose and jaw were throbbing, my knees felt as though they'd been hammered by an angry blacksmith.

People stepped around me. A few business types (I knew by their shoes and cuffs) chuckled as they passed. I tried to raise my head, but the pain prevented it. I wondered if I could stand.

A thin layer of ice was beginning to form on the nylon of my new coat which crackled any time I ventured even a slight movement. I concentrated on staying awake. My eyes focused on a small splatter of blood and I exhaled sharply as though I could hide it behind a cloud of breath. I explored my front teeth with my tongue. None of them were loose, but I tasted blood. It seemed as though I had been there for hours. In reality it was probably less than a half hour. All the while, they stepped around me. *Friendly, friendly Montreal*, I thought. *Friendly and classy.* I probably didn't need anyone's help, mind you. I just didn't want to get up. Finally, someone stopped. *Must be a tourist.* He wasn't.

*Monsieur? Êtes-vous mort?*

*No. Not dead yet.*

*You want to stand-up?*

*I suppose.*

He was older than me, but he was probably stronger, too. He pulled me to my feet and winced when he saw my face. He shook his head and mumbled some French patois I didn't understand. With a paternal tenderness, he brushed the icy crust from my back, straightened me out. People passing us averted their gaze when they saw my face. I figured that it must have looked worse than it felt.

*Can you walk?*

*Oui. Merci, mon ami.* I patted his shoulder and tried to look as grateful as possible, though part of me resented his kindness. The crazy part, I suppose.

He nodded. *OK. Salute.* He smiled his encouragement and turned to leave.

*Bonsoir. Merci beaucoup*, I said.

He waved without looking back. I watched him walk away and then hoped that I could do the same. I was weak and cold and so dejected I could hardly draw a breath. I looked down at my nearly dry outline on the sidewalk with its red accent and my first thought was that I could not face my mother. Whoever she was, she did not need anything like me tumbling into her life. Besides, if she had ever wanted to contact her first born, she would have done so years ago. I took the tickets from my pocket and tore them in two. I dropped the pieces and made my way home.

# { 6 }

The first conscious breath lit the furnace of my rage and I squinted at the midday light. My head was throbbing. Noticing the blood on the pillow, I felt my face to find the epicenter of the pain. It was in my chin, but the whole of my head ached. My legs ached, my back was twisted. Without thinking, I reached for the phone and dialed.

*Hello?*

*I think you're full of shit*, I told her. *It's my kid and I know it is. You just don't want me around.*

*Go to Hell, Spat.* She hung up.

I held the phone until I decided what to do next. I tossed it and went to the bathroom to inspect the damage. The bruise on my chin hadn't revealed all of its colours yet and there was a small cut in the middle of it. The left cheek and my nose were scraped up, the teeth were all right. The knees were bruised; my left palm had a scrape. All in all, it wasn't so bad. I smiled at myself, for a moment, almost laughed. Then I remembered the tickets. *FUCK!* I punched the wall and immediately regretted it all over. As I hobbled back to bed, I reminded myself (as I had so many times before) that I was, the biggest asshole taking up space on this planet. I stopped in the doorway of my Spartan bedroom and wept, briefly. That made me laugh. I eased my head onto the pillow and then passed out after whispering my age-old prayer to the world, *Go fuck yourself.*

+     +     +

I woke to the sound of the wind trying to peel the roof. It was vicious enough to make me get up and put on pants. Once I had gotten used to its ferocity and had seen the view from every window, I sat at the kitchen table. In the shaking streetlight, I rolled a joint. Self-pity crept all around me, its warm blanket open and waiting. I decided that the joint would put me back to normal and that a crawl through the gullet of despair wasn't necessary. I would call Linda tomorrow and she would fix everything. Then I'd get the visa and a new passport.

I lit the joint and went to the window that faces the alley. Everything had been lightly frosted and then blasted clean by the wind. There was no sign of life. I stared at the reflection of the joint's ember in the glass and tried to imagine my mother's face. I saw my brother as some slightly younger thing like me who didn't drink and worked in an office. I wondered what he would make of his Canadian sibling. Having never been the sort of ass who goes out of his way to please, I had to speculate as to what the criteria of likability might be. I heard a loud crack and felt bits of glass bouncing off my face. My eyes were closed. My first thought was, *You have not been shot.* Then, *Don't move.*

There was the coldness of shock through my body. My back was rigid. Heat pulsed from the middle of my forehead, despite the cold air blowing into the room. I wouldn't call what I felt pain. I opened my eyes. I had dropped the joint and it was burning the side of my right foot which carefully lifted itself from the floor. The wind was trying to fit itself through the apple-sized hole in the window. I could see the outline of my face in what remained of the ancient, rattling pane, but not well enough to know what was protruding from my forehead. I thought I could smell chemicals burning. Carefully, I made a small step backwards, keeping my face forward. A rill of blood fell in front of my left eye and onto my chest. A sympathetic tear on the same side followed it, but I held my breath. There were a few black drips in front of my eye, and then it seemed to stop. I turned, as slowly as my trembling legs would allow, and walked to the table. Keeping my head up, I sat and felt around for the scissors and a bud. I rolled quickly, forfeiting points for neatness.

Hands shaking, I smoked the joint and told myself that since I was still conscious, the damage couldn't be that bad. I failed to imagine what it was that had tried to get into my head. I wondered if a bullet fired from very far away could reduce its speed enough to pierce the skull, but not penetrate it completely. Maybe I had been only somewhat shot.

I stubbed out the joint and stood. I walked in slow motion to the bathroom. I remembered a Buddhist monk in a movie that Patty had made me watch who walked the length of a temple at that same pace. It was cool and boring. In the darkness of the hallway, I considered applying some meaning to the recent wave of accidental violence being done to me.

*Maybe it's a warning*, I thought, *to stay home*. I sneered at the notion and wondered, as I had for decades, why anything had to mean something else. Meaning doesn't increase value for those of us who don't accept it and I have never needed it to give mass to anything. Meaning diminishes reality by changing it to support the weight of connotation. It's a fearful blurring of the picture or else a retouching to satisfy the staid and sentimental. I just don't have the gullible mindset required to assemble it. If I were superstitious, everything could make sense; however, the randomness of the universe was always most apparent and so closest to truth. A few years ago, a brain at the library told me that he believes that there are others of us throughout every cosmos, living exactly the same life, doing exactly the same things, wondering about exactly the same shit. He tried to explain it, but I didn't get it. I felt somewhat comforted, though, by the idea that there were many Spats, light years away, having to deal with the same pointless garbage; lines of convergent evolution, weaving through the universe.

I faced the complete blackness of the bathroom and braced myself for the light. Positioned in front of the mirror, I told myself to count to ten. At nine, I snapped on the light. A bolt went through me when I saw the jagged metal in the dead center, just above my eyebrows. I leaned closer to the mirror and turned my head from side to side, but I could not identify the shrapnel that had lodged itself there. I dared to move my head a little faster and, gradually, in all directions. There was no jolt of pain to stop me. I tilted my head to the side like a puzzled dog and stared at the thin, jagged disk, wondering what it could be. I considered pulling it out, but I didn't want to deal with the mess and the pain that was sure to follow. Anyway, I had a more pressing question. I walked at normal pace, back to the kitchen, and dialed the phone.

It rang four times and Patty's recorded message started. It was interrupted by a loud click and her sleepy voice. *Hello?*

*Just tell me who the other guy is.*

*Do you know what time it is?*

*No.*

*Do you know what day this is? ... No. No, you don't, do you?*

*What day is it?*

*Never mind, Spat.*

*What? It's not your birthday. It's not—*

*No, there's no occasion, Idiot. I'm only pointing out that you don't know what day this is.*

I tried to think of it, but I really couldn't guess. It wasn't the weekend, but it didn't feel much like a weekday, either. Having no sense of time is the sole advantage of being unemployed.

*There is no other man, is there?*

*Oh, Spat, you're such an asshole.*

*It's a smoke screen. You just want to push me out of my kid's life.*

*If you're not the father, it's none of your business, is it?*

*But if I am—*

She hung up. I sat for a while, listening to the wind until it was too cold in the room. I got duct tape from the drawer and made a square of it to cover the hole in the glass. Looking out at the street, I scanned the distance as though there could have been a clue as to the origin of the metal in my head. Realizing that I was standing on bits of window, I stepped away and bent to brush the bottoms of my feet with my finger tips. I went back to the bathroom.

Gently, I touched the tip of the metal to see if there would be a sting. Besides the dull throb in my head from the fall on the Main, there was nothing. Without thinking, I snatched the shrapnel out of my face and let it clang into the sink. A thick line of red took the same path as before, over my left eye. A second ran down the side of my nose and to the right. I rolled toilet paper around my hand and covered the new coin slot in my forehead. I could feel it now. I went back to the kitchen and ripped two pieces of duct tape from the roll to make a square. I tossed the bloody toilet paper into the sink and grabbed a few tissues from the box on the fridge. I put the silver square of tape over the tissue and pressed it to make sure it was evenly attached. The gash sealed, I laughed out loud and was startled to not recognize the sound of my voice. I decided that I should sleep, but first, I had to wash the metal head accessory and inspect it.

At every angle, it was equally mysterious and threatening. It cut my finger without my realizing and I thought it best to be rid of it. I dropped it into the garbage, wrapped some toilet paper around my bloody finger and went back to bed. The wind howled to say, *That was just a warning.* I smirked at its vehemence and went quickly into a deep sleep as distant sirens began to wail, getting closer.

+    +    +

Cautiously, I peeled the duct tape bandage from my head. New blood appeared, but it didn't run as it had the night before. With a wet face cloth I cleaned the wound and the various other scratches on my face. A new bruise showed itself on my cheek and the one on my chin was now blue, yellow and green. There was a knock at the door. Though I had no reason to expect him, I knew that it was Hank. I dressed slowly, hoping that he would leave. When I got to the door, he was there with an envelope in his hand. He seemed less surprised by my battered face than he was at the mess of my apartment.

*It smells like the 70s in here*, he said and chuckled. *I used to smoke that stuff by the pound.*

*You want some coffee?*

*No, thanks.* He gestured to my face. *What happened?*

*I took a fall*, I said.

*Pretty bad fall.*

He sat and winced at the bloody finger prints on the table. His eyes roamed over the dirty glasses and scattered bits of weed.

*What brings you here, Hank?*

He didn't answer. He looked at me with that eternally accepting smile that Poppy had. It was impossible to imagine what Hank might have been thinking.

*Your forehead's bleeding*, he said. I took a few tissues from the box on the fridge and pressed the wound with them. Pressure stops bleeding. Finn taught me that the first time I had my nose bloodied by one of my fans.

*I thought I'd come by and see you … in case you want to stay down there.*

I decided to take the opportunity to get caught up. *So … You talked to Patty about my mother.*

He looked uncomfortable and I was glad.

*Well … I suppose I did … When you two were first married. Why?*

*She asked me about her.*

He didn't seem as afraid as he did the first time I asked him about his sister-in-law. I wanted to grab him by the sides of his head and split the table with his face. I wanted him dead, but in the silence, that wish had shrunk to unfocused hatred.

*You should try and get back with Patty*, he said. *She's a nice girl.*

I laughed hard, even though it hurt to do so. I wanted to remind him that he knew nothing about me, regardless of how much information he had about my missing mother. *Patty's a whore*, I said and smiled. That seemed to hurt him, so I was pleased. He took an envelope from his jacket and wiped a space clean on the table for it.

*I brought this for you.*

*What is it?*

*Some pictures. A letter.*

I didn't want to open it in front of him. I wasn't sure why. *If I punched him*, I wondered, *would his head burst like a water balloon? Probably*, I decided. Little walnut-sized brain would roll away, under the table. I stood very still. Everything was made of glass. Moving could have shattered it. Great slabs and shards of the glass world would come raining down and nothing would ever grow in the void left behind. The black hole universe.

*Spat?* He was gaping at me with that puzzled concern that always pisses me off. Even the norms hate that.

*What?*

*I said I want you to tell her something for me.*

I surmised, by his sour expression that I should have been showing some reverence for what Hank was about to say instead of imagining beating his brains in. I sighed and looked away to show him my disdain for that kind of grand-standing.

*What? What do you want me to tell her, Hank?*

*Tell her I'm sorry, but I'm going to rent a place in the Laurentians and spend Christmas there with some friends. Just tell her that for me, will ya?*

For a moment, I couldn't speak because there was simply too much to say. Seeing my mood darken, Hank folded his arms.

*Has she been coming here all these years?* My fists were tight and slightly behind me.

*What? No. That's just my message for her.*

*Did she invite you there for Christmas or—*

*No ... I haven't seen her for more than thirty years, Spat*. He wasn't lying. He looked lost.

*Have you talked to her? Recently?*

*Not for ages*, he said. *I'm glad you're going. It's long overdue.*

I liked him again. Just like that. Of course he wanted what was best for me. Why wouldn't he? Poor old Hank.

*Just give her that message for me, will ya?*

*I'll tell her. You want a toke, Hank?*

He laughed. I wanted him to stay. I was realizing how long it had been since anyone had come to visit.

*No, thanks*, he said. *I'll have a belt if ya got one.*

I found the remains of some gin and a couple of glasses. I sat across from him and considered how I would start a conversation with him without mentioning Poppy. Finn was listening, as he always was; sprawled across the ceiling, finally enlightened, maybe getting a kick out of our corporeal discomfort. I filled the glasses.

*Cheers*, he said and inhaled it, silently. I smiled at him, becoming unexpectedly fond of James Henry Ryan. Since he had such intimate knowledge of my beginnings, I wanted to know something about him.

*Tell me about your hands, Hank.*

*What?*

*Your hands ... and the stove.*

Slowly, his jaw lowered and his lips parted. He looked at me with amazement that grew to revulsion.

*How did you know about that?*

I didn't want to draw Poppy down by saying his name so I said that I vaguely remembered that he had burned them. It was too late. Before I could change the subject, Hank stood.

*My ...* His voice was gone. He swallowed and winced. He fixed his eyes on me with purpose. *My brother had a cruel streak*, he said. *But that wasn't the worst thing he ever did.* He seemed like an actor breaking character. He went to the door and finished his exit with a slam. I felt sick to my stomach for a few seconds. I told myself that Hank was blaming Finn for what Hank had done himself because he didn't want to look crazy. He was embarrassed. Hank was haunted. I reminded myself to avoid becoming like him as the clock runs out.

I picked up the envelope and considered it, briefly. I tapped it on the table to move the contents to one end and then peeled off the edge of the empty side. There were two black and white photographs, taken in the mid-sixties. One was on a beach. She was beautiful, dressed for a hot summer, holding a baby. It must have been me in her arms. No matter how closely I studied her face, it didn't seem to reach me completely. As much as I wanted to commit her to memory, part of me resisted even seeing her. There was a second picture of her seated next to Poppy, but he was blurred because he was standing up to leave as it was taken. She seemed to be deep in thought. She was half my age, a kid, with eyes like mine. I ran my finger across the picture's white, scalloped edges. At once, something had ended and something else had started, but I couldn't name either of them. I knew that soon, I would connect the missing pieces of my stupid life and things would make sense. I would stop being what I was.

The letter was in a small, pink envelope with matching paper. The tiny flowers printed on the back had faded, leaving only their outline. The edges of the envelope had yellowed and the return address was smudged. Dartmouth, Nova Scotia. I wondered what had brought her there. Maybe she was born out east. I didn't want to read her mail just yet. I studied the first picture again. She looked happy. Tired and happy. A drop of blood fell from my forehead and splattered over her. Immediately, I swabbed it off with my fingers and then wiped the photo on my shirt. I took a tissue, moistened the corner with saliva and carefully restored the image. Suddenly, her face seemed as familiar to me as my own. A sense of calmness came over me. I could not remember the last time I had felt that. Maybe I had only imagined the feeling to give the moment some relevance. I wanted it to be sacred, somehow. I opened the letter.

It was a single page, not quite filled with words that had been written slowly and carefully. A small drop of blood was inching its way into the corner of my eye. I dabbed it with the tissue and then pressed the wound in my head with the palm of my hand. As I read, I tried to imagine her voice. She was telling Hank about how the baby was doing. He was sick or something and she had been in the hospital with him for what seemed, to her, to be a long time. She told Hank that her Aunt, a nun, (of all things) had arranged for Ann and the baby to join her in a move to New Zealand. Ann had no one else in Nova Scotia and didn't want to be alone there. They probably hanged single mothers back then. She asked Hank to watch out for me, to make sure that I was well looked after, and to write with any news about me.

I stopped reading and stared at the table until my vision distorted. I could see her, young and scared, too immature to deal with what she had been given. She was sitting cross-legged on a bed, using a book for a writing table. I pitied her as much as I ever would anyone until I reminded myself that the letter was nearly forty years old. She signed her name without a closing, *Ann*.

The last item in Hank's envelope was an index card with her name, address and phone number on it. I considered dialing the number, but couldn't think of a single thing to say. Nor could I let go of the card. I decided to wait until the evening to phone her, that way, it would be morning where she was and she wouldn't have to lose a night's sleep wondering about her idiot son on the other side of the world.

*Ann*, I said. My forehead started to bleed again. I reached for the duct tape to make a new bandage.

+   +   +

I had started to call her several times during the evening, but I couldn't do it. I put the phone on the kitchen table and watched it like a sad vulture ogling a lame deer. I smoked a few joints, had a few drinks and listened to Maxinquaye twice. For an hour or so, I considered the worst case. If she hated me, I would get over it. After all, up to that point, she had been little more than a few vague images in my world. I had trouble convincing myself that her rejection wouldn't matter though, so I did push-ups to failure. That didn't take long. There was nothing I could do, no attitude I could adopt that would stop the stakes from rising. I tried to talk myself out of going, but knew that canceling was impossible. It had been decided. Anyway, I was due for a growth spurt.

That's how I ended up with Hitler—backing myself into a corner. I asked her to marry me in order to win a boozy argument about who was more committed to our doomed coupling. I just decided that it was what I had to do. If I had been honest, which was out of the question until very recently, I would have admitted that she was a drinking buddy with whom I had great sex. She was a good friend. When the novelty of the wedding and its spoils had worn off for her, we still liked each other well enough. I bided my time through the early part of it, perpetually baked and nodding in agreement to whatever she happened to be saying. I lied a lot, as though I were deeply in love and trying to keep her. She knew, a few years in, that she had picked the wrong man, so she only lied when it favoured her. Otherwise she spat bitter truths like, *You think you're it!* Despite all of the squabbling, there was no denying that we would never know anyone as well as we knew each other.

Patty made me swear, years ago, that I would never tell this secret, so here goes: When she was in her early twenties, she went out with her friends from school and got drunk. It was a blistering July night. Patty and her girls were causing a ruckus on a crowded terrace. She went inside for a fresh Margarita and ended up hitting on a guy at the bar. He was reading a newspaper, pretending to be oblivious to her. She wouldn't give up. She'd fuck him or else kill him to insure his silence. She was a predator and didn't mind making her objective obvious. She flashed the tits, gave his crotch a grab and stuck her tongue in his ear. It was a poem to grace, to subtly itself.

In a men's room stall, they used each other up, not even trying to be discreet. She rode him until they were exhausted and the news of their copulation had spread throughout the bar.

Two rounds without a condom. It was in the days before the plague had spread into the hetero population, as far as anyone knew. When it was over, he would not let go of her. She was moved by the way he held her on his lap, pressing his face into her moist skin. He didn't have the usual post-coital need to flee and that was new to her. She laughed and kissed the top of his head, deciding that he was, at least, worth talking to. She took his face in her hands and studied his eyes to be sure (as sure as anyone that drunk could be) and said, *If we ever have kids, promise me we'll tell them we met in church.* She and the man laughed and stayed seated together until a bouncer rapped on the metal door and told them to get out. When they stepped out of the bar, her boisterous friends applauded and then protested when she began to lead the man into the street. She hailed a cab and waved good-bye to them, mouthing words that the man couldn't see. In the cab, she told him, *I'm serious. Promise me you'll never tell anyone how we met.*

I've told lots of people. The would-be secret of how we found each other was, to my mind, the only interesting thing about us. I would remind her of it whenever she would adopt that rich bitch intonation that she used sometimes or spouted phrases that could only have dribbled out of her absurdly conservative parents. That was always her defense of them whenever I'd point out her family's bigotry and how she had been warped by them. *They're conservative!* She would say it in such a way as to suggest that it could not be helped, that it had befallen them somehow. The word "conservative" had always seemed like a polite euphemism for the word "cowardly". Any differences between their cluster and the rest of the world terrified them, so they built a cocoon of shit around themselves and painted it gold. *Life is change,* I would say. *That's why your creepy parents are so fucking creepy. They don't change.*

*You're just mean!*

*Touché ... They made you insane, you know, Patty.*
*Fuck off.*

Throughout my thirties, I was never off of my high horse. I felt it was my calling to repeatedly point out what was wrong with everybody. It was just one of my many charms, which is why I often thought that Patty should have stuck it out with me. For the fun of it. It wasn't boring when it was going badly. I miss the yelling.

Sitting at the kitchen table, absentmindedly crushing toast crumbs with a spoon, I realized that my thoughts had become divided between two women. Ann was a complete unknown and Patty was known far too well. Neither brought any comfort. I tried to focus on the baby but, out of the bath water, it did not yet exist for me. It was still just a tiny cloud of potential, approaching from far in the distance. I knew it was mine. If there were any doubt, she never would have told me about it.

+    +    +

I had weeks to wait for the face to heal well enough to have a passport photo taken. Linda managed to replace the ticket that I had told her had been lost and pushed the departure date back by a month. I tried to keep up a good front when I saw her, but I was preoccupied with the reaction the foreign half of the family might have to my impending arrival.

*Are you OK, Spat?*

*I'm good. I just had a fall.*

*Are you sure you're all right?*

*I'm sure. Could you put a rush on this somehow, Linda, I have to be somewhere.*

*Sure!* And she raised her eyebrows to sustain an air of efficiency as she typed. She glanced at my face, repeatedly.

*All I have to do is print it ... Is that duct tape on your forehead?*

I peed a little. Just a squirt, but it startled me and I began to dread some sort of middle-age bladder condition. I had forgotten about the square of tape on my forehead.

*That's what I said to the doctor. It looks like duct tape.*

*It's printing now.* She folded her hands and made a half smile.

If Ann didn't want to see me, I decided, I would go anyway and meet my brother. I would, at least, get a sense of who they are and find out if I had inherited any noteworthy diseases.

At about midnight, I surprised myself by grabbing the index card with her number. I dialed quickly. A woman answered and my heart raced. She said hello twice before I answered.

*Hello. It's ... I'm Spat. Spat Ryan.*

*Spat? ... Ann's son?* She sounded British.

*Yeah. Who's this?*

*I'm—*

The line went dead. There was silence and then a dial tone. It was a young woman's voice, I thought. A housekeeper, maybe. My phantom mother might have been rich. Maybe she had married money and had been living the high life all these years. I re-dialed.

*Hello?*

*It's me again.*

*Sorry about the telephone, Spat. We've been having a bit of a time with it.*

*Is Ann at home?*

*She's in Melbourne, I'm afraid. She'll be back on—*

Again, the signal was lost. Though our exchange was brief, I liked the woman's voice. She sounded familiar, friendly. I imagined her to be younger than me, with dark hair and a graceful frame; one of those long limbed women with olive skin who does yoga and likes Thai food.

It occurred to me that I could be anyone when I arrived there. Even if Hank had given them a warning, how hard would it be to insinuate that he might be getting crazy? I thought, briefly, about a health regime, getting into better shape before arriving there. I considered buying a suit, inventing a profession. The thought of how much fiction it would take to fill the blank spaces was sobering.

I considered phoning again, but decided to wait until I was sober. All night, I sat up, considering my story and how I would tell it to her. For a while, I watched the only lit window across the street. There was a couple, in their cramped kitchen, having an argument. I felt pity for them, whoever they were, and then envy. The night had been exhilarating and wouldn't allow sleep. That calming seriousness came down and made me feel relevant for the first time in years.

I went to the window with the bulging duct tape bandage. The sun was rising behind the grey gloom. Down in the yard across the alley, sparrows knocked snow from forgotten towels on a grinning line. The alarm to move cars before the plow was getting closer. In the alley, two men in somber clothes were walking; arms tight to the body, heads pitched against the wind. I stared into the wood smoke sky above them for a long time and considered the inexorable facts of my life.

After combing through the past for the root mistake, I had to accept that it might not exist and that my failings were only the natural result of countless bad choices. I didn't start out on a sour note, but my intended symphony was, in the end, a long-winded fart. I did not dare. Things had almost happened. There were clues and insights, from time to time, lost like keys.

I went to the bedroom and closed the blind to keep what was left of the night in. I fell into the bed and shut my eyes.

For the first time, autumn had come to the jungle. Not dead, but sleeping, once lush ferns and vines had faded to the colour of camels with veins of tobacco brown. The canopy had gaping holes at the top. The birds were gone. Where the dried, yellow leaves did not cover the ground, the earth was black and cracked. I was naked, standing close to a massive, vine-entangled tree. I listened, but there was no sound. I began to climb the tree because it seemed expected. It was not hard to do. As far up as I would reach, there would be another perfect branch. I stopped my climb on a wide, lichen covered limb. It was warm. I felt a faint pulse beneath the bark. I pressed it with a finger. To my amazement, it cracked like an egg shell. There was flesh beneath it. I peeled away enough of it to discern the abdomen of an infant. It was too frightening to stay up there any longer, but when I looked down, the branches I had climbed were gone. I stood and jumped to the earth. In mid-air, I realized that my legs couldn't possibly survive the landing. I shut my eyes, but I could still see the earth approaching. I titled my head back and thought the words, *Crash Test Dummy*.

# { 7 }

At the intersection of Cleveland and South Dowling Street, I pushed the walk button over and over and counted the slow, steady beeps. I could have built a house waiting for the light to change. Lingering in the heat, without sunscreen or a hat, I baked. The sudden summer and lack of sleep was nauseating. People seemed to be smirking at me as they passed in their reversed shit boxes. Maybe I looked too white or so much like a tourist that it was laughable. There were unexpected palm trees here and there and banana trees dominating the tiny front gardens of huddled houses. Bizarre birds with long, bow-like beaks picked at the grass in the park across the street. When the walk light appeared, a noise signaled the change for the blind. It sounded like the beginning of a bad techno song. When I came to Arthur Street, I stood for a moment and reconsidered what I was about to do. I stared down at the words "Look Right" that were painted at my feet. Eventually, I started down the narrow street that was lined on both sides with small, ugly cars. Each stone house had wrought iron gates on every door and window and the neighbourhood was silent. I came to the address Hank had given me and stood in front of the house, unable to move. After a minute or so, the front door opened and I walked away. A woman's voice called behind me. *Hello.* I didn't look back. She called out my real name and there was no doubt as to who she was. My heart was pounding and I felt as though I might pass out.

I kept on to Albion and up to Flinders, replaying her voice in my head. I decided to find a bar and followed the signs to King's Cross.

Porn shops, strip clubs and homeless addicts, were packed into the tiny sleaze district. I found a bar and inhaled a few Victoria Bitter's. I thought it was weird to name a beer after some anal-retentive, sexless monarch, even if she did smoke grass to relieve her menstrual pain. Seeing the old pothead's name on the bar taps, I wondered about the local weed prices and availability. More and more, as I drank the magnificent beer, I began to feel that going to the other side of the world was a mistake. I realized that I was in no way prepared to go back to my mother's house. What if she turned out to be some drugged-up piss tank with a foul mouth and a Men at Work record? I felt tightness in my chest. I decided to keep drinking and to postpone what was sure to be a disturbing reunion. I thought about Poppy and felt almost queasy with guilt. I knew that if I were to hear Ann's story, the memory of my father could be permanently altered, ruined.

Aussies like their beer and so I liked the Aussies. I chatted with a few early morning drinkers in the dim tavern and frequently struggled to understand what they were saying. To me, they sounded like British hillbillies, but I didn't bring it up. They seemed friendly enough, but indifferent, too.

I figured that I had not slept for about thirty-eight hours and everything had taken on the air of a vivid dream. The first flight from Montreal to Toronto went by in what felt like a few minutes. Toronto to Vancouver took about five hours after a three hour wait. From Vancouver to Honolulu was another five. By then, after an eternity on Screaming Baby Airlines, I would have been happy to take up residence on that island state and live out my life working in a poi factory. I stood opposite the angry smokers on a pedway and wilted in the thick, moist night. I surveyed the tropical vegetation in the quiet darkness and realized how far away from home I had come. The flight from Honolulu to Sydney was another ten hours. They kept offering food and shitty movies to distract us from the ruthless boredom and ass crunching seats. It didn't work. The exhaustion and tedium had transformed some small part of my shrinking brain. The sound of the crying babies blended with the rush of air and distant headphone tweeting to make strangely beautiful music. The fatigue gave me a welcomed mental distance from the world. I thought about Patty, wondered if she was all right.

Beyond weary and missing a day, we—the other zombies and I—descended over Sydney. Below us were bunches of brick houses, all but enclosed by trees. The city looked smaller than I had imagined. After the initial sight of it, it was just another tick in the feathers of the world: a momentary shield against nature, like any city.

A few minutes after we landed, we sat on the tarmac as flight attendants came down the aisles, opening all of the over-head compartments. An announcement told us about Australia's delicate environment and how it had to be protected from alien insects. The voice assured us that the chemical spray they were about to use was completely harmless. The insecticide was non-toxic and non-staining, we were told, so no one said a word. Of course it wasn't only the luggage being sprayed by the perfectly safe chemical mist. We sat, silently, while it fell over us. The insecticide had been given a sweet, cherry scent which only made it more suspicious. As we waited the required five minutes during which the tiny stowaways were supposed to die, I tried to hold my breath for as long as possible. My head was pounding, my back was rigid. Welcome to God's Great Garden.

Drunk and suddenly enjoying my over-seas adventure, I asked the bartender where I might find some weed. He eyed me for a moment and then said that I should meet his mate, Dick. *He'll be by 'round noon.*

I told the barkeep I would be back and set out to find something to eat. Walking in the heat, I began to feel every inch of the distance I had traveled. There was undeniable excitement, but my prudent dread kept it in check.

Sitting in Hungry Jack's, I had an urge to phone Patty. It would be night back home, I decided. By now, she had probably talked to Linda and knew the particulars of my trip. I didn't want her to worry, even though she would never admit to being at all concerned. After devouring a chicken wrap and fries, I went back to the room I had rented.

My hotel, The Mildew Arms, seemed to be operated by art students and reformed junkies. One of them, Brent or Brad or something, spouted as many Aussie clichés as he could through a tight smile.

*G'day, G'day! The sun's on, I reckon.* And he winced upward as though we were outside. I thought that only cowboys in movies used the word "reckon". I forced a grin and felt an unexpected pang of love for Canada.

+    +    +

When I woke, the sun was going down. My head was still throbbing and all at once, I knew what I had to do. I showered, changed clothes and started back to the house on Arthur Street. I would tell her, I decided, that I didn't hear her calling to me. I would be polite and civil, someone entirely new. I vowed to stay calm no matter what.

When I arrived at her door, I rang the bell and hoped that she had gone out. What if she had remarried? What if her replacement husband was a crusty old fuck with scales and webbed hands? The door opened.

Seeing her face, my plan to play it cool and my rehearsed greeting left me. I hoped that I smelled all right. She regarded me with what seemed like wonder, but there was an obvious air of regret. Her sad eyes opened and closed as they filled. I thought to myself, *I wanna go home.*

*Come in.* Her voice was faint. I couldn't speak. She led me to the kitchen where a beautiful woman with dark skin was frying fish. Ann introduced me to her, calling me by my old name. I shook the beaming woman's hand and said, *My name is Spat. Spat Ryan.*

Ann seemed puzzled by this, if not slightly wounded. She managed to smile. She was surprisingly familiar. She was about sixty, I guessed. She was dressed like one of those women who work at the health food store that Patty used to drag me to on Saturdays. The lines around her eyes betrayed a long history of concentration and confusion. Her grey and white hair was long enough to qualify as eccentric. Her skin had been browned by the Aussie sun. She had long since adapted. As the younger woman, Caz, grinned and invited me to sit, I began to plan an escape.

*Have you eaten, Spat?*

I shook my head no and wondered if it was fatigue or the beer or the climate that was making me weak. Ann began to cry, but fought it as best she could. She embraced me and held me as though I might get away. Sensing the awkwardness, Caz took over.

*Have a seat, Spat,* she said. *You must be knackered.* Ann released me and left the room. Caz whispered, *She's all right, Darling. Just a bit overwhelmed.* I wanted to run to the airport, empty my pockets and beg for a seat on the next plane out of there.

*Sit.*

While we waited for Ann to return, Caz and I ate the supper that I didn't want. It was delicious but, with every nerve in my body firing, impossible to enjoy. She asked about the trip, about the weather in Montreal. She seemed pleased by my arrival and assured me that everything was as it should have been. I stole glances at her breasts and her lips. She had deep, black eyes that failed to conceal a wicked sense of humour. She was about my age or a little younger. I wondered why Ann needed a housekeeper. Just as I was about to ask about him, Caz said, *Mick's sleeping. He's really excited about meeting you, though. Where are you staying, Spat?* I told her the name of the hotel and she nodded and smiled at me. She thought I was handsome. I could tell. She called to Ann, *Where are you hiding, Ann?* She grinned and winked at me. That was enough. Ann called for Caz. *Excuse me, Spat. Help yourself to anything, Darling.*

I wondered if she was flirting with me. I hoped. After a hushed argument in another room, Caz returned.

*Ann's having a hard time with all of this, Spat, as you can imagine. I mean, she's thrilled that you're here. Just a bit... emotional. That's all.*

*I should go,* I offered.

*No, stay and maybe Mick will wake up.*

I stood. I apologized and made my way to the door. It wasn't until then that I noticed the framed spiders all over the living room walls. Caz followed, assuring me that Ann was fine and that our next meeting would be better.

*I'm really glad you made the trip, Spat,* she said. *All the way from Montreal in one go. That was full on.* She smiled and shook her head.

*Thanks for dinner,* I said. I wanted to say more, but nothing came to me.

*You'll come back for breakfast,* Caz said.

I nodded and left her, making up my mind to never return. An explosion of rage made me shudder as I walked. Anything that my eyes managed to focus on developed a red haze around it. *Fuck you, you fucking bitch,* I thought. Walking faster, in the wrong direction, I stopped and vomited on the base of a tree that had bark like military camouflage. *Why did you come here?* I asked the question repeatedly, waking from the hope-induced dream. I could no longer imagine what the answer was supposed to be.

# { 8 }

Days could have passed while I slept. Birds, the likes of which I had never seen, were arguing near the window. I sat up in the sweaty bed and replayed my brief meeting with Ann, whoever she was. I turned on the TV and watched an American style morning show hosted by chipper robots whose banter was so dull, it became almost hypnotic. Then, suddenly ravenous, I showered, dressed and made my way down to the comically cramped dining room.

Bloated with a bad breakfast, I walked to the harbour. Tourists and locals alike seemed vaguely pissed about everything. Hung-over. Out of ideas, I paid way too much for admission to the aquarium. I made my way past gaggles of yelping children on a field trip, to a transparent tunnel in the shark enclosure. I watched them swimming overhead and wondered if they knew that they had been trapped. They seemed to be looking for a way out. Alive, but dead in the eyes, their every move seemed to have a malevolent purpose. *Misunderstood.*

I remembered going to the Biodome with Patty, once, when we were still friends. She had a laughing fit, watching the lone capybara sitting in its fake environment. The large, South American rodent seemed resigned to his fate and sat, motionless, in the center of its pen. Patty laughed until she cried and then became incensed that the animal was so far from home, separated from its own kind. When she settled, we took the metro home and didn't speak for hours. I suspected that the mood swings were about something other than the misfortunes of an over-grown rat. That was when she first started talking about procreation. I said nothing because I couldn't think of an acceptable lie. I didn't have to put my resistance into words. She knew. Like everyone, everywhere, she knew everything.

I wanted to phone her, to have a real conversation. I wanted to tell her that she wouldn't have to raise our child on her own. Meeting my mother seemed trivial when I considered that I was about to become a father. What was I doing on the other side of the planet, obsessing on the past when the future was about to burst? I decided to phone the airport to have my return date changed. *Tomorrow*, I thought.

Walking up Liverpool Street, I thought about Poppy and what he would have to say about the situation. I thought about the biggest secret and the horror of having to hear it from her. Ann could have many other truths, land mines waiting to bring me down.

Sweating, I sat at a table outside a gay bar on Oxford and drank until I had convinced myself that leaving was the wisest decision. The skinny bartender called me "Dear" and kept giving me my change on a small white plate. I played with the bloated coins and wept, quietly. It was less like crying than it was like leaking. The tears rolled down and I didn't bother to wipe them away. I wasn't embarrassed. I wasn't even interested in my own misery anymore. Though getting on a plane was the very last thing I wanted to do, I knew that it was the only sane option. At my age, what difference would it make to know the woman who gave birth to me? How would knowing more about my father change anything for the better? No one else seemed particularly attracted to reality, so why was I running toward it? I asked the bartender where I could get some weed and he brightened, considerably.

*Come with me, Dear.*

We sat on an old crate in the alley behind the bar and shared a joint. The bartender was talking non-stop, but I was tuning in and out. Time was dragging and the cement at the base of the bar's foundation had thin cracks in it that formed an ancient code. Just as trillions and trillions of accidents over billions of years had led to our existence, the cement just happened to be cracked with secret symbols that spelled out the greatest mysteries of the universe in three simple sentences. If I hadn't been so baked, I would have deciphered that code. The young bartender stopped his chatter and looked me over.

*You're not queer, are you, Dear?*

*No.*

*Well. Nature is cruel … What brings you to Aussie?*

*Business*, I said, hoping he wouldn't ask what kind.

*What kind of business?*

*I'm—I do freelancing*, I said.

He smiled at the vague lie and told me about a local DJ I had to see if life were to be worth living. He seemed happy; not just high, but truly happy. This made him look stupid in my eyes, but it was hard not to envy it. *I'll be happy when the baby's born*, I thought, nourishing the new truth.

*I don't know why I'm here*, I said.

*You don't need a reason, Baby. Have you been to the beach?*

*No.*

*Go to Bondi. Have a swim. That'll fix ya.*

The joint consumed, I stood and thanked him.

*No worries. Enjoy yourself, dear. That's why we're all here.*

I made my way through the alley toward Flinders Street and he called to me. *The beach, Mate!* I smiled back at him and nodded. I realized that I had left a full pint in the bar, but didn't want to go back. Starting toward the hotel, I felt grateful. My tongue was thick, my mouth dry. I stopped and stared at a sign outside a church that promised salvation to the people of Surry Hills. *Salvation from what*, I wondered. The stained glass was obscured by a mesh of rusted wire. It was hard to look away.

+    +    +

When I got back to the hotel, Caz was there, waiting. Immediately, I hoped that there would be sex involved, but I suspected that her intentions were not quite so pure.

*Sorry about the ambush, Spat. When you didn't come by for breakfast, Ann was ...* She decided not to finish her sentence and smiled, encouraging me to do the same.

*I'm going back to Canada*, I said. She looked as though she might panic and wrestle me to the floor to prevent my escape. I felt a stirring in my crotch.

*Try to understand. This is really hard for Ann. She's doing her best.*

*I don't care*, I said and immediately regretted it.

We stood there, silently, for what felt like ten minutes. I suppose that if I had really wanted to bail I would have gone to my room to pack. Instead, I waited for her to talk me into going back to my mother's house. I was disturbed by how I could want and not want something with equal intensity. I was embarrassed by the drama. Finally, she asked me to go back to the house with her and I agreed. Besides, I figured, now that I had a decent buzz on, it would be a lot easier.

As we walked, Caz told me about her admiration for Ann as though she were selling a candidate. *She's done heaps for my people*, she said. Before I could ask who her people were she explained, *I know I don't look it, but I'm a Blackfella. Aboriginal*, she clarified.

*Oh*, I said.

*I'm not pure, mind you. Dad was a Leb, but me mother was born in Cowra. She was Wiradjuri.* Though the local names meant nothing to me, I assumed that "Leb" meant Lebanese. In her country, political correctness had not yet grown a forest of euphemisms in which the freedom fighters and bigots alike could hide. Ann, she explained, became interested in native rights after her husband died.

*What was he like?*

*Dennis was all right. Bit stuffy. He was an entomologist.*

*That's bugs, isn't it?*

*Yeah. He was mad for bugs. After he died, we went through a rough patch. We were on the bones of our arse for a while there.*

*What does Mick do?*

*He does what he can. Our Mick is ...* She smiled and shook her head. *Well ... There's no one like him, really.*

When we came to the house, Ann was gone. Caz assured me that she would only be out for a short while.

*Come and meet your brother.*

In the second before she pushed open the bedroom door, a nervous jolt shot through me. Dread welled up and I didn't know why. When I saw him, that first time, I knew that my life would never be the same. He was sleeping, head cocked in an odd position, thin arms folded across his chest. His flesh was wasted; his skin was so pale it looked nearly translucent. His long fingers seemed almost fused and were cocked at strange angles. His dry, chapped lips were parted, drawing in shallow breaths. The bed was like a hospital bed, but wider, simpler. Next to it, there was a futon and on the other side, a small table crowded with pill bottles. An over-stuffed bookshelf loomed over him, an avalanche waiting to happen. I whispered to Caz, *What happened to him?* She tried to hide her shock and said, *Ann can fill you in on all of that.* Pretending not to know the things that I could not deal with was a standard response for so long, even I was unnerved by my performance. I felt my version of our shared history fall away. There was no more defense against that sickening truth. I wanted to get out of that room.

*We shouldn't disturb him*, I said. She didn't seem to have a response and bit her lower lip, watching my face for a clue. *Yeah*, she said, *Let's let him sleep.* A nervous malaise grew in my gut. My mind raced. I got quietly angry to avoid thinking too deeply. *What's going on here? What the fuck is this?*

I didn't hear Caz's words through the fog that had grown around me. By her tone, it was small talk. I made no effort to hear her. Ann returned with a bag of vegetables and bread. She smiled at me and said my real name.

*Please call me Spat.*

She nodded. She seemed more at ease than she had been at our first meeting. She embraced me and I hugged her back, playing along.

*You must have a million questions,* she said.

*A few.*

*Have you talked to Mick?*

*He's sleeping,* I said.

*He's not looking too flash, I reckon,* Caz said. *We don't really see it anymore. But he's fine, really. He is.*

Ann explained that Mick was getting over pneumonia, a common ailment for people in his condition. She spoke with the calm certainty of an expert who had seen it all. She led me to the kitchen. Caz made tea.

*I was sorry to hear about your father,* Ann said, and it sounded like something she had been meaning to say.

*Thank you.*

*I was always sorry that Hank couldn't* ... She lowered her eyes and swallowed hard to subdue her grief.

*Sorry that Hank couldn't, what?* I wanted to ask, but I had decided to let her do most of the talking.

*How is Hank?*

*He's all right,* I said. I remembered his message for his sister-in-law. *He wanted me to tell you that he's going to spend Christmas in the Laurentians with some friends.* Her lips parted and her eyes grew large. The change in Ann's mood was so startling, Caz turned to us as though her name had been called.

*When ... When did he tell you that?*

*Just before I left ... Are you OK?*

She went to phone and fumbled with an address book. Her hands were shaking.

*What's the matter?* Caz asked.

*I have to talk to Hank.*

Caz took the book from her, found the number and dialed.

*What's wrong?* I asked, with a little more urgency.

*I'll explain when ... I just need to talk to him.*

I tried to calculate what time, or even what day, it would be in Montreal.

*It's ringing,* Caz said and handed the phone to Ann.

Caz and I traded a look of bewilderment. With each unanswered ring, Ann became more distraught.

*Hank doesn't have friends in the Laurentians,* she said.

*So ... I guess he lied,* I said, shrugging.

*Years ago, we knew this girl.* Ann let out a short, anguished breath and tilted her head. *She was ... Anita had a lot of problems. Family problems. She was always ... battling this awful depression ... It was around Christmas and she told us that she was going to the Laurentians to spend the holidays with some friends. We knew it wasn't true, but we went along with it ... And she killed herself. I found her. She was ...* She focused on the phone. *There's still no answer.*

*Hank wouldn't ...* I thought for a moment.

*I'm the only one who would know what that message meant,* she said.

*No, I don't think he'd do that,* I said.

*Is there someone you could call to check up on him? Could Patty go by and see if he's all right?*

I couldn't think of a way out of it, so I agreed to phone Patty. She changed her surly tone when I told her that I was calling from Australia. She asked about Ann and I gave her short, positive responses. She kept saying, *I'm glad* and that was pissing me off.

*Listen, we need you to swing by Hank's place and see that he's all right.*

*Is he sick?*

*No, we just haven't heard from him. So go by and see him, will you?*

*OK. Give me your number there.*

While we waited to hear from Patty, Ann talked about Hank. She had obviously loved him. I worried that Patty would be walking in to find Hank's brains all over the walls. I would have never heard the end of it. Caz disappeared into Mick's room.

*Hank was my savior ... He wasn't like Finn.* She looked at me, her eyes serious, defying the ghost in the room. *I'm sorry.* She wasn't. *He was your father.*

I said nothing. Her beef with him, I told myself, was none of my business. Finally, she asked me what it was like, growing up with Poppy. I fought the urge to defend him and told the truth as I knew it.

*He was a great father. I loved him a lot.*

She smiled and said, *I'm glad.*

My thoughts drifted to the brother on the other side of the wall. I suppressed the urge to flee and swallowed what was left of my cold tea.

# { 9 }

We were in her cramped living room, discussing possible reasons as to why Patty had not yet phoned. I surveyed the framed insects that covered the walls. There were small deadly spiders, harmless spiders as big as hands, and tiny winged creatures too weird to be real. There were simply too many of the ugly fuckers behind too many panes of glass. I wondered why Ann didn't take them down when Dennis died. There were no family photos except for one loose, bowed photograph of Dennis and one of Mick and Caz in party hats.

*I could call Patty back,* I offered.

*No,* Ann said. She had resigned herself to Hank's demise, though I found it hard to believe that he was dead. He wouldn't have had the guts to end it himself.

*How was school?*

*School?*

*Did you like school?*

*It was ... fine.* I shrugged.

*You must have been...angry. You must have wondered why I left.*

*I hardly remembered you.* I wanted that to hurt, but then felt sorry for it. I dared to say, *I know why you left,* hoping that it would close the subject. She nodded.

*I had always planned to come back for you. Hank didn't*

*have the heart to steal you away from Finn. He tried once, but he couldn't do it.*

I was a little sick as I remembered sitting in Hank's car, near the mountain, wondering what could make a man cry. Though I didn't have a brother until a few hours before, I found it impossible to imagine stealing his son from him.

*Poppy loved me. He raised me the best way he could. I know ... It was different for you.*

*I was very young. We both were.* Ann went to a shelf and returned with an over-stuffed photo album. Seeing the school pictures, report cards and letters from Hank, I began to resent her. It felt bizarre and intrusive; seeing these flakes of my childhood, my sad evolution, sent around the world to a collector I didn't know. It was depressing to see the class photos. In each of them, I'm in the back, trying to disappear. It all looked worse than I had remembered.

*Hank sent me everything he could get his hands on.*

Something changed in my head. Small confessions rolled away from their newly opened compartment and out into the world.

*When Finn died ... I thought I might hear from you.*

*I wanted to,* she said. *I wanted, more than anything, to see you ... But I had no right ... I had abandoned you ... And I was afraid.*

*I was scared to talk to Poppy about you. Hank never said anything. You were a secret ... The worst kind.*

*I'm sorry.*

*Don't be. There's no point.* I meant that.

Her eyes settled on the carpet and she folded her arms.

*Is your life ... Are you happy?*

*No.*

*Me neither.* Patty called, finally. She told me that if Hank were at home, he wasn't answering the door. She said she'd go back tomorrow. Ann took that as proof that she was right about his self-deletion. This time, Patty could tell by my tone that things were uneasy in my mother's house.

*Are you all right, Spat?*
It was strange to tell Patty the truth. *No.*
*Stay until you work it out.*
*Are you OK?*
*I'm fine. I'm eating a lot.*
*That's good.*
The silence between us was slightly elongated by the delay in transmission, making it all the more awkward. I didn't want to hang up.
*Take care, Spat.*
The line went dead.

+  +  +

Over supper, Caz and Ann talked about their idiot government which sounded very much like the idiot government back home. There was a treaty called the Black GST which, if ratified, would acknowledge the slaughter of countless Aboriginal people and return their stolen land. Of course, the government had no intention of changing anything. Ann had been a local celebrity, known for her quotable jabs at the Prime Minister. She led rallies and protests, demanding that Aboriginal people be given control of the money intended to rescue them from astounding poverty, early death, blindness. *You have to fight the darkness*, she said, *or else you're just a hole in the world*. Ultimately, she wasn't fighting the seemingly indomitable racism, but a long-lived scam. White people controlled and pocketed most of the funds that were meant to repair many decades of damage. If Hank had managed to pull me out of the life I had with Poppy, I would have been on the front lines of that protest. I would have had a purpose and an accent. I told them about the day in 1990 when Natives outside Montreal were pelted with rocks and chunks of cement as they crossed the Mercier Bridge. Dozens of Police standing by, doing nothing, the shower of venom and stones poured down on cars full of Mohawk families. On the news, it seemed like an actual celebration of redneck supremacy. The story didn't seem terribly comforting to Caz and Ann already knew it. I regretted bringing it up.

This is a secret. I don't know why, but as the subject returned to Hank, part of me hoped that Ann was right about his message. The idea of his being dead was, somehow, comforting. One less witness, one less accuser, I suppose. It was a relief.

*What made you decide to make the trip, now, Spat?*
I considered how to answer Caz's question.

I asked Ann, *Do you remember Polly Beene?* She arched an eyebrow and nodded. *There's a name I haven't heard for about a hundred years. How did you know about her?*

*I met her on the Main one day.*
*I'm surprised that she's still around.*
*She's not*, I said. *She died.*
*Oh.* Ann continued eating.
*Anyway. She told a lot of stories about the old days. About Poppy.*

*Right*, Ann said. Clearly, she wasn't interested in hearing about it.

*I thought … that maybe you could fill in some of the blanks.*
*About Mick*, Ann said, without looking up from her plate.
*Yeah. About Mick*, I said, my voice waning.
*He must be awake by now*, Caz said.
*I can't …* I didn't want to offend, so I tried to sound a bit wounded. *I can't talk to him just yet.*

I pretended not to notice the look exchanged between the two women. If Patty were there, she would have driven the conversation, keeping everything within the margins. I missed her more than I had ever thought I could.

*What do you need to know?* Ann's voice had deepened somewhat. She wouldn't look at me. I had no words. A faint voice called from the bedroom. Caz stood, immediately.

+ + +

Ann held my arm as we entered his room. Mick stirred and smiled a crooked smile at me. I tried to smile back, but I couldn't manage it. I couldn't move. He mumbled my old name and raised a hand.

*Call him Spat, Darling*, Caz said.

Ann nudged me forward. I approached him and took his frail hand. My face was wet. His eyes searched mine as though they were reading a report, getting caught up on what had happened.

*He's tougher than he looks*, Caz said. *Just when we think he's gone for all money, he comes roarin' back.*

I sat on the side of his bed and cried like an asshole over everything that could have been and wasn't. He squeezed my hand harder and I was surprised by his strength. I turned to see that Ann and Caz had gone. The door was closed. I lurched forward, stunned by a surge of grief. I lay next to him and neither of us said anything. Language could not have contained it all. The child I hardly remembered was closer to me than any other person. It was as though I had only then realized how lonely I had been. I had lived for both of us, I thought, while he wasted away. I imagined that he would have killed to have half of what I had squandered. I shut my eyes as tightly as I could and tried to hold my breath, but there was no stopping that flood of despair. His voice rose like a wisp of smoke from his delicate body.

*It's all right, Spat.*

+     +     +

When I woke, Mick was sleeping and the house was silent. I went to the kitchen and spotted Caz in the backyard. She was reading. I went out and sat across from her on a wicker chair that tilted left and creaked with the slightest movement. A trio of strange birds perched on the fence.

*Poor Spat*, she said and pressed her lips together. *It must be hard.*

*Do you know how ... Do you know what happened to Mick?*

She nodded. *You didn't talk about it, did you? With Mick, I mean.*

*No.*

She seemed wholly relieved. I realized that he had never been told. I was too exhausted to be suitably incensed and was still averting my gaze from the biggest secret. I was about to tell her that he had a right to know everything, but Ann arrived home with newspapers.

*We're out here,* Caz called. The birds flew away. *I'm going to check on Mick.*

Ann took Caz's chair and folded her hands across the papers on her lap. The sun was setting.

*Patty hasn't phoned?*

*Not yet.*

She thought for a moment and said, *I should tell you that I had planned a trip to Canada when Finn died.*

*Oh?*

*I almost made it, but Mick had a fever.*

*It was a small funeral,* I said. *No one came.*

We said nothing while, inside, Caz's laughter filled the house.

*Your father ...*

I braced myself. She smiled the way people do when they're feeling sentimental.

*On the street, his loyalties could change in mid-sentence. He always took the easy way out ... so he could never dominate as much of his world as he wanted ... But he wore a suit well. Good disguise for ...*

She realized that she had gone too far.

*For a thug,* I said.

*I'm sorry ... I know he'd been in an accident, but he had a heart attack, didn't he?*

*No. When he was hit by the car, they gave him the wrong meds in the hospital ... and his heart stopped.*

She winced at the old news and I hoped that she would cry; that she had some remnant of love for my father. Instead, she thought for a long time and said, *Poor Finn.*

The way she said it suggested that he was better off; a mad dog put down for its own good as well as ours.

+    +    +

Both Caz and Ann had gone out when the call came. Patty had talked to one of Hank's neighbours. There had been no funeral. Hank, the stupid fucker, had swallowed a mixture of old medications and then phoned the couple next door to drop over for a drink. As per the directions he had left in a note, he was cremated and swept out of the world without a fuss. The neighbour had given Patty the number of the lawyer who was handling the will. I wanted no part of it.

*I'm really sorry, Spat*, Patty said.

*It's all right, I told her.* It was.

*How long will you be there?*

*I'm coming back in a few days*, I said.

*OK.* She said nothing about getting together when I got home. She couldn't say much more without sounding connected to me. Though her tone had been sympathetic, I knew that she would revert to her usual spite as soon as she saw me again.

After hanging up, I remembered drinking with Rob and Linda during the ice storm. The city was frozen and thick layers of ice covered everything. Huge sheets of it slid from buildings downtown, all of the trees bowed as if to show their submission and then many succumbed to the weight of the rime. After a few days, pumping stations failed and we were without water. Fires, hypothermia and the trauma of it all took twenty-eight lives. Thousands of us went without power for more than a month.

Rob and Linda had us over for a barbecue. Both were pack rats by nature and had enough bulk food to last until spring. The shrubs in their backyard looked like a tangle of glass cables and Patty kept saying how beautiful it was. Linda and I went inside to search for candles in a box of Christmas decorations.

When we returned without them, I wasn't sure, but I thought that Rob had his hand on Patty's ass. I said nothing, enjoying the tension and a brief stroll across the moral high ground. Rob talked too much and too loudly, covering something to which Linda was oblivious and by which I was, strangely, pleased. Suddenly, Patty was like me. It made me appreciate her more, though I wasn't absolutely sure of what I had seen. I could have imagined it.

The four of us refused to give in to the fear and frustration of the winter's attempt to smother the city. We stayed drunk, stayed high and waited for the thaw. When it was over and the power was finally restored, a weighty sadness silenced us for days.

Caz and Ann returned home with bottles of wine and beer. I told them that Patty had called.

*He's dead, then?* Ann was still, readying herself for the news.

*Yeah. I'm sorry.*

Her eyes were unfocused. She leaned on the table and shook her head. Her voice was weak when she whispered to Caz, *I have to tell Mick.*

Caz winced at the idea and folded her arms. *I don't know, Ann.* She was barely audible. *Is there really any need?*

*He has a right to know his father's dead.*

I felt my face flush. A sharp ringing filled my left ear. For a second, I saw myself beating Hank into a pulp.

Ann caught my eye and realized that she had revealed a truth that would eventually make sense of everything I had been dragging behind me for decades. I drew a deep breath and left without a word.

# { 10 }

A beautiful girl in a wet suit, surfboard under her arm, waited for a bus on Pitt Street. I decided to wait for the same one. I looked forward to seeing the beach. As I lingered near her, I wondered how sweat-stained my shirt was. She was probably too young for me chronologically and too old for me emotionally. This was, and probably still is, true of any woman who ever made me want some.

*Hey*, I said and did that stupid, simultaneous head nod that I used to do. She ignored that, but gave me the sideways glance to judge my distance from her. I wondered what I looked like and watched my reflection in a car window, as it passed. It wasn't a good enough look to judge the scum level, though. When her bus came, I had already considered every approach and rejected all of them. When the bus pulled away with her on it, I walked, for no particular reason, to George Street.

I stopped at a sunken pub with a street level window where I watched the monorail and imagined flamboyant disasters. I drank fast and kept the seal around the mental hatch against which my family members, living and dead, were crashing. I resisted well into five pints of beer, but it was impossible not to envision Ann and Hank's guilty pairing in the sixties. If you fuck your brother's wife and there are no hallucinogens involved, there's more than simple lust at work. Did they hate

Finn that much? *Fuck you, Hank,* I mumbled to myself. In a single moment, my long lost brother had been demoted to half-brother and my mother bore yet another red X on the record that all we obsessive types are keeping. A few more pints and I wondered if they actually loved each other. It could have been entirely one-sided. Ann had a husband and a life here, while Hank had nothing but his money. Maybe he had been waiting, all those quiet years, for her to come home.

Like all well-intentioned liars, I decided, my mother and Hank had their reasons for letting the fiction continue for decades. With time, though, all of the reasons expose themselves as the excuses they've always been, so why fight it? The truth hovers, following and accusing, a rare constant in the ever ending dance. No one gets away with anything.

Drunkish, I made my way back to the King's Cross. The atmosphere seemed familiar and safe, now. It was getting dark and the pressure was off. Another day down. I picked the wrong bar and met Dave.

*Pot of good cheer for your brother, Mate!*

*What?*

*I'm just a Westy with a hops deficiency, Mate. Not the full quid, I reckon, but who among us, eh?*

*What?*

*You a Yank?*

*Canadian.*

Hearing this, he opened his mouth as wide as he could and growled until he laughed. He patted my shoulder and shook my hand.

I mumbled, dutifully, *Can I buy you a beer, man?*

He didn't waste time by signaling the affirmative. Instantly, he was seated beside me and calling for the bartender. I knew Dave would be hard to shake; a human barnacle whose mug repelled soap as well as it did the razor. He was probably in his forties, but he could have been younger. His facial features were bunched together around a sharp nose and his clothes might have been found in a dumpster. His drinking character—the comical rogue with nothing to live for—was so deeply rooted in the immediate, that it gave him the air of a young child.

*Canada's fuckin' cold, I reckon.*

*In the winter*, I said. *Yeah.*

*What brings you to paradise?*

*I'm a hit man*, I told him and he seemed delighted by that.

*For the Mafia?*

*Yeah.*

*I didn't think Canadians killed people.*

The bartender delivered a couple of VB's and Dave's grin was so wide, his skin stretched into folds under the strain.

*Who's the target? It's not me is it?*

*Not yet*, I said. He laughed hard and pounded on the bar. He thought, seriously, for a moment and then declared, *Murder's not really worth the aggro, is it? It's a thief's life for me. Nick what you need. Live, let live. I'm a bit of an ear-basher, I should warn ya.*

From what I could understand of our conversation, Dave was a chronically unemployed iron worker whose entire family had been killed in a fire several years before.

*It freed me! It freed them! We all got what we wanted. That's the horror of life. We all get what we want, Mate.* His glib remembrance of those he had lost seemed genuine and so all the more unsettling. He threw an arm around my neck and yelled for the barkeep. His flimsy grip made me feel as though I were made of marble. I must have been drunk because nothing about Dave was getting on my nerves. The beer kept coming, I kept paying and Dave became increasingly incoherent.

*Bloody old, bloody bludger. That's what they'd call me, now. Been gone for yonks, though. Hardly remember them ... I'm a man of simple means, Spat. It does not mean that I am a simple man.*

*Right on*, I said and decided that I had had enough. When he went to take a piss, I considered ducking out, but the bartender got chatty.

*You gotta watch Dave, Mate. He's a bloody nuisance. Steal the nuts off a tiger.*

*He's all right*, I said.

*No, Mate. He's a skater.*

Just as I had decided to bolt, Dave returned with a wet face. He was shaking water from his still dirty hands. I wondered what a skater was in the local vernacular. Dave shoved his hands under his arms to dry them and smirked at me. *Can't polish a turd, I suppose.*

I made my way to the men's room which smelled like summer in the slaughter house. Shiny dots of urine spotted the floor. I chose the least offensive stall and pressed the button to flush the toilet with my foot. A toilet should have a handle as nature intended, but everything down under evolved in isolation.

As I approached my seat at the bar, Dave was taking a swing at the bartender. As the brawl erupted, I walked into the bustle of the street where rowdy packs of students whooped and chanted gibberish. Something about football, I imagined.

Walking back to the hotel, I had two offers for a fist fight and declined them both. It made me feel young again, just being asked.

*Sorry about all that, Spat.* He was behind me. *Had a bit of a blue with Tom so we can't go back, I'm afraid.*

*I'm done for the night*, I told him.

*Pish posh*, he said as a drop of blood peeked out of his right nostril. *I know a place we can go.*

*I'm done, Dave.*

*Come on, ya big poofter!*

*I'm done.*

*I'll tell ya me life story and leave out all the true bits. Come on!*

*Fuck off.*

He took my arm and tugged. I suppose that I was drunk enough to be led anywhere by anyone, but being with a mongrel like Dave made me feel closer to sober and, when I dared to look at him, nearly respectable. I was the sensible one.

*There'll be tits*, he promised. *Besides, it's your shout.* I had no fight left. We stumbled, together, down into a strip club that couldn't have been more humid if it were underwater. The stairs were so steep that it was less like walking than it was like falling vertically. There were men, hostile strays, here and there. Their eyes remained fixed on the strippers, even as they walked or drank. They seemed to be entranced less by the show than by their own reverie. Two women danced on the blue translucent stage in G-strings and enough make-up to cover both ends of a rhino. The blaring, shitty pop music was giving my stomach a turn, the bass pressed into my gut.

Hands shoved into the pockets of his jeans, Dave stared up at a bored goddess who slashed the air with a riding crop. Drool glistened at the corner of his startling smile and he seemed to have an even more objectionable odour than before. But, there were, as he had promised, tits. A gruff doorman with the arms and probably the wit of Popeye gave me a warning.

*I'd think twice about the company I keep, Mate.*

I slurred something in response and made my way to the bar where the doorman's identical twin was waiting. I wondered, for a moment, if I were hallucinating but decided that it made no difference. I was out to obliterate.

A new dancer, dressed in a red rubber bra, a red holster and tall, transparent heels tiptoed onto the stage. She had trouble keeping her balance and clung to the pole. Concluding that the floor was a safer place to be, she squatted and then leaned forward on all fours. She did the classic cat skulk to the lip of the stage, losing one of her plastic shoes on the way. Dave stood, knocking his stool over, and applauded.

*They'd have to burn me off of that. Bloody hell!*

*Sit down, Dave.* The bouncer was not to be fucked with and it was apparent even to the remains of my new friend. The evil twin waited for an excuse to pound on him, but Dave knew better than to start something. He offered no resistance. The bouncer wandered back to the door, keeping an eye on us.

The music mutated with my vision. The spots of light sprouted long, fading tails. Fragments of memories, lies and curses fell like volcanic ash in my head. My thick blood slowed its progression and my skin melted. I threw my head back and laughed. My muscles tensed and I could hardly breathe. I focused on a single light, keeping my head still so that the speck of illumination would not sprout a tail and get tangled in the others. Gradually, I stopped laughing and my shallow breaths became deeper.

Dave had leaned against the bar, facing the stage. His bent cock in his hand, he stroked it as though he were scraping rust from a pipe. His eyes were fixed on the woman who was subtly signaling to the bouncer for Dave's removal. The evil twin, who had stepped outside, was back and moving fast. He grabbed Dave by the back of the head and his enormous hand squeezed the skater's greasy hair into a tight clump. By the time I stood, the bouncer was already at the bottom of the stairs. Dave was screaming like a rabbit in a snare, struggling to put his works away. No one seemed to notice as the doorman dragged the unwanted customer up to the street with one hand. I followed, struggling to keep my balance on the narrow steps.

On the sidewalk, Dave took pathetic swings at the younger, bigger man who held him by the throat. The gurgling growl that issued from his clenched neck almost reignited my laughing fit.

*Let him go*, I said, calmly. I was sure that he would comply.

*Rack-off, ya fuckin' Yankee shit.*

*Yankee!* I felt my fists grow heavy and the old chain on my hostility begin to break. Before I could come to his rescue, Dave had managed to get hold of the bouncer's balls. He squeezed as hard as he could while the huge man folded in two. His arm caught, nearly eye to eye with his enemy, Dave laughed nervously. He tugged his hand from the vice of muscle that had formed to protect the jewels and ran. Watching him go, I was amazed by his energy and relieved to be rid of him.

As I staggered in the direction of the hotel, I became so tired so quickly, I had to fight the urge to curl-up under a hedge or stretch out on a bench. Everything was a bed.

About an hour had gone by when I realized that I had taken a wrong turn. Having no idea where I was or how to get to my hotel, I sat on the side of the road and tried to think of a game plan. My eyes longed to close and my head was heavier by the minute. Sleep began to coil around me and I could not resist.

+    +    +

Poppy used to give me an orange every morning, sliced into wedges. He made oatmeal with brown sugar and toast that was always darker on one side. I would watch his hands and listen as he sang sweetly dirty songs or else shared another chapter of his childhood. He softened the jagged edges of his early life and fictionalized the worst of it until it was an adventure story suitable for a child. It wasn't until long after his funeral when I realized that altering his history was as much for Poppy's own peace of mind as it was for my entertainment. He was replacing his memories, filling the black cracks in his morbid youth with light. Even when the memories contradicted each other or sounded completely implausible, I accepted them as truth. Of course, I knew some of the real story. I had overheard him talking with Hank more than a few times. Once, they had been through a flat of beer and Poppy recounted the story of the day his mother had tried to drown Hank in the bathtub. Poppy pulled her arms from the back of the struggling boy's head and was able, at age nine, to drag her from the bathroom and lock the door. He put a towel around Hank and they waited for her to fall asleep. So they wouldn't think about being hungry, Poppy made-up a song. When he began to sing it at our kitchen table, keeping time with a stomping foot, Hank let out a cry of recognition and laughed until he wept. He said that he didn't remember the attempted murder, but knew the song from start to finish. It was about a rat that had lost its tail. The melody left much to be desired, but the lyrics were clever. Poppy was a clever man. He had to be.

I thought of the daily orange when I woke up under a bench on Bourke Street. There was a white flower a few inches from my face that had an orange center. My brain was pushing against my skull, bloated with unwanted information and poison. As the morning light pierced my eyes, I could not shake the image of Ann and Hank together. My thoughts, angry wasps in a jar that they would never escape, were moving so fast it was nauseating. I wanted weed and wondered if I could find my generous friend on Oxford. I stood as slowly as possible and my skull contracted, adding to the strain.

I walked to Liverpool and up to Oxford. I couldn't remember which place had the bartender with the dreamy weed. After several passes, I gave up and went back to my room.

There were messages from Caz, an invitation to dinner. I splayed on the bed and considered the situation. I didn't really know those people on Arthur Street. What was the point of getting to know them when I would probably never see them again, anyway? It was unlikely that they could travel with Mick so there was faint hope of them ever coming to Canada. If Ann came alone, what would we do to fill the time? My mission to meet her was over. We didn't like each other. I phoned and had the return ticket changed for the day after next. This would give me time to buy something for Patty and to track down a toke. Maybe have a swim. I undressed and turned on the shower. The phone rang.

*Hello?*

*I'm sorry I blurted that out about Hank and Mick. I thought you knew.*

*It doesn't matter, Ann.*

*Of course it does. I'd like to explain.*

*There's no need.*

In the silence that followed, I began to remake her in my head. She was a manipulator, a cheat. She used her sorry past for sympathy and had used anyone she had ever met. How long before I would become one of the servants? What was she paying Caz? Nothing? She probably took care of Mick in exchange for room and board. And what about Dennis the bug man? He must have left her something.

*You look like your father, but you're definitely my son.*

*How do you figure that?*

*You're stubborn like me. You can hold a grudge.*

*What is it you want?*

*Come for a walk.*

Hung-over and getting hungry, it was the last thing I wanted to do. I thought about Patty for a moment and what she would suggest for an answer.

*I'll be over in an hour or so.*

+   +   +

Three hours later, as we strolled in Moore Park, Ann told me about how her romance with Hank had started. She'd been fighting with Finn about his drinking and he had hit her. It was the first time that had happened and the shock of it sent her into the street in her housecoat. Hank had a small apartment in Verdun at the time. She took a bus there to hide out.

*Hank was gentle. He was ... I loved him. You understand that, right?*

I didn't care. It was eons ago and it didn't concern me, but I kept up my side of the discussion out of courtesy.

*So why did he stay in Montreal while you were here?*

*He had to. He had to watch out for you.*

I scoffed.

*If I had gone back, Finn would have killed me. I was afraid. And we were both afraid to leave you alone with him.*

*I doubt if it was as serious as that.*

She stopped and studied my face.

*Do you know what he did for a living?*

*Yes.*

She said nothing more for a while. We continued our walk to nowhere. I watched a man chasing a dog, running in circles near a cube of public toilets. The dog's bark sounded like choking.

*I don't understand you, Spat.*

I liked that she called me by the name Finn had given me. It pleased me until I felt the distance growing between us.

*What's to understand?*

*Finn was a violent man. If it wasn't for his temper, none of this misery would have—*

*I know*, I said, before she could finish.

Again, we said nothing for a while. I watched the palm trees near the road and felt homesick. Out of nowhere, my defensiveness rallied.

*Hank didn't watch over me, Ann. I hardly ever saw him. He sent you my report cards and pictures and shit because he loved you. Not me.*

*Spat—*

*It's true. Me and Poppy were happy. Hank was just ... He was nothing to me.*

That hurt. She watched me for a moment. I imagined that she saw only Finn in my face.

*Caz wants you to come by for supper.*

With that, she turned and walked home. I watched her go and resisted my regret. I realized that the cliché about mothers and guilt must have been true. Hadn't she suffered enough?

Lying in the field, I watched the sky clouding over and wondered what normal people would do in my circumstances. I had no idea which of us was in the right, but I suspected that none of it mattered. I stood and walked in the direction of the harbour. I wanted dog hair and weed. I wanted sex and I wanted meat.

+   +   +

A young lesbian couple in the corner of the Maggio Hotel Bar were enjoying the scowls from a table of nearby business types. The necking women were all in black with dyed black hair and black fingernails. They made a big show of their love, moaning, wagging the tips of their tongues together. Clearly, they were tickled by the hetero chill in the air. I was in love with them, getting normal with a pint in the corner. I fantasized that they were bisexual and that the three of us could spend a few hours bridging the gap between our worlds. One of them glanced at me and said something to her partner who turned and took a long look. I smiled at her and she smiled back. They giggled and continued their show. I was an old pervert, I supposed, but it was impossible to give up on the dream of a three-way. I was hard, ready for anything. I tried to look as though I were staring out at the street, lost in thought, while repeatedly glancing at the giggling women. The one facing my direction caught me and alerted her mate. They laughed and waved a little. I smiled broadly and waved back. This inspired sneers from the suits. They were just about finished their lunch. There was something quaint, almost cute, about their supposedly moral indignation. Old before their time and angry at the world, they enjoyed the elevation they felt in their disgust. One called to the gothic dykes, *You belong in a brothel! Why don't you go find one?* This, of course, was met with more laughter and more exaggerated gestures in the Sapphic performance. Hard as a rock, I squirmed on my wooden chair, trying to adjust for comfort. Nothing worked.

Eventually, the irate suits made their way out, smug in their jealous outrage. I felt pity for them, but it was that sort of half-hearted pity offered up for far distant disaster victims and the long dead.

The giddy women took the table the business crowd had occupied and smiled at me. *I thought they'd never leave,* the more buxom of the two said. I raised my glass to her. Her friend sighed and stretched out, slouching on a newly vacated chair. It was the table with the best view of the outside. I was disappointed when the glorious brats turned their back to me and focused on the street. The show was over.

I ordered more beer, feeling the smog of sadness coming down. Without warning, my thoughts became stuck on Mick. Poor Mick. I tried to imagine his life in bed, the world through his eyes. I wanted to die. This mood swing made me queasy. I was finished. It was time for me to be erased from the nonsensical equation; the one that we all suspect has a solution of zero, anyway. I let that sink in, even as the future baby back home was pulling me back into the world. I needed to talk to Patty. I downed the beer in my hand and ordered more. Hard-on gone, I stared at the table and felt my will to live evaporate even further. I wanted to feel rage, but could not revive it. That was a first.

The more I drank, the more sober I became. I felt the scar on my forehead and thought about the metal surprise that had exploded through my kitchen window a little more than a month ago. The accidental part may have been my survival. I had missed my stop and now the train was going somewhere I was not supposed to go. Had the mysterious projectile penetrated my brain, all would be as it was supposed to be. If I had sustained that brain injury and lived, though, I would have been like my half a brother: waiting for the end of my sentence, dreaming away the endless days and being grateful only for sleep. That curious accident, like everything else in my jerry-rigged existence was an almost. I was an unintended chemical flare-up and I had no doubt that my extinction would go all but unnoticed. Knowing just how imperceptible and trivial I was, I shut my eyes and called for another glass.

I remember the largeness of the hand on my back as I was shoved out into the night. I don't know what I had done to get myself thrown out of the Maggio. I remember laughing, so it must have been something crass. A man in a black suit was pointing at me and shouting, telling me to never return. Finished threatening me, he went back inside and the door closed. I looked to the table where the cool women had been, but it was full of wincing tourists now.

I was sweating and staggering, looking for a place to sit before the long walk back to my rented bed. I found a bench where a homeless man was smoking a cigarette. He repeated the same phrase to me several times, but his words seemed to be coming out backwards. I shook my head and fought to keep my eyes open. As pounded as I was, I knew that if I didn't stand I would be there until morning.

Defying spiteful gravity, I stood and thought about which direction to take. I recognized, albeit vaguely, a canopy over a kiosk that I had seen earlier. I walked toward it, focusing on my balance, trying to keep a steady pace.

After what seemed like hours, I was in the familiar neighbourhood. I stood at the top of Arthur Street and thought about Mick. I wanted to tap on his window and tell him everything that was swimming around in my head. Even if he could not understand what I told him, in my liquefied brain, it was a great idea.

Climbing the fence was harder than I thought it would be. I landed with a thud and laughed. I heard a woman's voice—not speaking, but moaning. It was Caz. On a date, I thought. I was jealous, of course, until I realized that her voice was coming from Mick's room.

Approaching his window, I felt my stomach clench. The image was so shocking that I felt a physical jolt. They were naked. She was straddling his thin body, riding him. Using him. I backed away from the window and into the fence as she let out an ecstatic growl and then pushed out a series of progressively softer breaths. In the corner of the garden, I tried to be quiet as I emptied the contents of my stomach. I covered my ears and shuddered. I scrambled back over the fence and vomited again. I tugged at my hair, briefly, as though I could pull the image out of my head. Trying to sprint, I stumbled, fell, and immediately stood again. The earth sliding from side to side, I ran as best I could. When I got to my room, I struggled with the key and could do nothing to stop my hands from shaking. I sat on the bed and felt something I could not name. It was a disturbing amalgam of fury, pity and shame. I sat silently for a long time and wished for my heart to stop.

# { 11 }

Before the knock at the door, I knew who was on the other side. I stayed perfectly still and waited for her to give up.

*Spat? ... I know you're there.*

Did she? Or was that a classic trick that mothers use? I had no way of knowing. The maternal world was still a sad mystery. As a young child, I endured frequent phases of silent envy whenever I saw other boys with their mothers. Most of those women seemed so impossibly kind and yielding, I would become mute if they spoke to me. I reveled in their sympathy. I loved breaking those hearts and being, for however short a time, one of their own. They could tell mine wasn't dead. She simply ran off and left me in those clothes, with that unkempt hair. As I got older, of course, all of that changed. I was the bad influence, coming to introduce their now gangly joy bundles to beer, weed and cunnilingus.

The knocking continued, getting louder each time. A massive *fuck off* yearned to blow past my tight lips, but I held it in. I was still raw with the horror of what I'd seen. I was thankful for having been as drunk as I was at the time. Sober, the image of it could have shredded me. I shuddered at the memory of his white skin, his frail limbs and the strange contortion of his body as she exploited him. And how could Ann not know about it? She must have heard. I began to feel another malaise beyond the hangover. What kind of people were they?

Ann's knocking ended with three short blows of her fist. I listened to her angry descent on the stairs and whispered, *Fuck you*. I wondered if she had come by because I had missed dinner or because I had been spotted going over the fence the night before. Whatever her reason, I didn't care.

How to deal with Mick's situation occupied my thoughts for the rest of the day. The notion of confronting Caz made me nauseous. If she were a male rapist, it would be simple. A few kicks to the head, a few broken limbs and the threat of something worse if he ever showed his face again. But this was different. Maybe she thought it was her right to exploit him. After all, she must have dealt with lots of his bodily horrors over the years. She must have felt, at times, as immobile as her patient. Being trapped with him, maybe what she had done— had been doing—was inevitable. I struggled to repel the image I had of choking her to death. I wondered if I could get Mick out of there, take him home with me. It would give my sorry existence a direction. Of course, I knew that I was far too mangled psychologically to care for him myself. But there was Poppy's death money and that could pay for a nurse, a real one. Mick deserved that money more than I, anyway. I wondered how much he understood of what was happening to him.

I walked along Darling Harbour where I saw a pair of cops sneering at each other. I considered asking their advice. I thought better of it, though, when it occurred to me that they might be like the cops back home. Besides, crime or no crime, this was a family matter.

I sat under a tree and, to my amazement, had a quick cry for Hank. His death seemed relevant for the first time, but I didn't know why. Poor miserable fucker. The religious thugs would say he was in Hell because he had taken his own life. So there. I wondered if I had spent more time with him, if we had been at all close, would things have turned out better. Probably not. We're all doomed, however differently.

Seagulls, whiter and cleaner than the ones in Montreal, mingled with lean pigeons near my feet. Across the water, children screamed and shouted as they climbed over a play area made of fiberglass cartoon characters. For the first time, the future baby seemed foreboding. What if he didn't like me? What if there was something wrong with him and he needed constant care for the rest of his life? I worried about Patty until I reminded myself of what a hard ass she was.

As queasy as my meandering thoughts had made me, hunger was becoming an issue. I found a Greek restaurant and stuffed myself with saganaki, loukaniko, a mound of kalamari and a half a bottle of ouzo. Suddenly, the world made sense.

Caz was no longer a demon, but a pest to be driven away with little, if any, effort. Mick would come to live with me, since his mother seemed tolerant of predators and was probably mentally disturbed. Problem solved. What had begun as a trek for closure had become a rescue mission. I made my way to Surry Hills, rehearsing what I would say when I got to Ann's house.

+ + +

When I arrived, Caz was laughing so hard she seemed to be having some sort of attack. The sound of it made me angry. I didn't knock. I walked in ready to take charge. Beaming, Ann approached and embraced me.

*I knew you'd be back*, she said.

*We have to talk*, I said, as seriously as I could over Caz's waning cackle. Ann studied my face for a clue, but didn't seem too concerned. Caz wiped her eyes and approached me with her arms open. My determination was beginning to wane. I tried to sure it up by looking grave, but both she and Ann seemed oblivious to my mood. Mick called from his room, *Spat! Come here!* I went to his room where he was sitting up, dressed in sweats. *Come here*, he repeated. I went to him and he put his thin arms around my neck. He kissed my cheek and I thought that I would die of heartbreak. He released me and told me to sit.

I pulled a chair from the corner and sat next to him. I thought about how to begin, but not knowing how much he could understand, the sentence wouldn't form.

*Mick ... Are you ... Do you know ...* Of course he didn't know what was happening to him. His life was completely contained in that room. He was at her mercy. For helpless people, necessity always takes precedent over trivia like morality. He had to be compliant or else he would lose her. Having grown in such a confined space, he had taken the shape of it and probably didn't know of any other way to be.

*What's the matter?*

I thought for a while and then I asked him, *Are you all right, Mick?*

*She's sweet, Spat. Me and Caz are having a go at making a baby again.*

He smiled his crooked smile and his head rocked from side to side, slightly. My eyes scanned the books on the shelf above him as I managed to utter a positive response. I could feel my face flush. The titles on the spines of the books were familiar. I had read a few of them, but some were a long way out of my league. Most were about history or physics, few of them were novels. I studied his face, which was constantly in flux. Nerves firing at random, his expressions revealed nothing. His was a kinetic poker face, impossible to read unless he smiled. To my deep and sickening shame, I realized that there was a whole and intelligent man in that ruined body. He was not a poor unfortunate thing. He was, I could see it then, far more highly evolved than I.

*She's a pain in the arse, lately, but I think just the chance of a pregnancy does wonders for her. You never had kids, did you, Spat?*

I tried not to let the silence persist, but there was a lot to process. Finally, I told him about the baby. He smiled, thought for a moment, his chin jutting forward for no reason. He took my hand and squeezed.

*Well done. Will you get back together when he's born?*

*I think so*, I said. I told him that I had to take a piss and went to the small bathroom off the kitchen. Alone, I began to realize that those people knew a whole lot more about me than I did about them. I should have kept in touch with Hank more. I should have learned something about them before arriving on their doorstep. I heard the old nun's baritone again, as clear as I had heard it all those years ago. *You big dummy!*

I was, more than anything, ashamed to have made so many assumptions about Mick, about Caz. I stared at a framed spider above a small plastic shelf and time slowed to a drip. I didn't move and didn't want to. I kept perfectly still and tried to imagine what I should have been for them. Finally, Caz called to me.

*Are you hungry, Spat?*

*No. Thank you*, I answered, trying to sound relaxed. I flushed the toilet and ran the water in the sink. I left the bathroom, realizing that I should have used it. I went back to Mick's room, where he was struggling to open a worn paperback. He tossed the book when he saw me and smiled.

*Tucker's her answer for everything.*

*You read all those books, Mick?*

*Most of them. Some belonged to Dad. You remind me a bit of him.*

*Really?*

*Yeah. He was a real serious type, too.*

I had no response and it didn't seem to matter. The silence was comforting. The rage, that had burned so hotly for so long, had dissipated. I felt, for the first time in years, that everything was as it should have been. The silence was not the absence of anything, but rather a warm and calming relief. It was broken, moments later, by Caz. She appeared in the doorway with a pan of fried fish.

*You're sure I can't tempt you, Spat?*

*He's not hungry*, Mick said. *Nick off.*

She stuck her tongue out at him and went back to the kitchen.

*She wants to get married,* Mick said. *I'd rather be eaten by rats.*

*Marriage is a death sentence,* I said. Mick's laughter erupted from his twisting body like the blast of a Roman candle.

+    +    +

My mother and I sat in the back garden while Caz gave Mick a sponge bath. Ann had been thinking about our exchange the day before. It was apparent in the way she spoke to me.

*I'm glad that he took good care of you. Finn, I mean.*

I had no response. I asked her about Caz and Mick. I was curious to know how long they had been together, how they had met.

*I knew Caz from the rallies. She used to come by and help Dennis with his work. I suppose she fell in love with Mick for the same reason everyone does. He's one of a kind.*

*He is that,* I said.

*I wish you could stay and get to know him better.*

*I can't,* I said. *Patty's pregnant. She'll need me.*

She lit up and almost stood. *That's wonderful! Congratulations!*

*Thank you.*

As she hollered the news to Caz, I had a nagging feeling that nothing would turn out the way I had been hoping. In my sick internal life, feeling joy was only freeing up space for misery. What if Patty wasn't lying about the other man? What then? I denied that idea and all of its terrible implications by clenching my feet and smiling back at Ann. For the first time, it was easy to be in their house. I began to sense their contentment. I envied it. But then, without words, maybe not even a look, we both remembered Finn and the biggest secret; the one I had always kept from the world and from myself. The immovable regret and the enduring anger muted us as Caz and Mick laughed in their bedroom. At last, Ann said what she had always wanted to say: *I hope he's burning in Hell.* I had no response. I had no desire to defend him, but I knew that it was time to leave. I went to Mick's room, to say good-bye. Caz was stroking his hair and whispering to him. He was laughing, quietly. When she spotted me, she smiled and stood.

*I just came to say good-bye. I'm going back tomorrow.*

*No!* They said it in unison.

*I'll stop in again on the way to the airport.*

Caz said, *Well, it's some hard yakka getting to know you, Spat. You're a real Harry-have-a-chat.*

I didn't know what she meant, but I assumed it was part of a standard send-off. I left knowing that I would never see them again.

Outside, I realized that there was no closure to be had. Nothing real could be so tidy. Ann's life was her own business and though I wanted to get to know Mick, it was unlikely that we would ever be friends. I felt guilty for having lusted after his wife. Since nothing came of it, I suppose every generation does a little bit better.

The ouzo's buzz had faded, so I decided to find a bar. As I walked, I thought of question after question I would have liked to have asked Ann. As they occurred, I dismissed each one as pointless. Time had so diminished the significance of the great reunion, that the loss felt minimal and expected. Though there was lots of shit to mull over, I was returning to my default setting and vowing to stay drunk until Vancouver.

# { 12 }

I kept opening my eyes wider and wider, forcing them to focus. There was still music blaring; but by the light outside, it had to be six or seven in the morning. People were still dancing and fighting, trolling for sex. They were all younger than me. They moved through the dark room like newly escaped mental patients, enjoying their baffling freedom. Lost party people would climb the stairs to the place, have a look, and then leave.

The tribal music took a sinister turn as the DJ started mixing some vintage disco with a speech by George W. Bitch. His voice was sickening; the sound of ignorance itself. I staggered to the bar and got the look from a girl in a silver skirt and bra. She also sported a bowler hat. When I attempted to charm her, she cackled and stumbled off into the shrinking fray.

Much of the next beer spilled as I worked to consume it. The coldness on my shirt felt good, though. I heard his voice behind me and didn't have to look to know who was there.

*Spat, you fucking glorious ratbag. You are well and truly fucked.*

He was hyper and nattering non-stop about anything that zipped through his perforated brain. Dave was my intoxication opposite: sharp and incoherent, while I was dull and incoherent. He put an arm on my shoulder and yelled over the thumping protest, *Allow you to buy me a beer, Mate.*

*Fuck off, Dave,* I muttered.

*That's the spirit.*

I remembered the warnings from the bartender and the doorman about him on the night we met. Though obliterated, I was still cognisant enough to know that I should have avoided him.

After this point in the revelry, there's a large gap. I know I bought beer for Dave and at least one more for myself. Almost everything in the next couple of hours has been deleted, perhaps mercifully, by alcohol. There is a clutch of clear images: being on the street with Dave, trying to stay upright as we walked and then a shoving match with fucking yabbos. That's what Dave called them. That word "yabbos" stuck, but the rest is still a mystery.

I remember the cab ride. It was a long one and took us far outside of the city. Punishment for everything I had ever done was on its way. I surrendered a wad of cash to the driver on Dave's insistence. After that, I remember the feet of men, including Dave, scuffing past my head. I was under a table, shutting my eyes as though it could have lessened the impact of the thunderous metal spewing from an archaic stereo. As loud as it was, I could still hear Dave's voice. His bellowed words were lost in the din. I knew that nothing good would come of them. I dipped in and out of shallow sleep until the music finally stopped and then I passed out.

When I woke, I could hear Dave slurring defiantly as a man threatened him. I hoped that the stranger would pummel my parasitic friend so that I could get out of there without him. I got my wish and then regretted making it. Dave hit the floor and I could see that he had taken a few shots to the head. His mouth was red and his eyes were wide. He was back on his feet in seconds. A voice said something threatening that I couldn't comprehend and then Dave was ejected from the bar. He was still bold, out there yelling about how brutal his revenge would be. His voice faded as he walked, but his fervor remained even when he was too far away to be understood. Now there was only the muttering of two deep voices. I went under again and came to an hour or a minute later. Standing took more effort than I cared to make. I wanted a beer to level off and then bed.

Upright, I scanned the place for something familiar. I could have been anywhere. The small dive looked as though it had been decorated and frequented by apes. There was a blue band of neon around a cracked mirror and battered road signs with black silhouettes of indigenous animals. The two gangsters at the bar smirked at me and chuckled.

*Fuckin' skaters*, one said.

*Your boyfriend's gone, Sport*, said the other.

They looked as though they had boxed every second person they had ever met. The larger of the two had obviously had his nose broken more than once and was missing a few teeth. His friend had a scar that ran the length of his face and an elaborate neck tattoo that looked to be the top of a much bigger mural. I focused on walking a straight line to the bar, but the one behind it read my mind.

*We're closed, Mate. Go home.*

The power of speech had left me. I eyed them both for a moment to show them that I was not, in the least, intimidated. Out of ideas, I made my way to the exit. They continued their conversation and the words sounded like gibberish. Then a phrase from the bigger of the two stopped me, cold:

*... Spat the dummy ...*

I turned, amazed. I moved toward him as my life-long rage reached its apex and my head began to throb.

*What did you call me?*

*Fuck off.*

I was astounded by how hard I hit him, but even more surprised by his reprisal. His fist was made of steel. I was sure that he had cracked my skull down the center. As I fought to stay on my feet, the one behind the bar leapt to the aid of his esteemed colleague. Another punch hit my jaw and the pain was more than I could have imagined. I went down and their enthusiastic feet began to pulverize. If I could, I would have pleaded for leniency. There was nothing that would have diminished their enthusiasm, though. All at once, I thought of Patty and the baby and Poppy and hard truth. A heel caught my right cheek bone and I escaped into unconsciousness.

+   +   +

I rose out of the tar, back into the world, my brain restarting. Everything had changed while I was out. This new plane of existence had a slight downward tilt. The mid-day heat seemed to intensify the pain that inhabited every cell. I squinted across the sand with my good eye and tried to imagine what it would be like to stand. I began to count to ten. At eight, I pushed away from the ground with my working arm and sat up. My head had become too heavy to carry. My dry mouth ached and the eye that had swollen shut felt as though something sharp were trying to pass through it from the inside. It burned. Everything burned. Raising my head to see where I was took more effort than anything I had ever done.

The bar was gone. There was nothing. Dirt, low shrubs and infinite sky. I assumed that I had been dumped on the road because I could not have walked very far. By the way I felt, I had been dragged to my resting place. A bicycle with no one on it approached. It passed silently and I considered the prospect of dying. In the distance there were lounging kangaroos; half men, half deer. I began to think about the various reptiles and insects that might want to make a meal of me. I knew that I had to stand, but it was impossible. I'm not embarrassed to say that I thought of Poppy and asked him to help me. It was the closest thing to a spiritual experience I had ever induced.

*Help me ... Please, help me ...*

I repeated the words at steady intervals, but nothing changed. I leaned toward the dirt, propping myself on my good hand, and moved my good knee forward. The good parts pulled the bad upward and I was standing. Spiteful gravity made every nerve end fire at once and the agony made me want to repel from the hard earth and float, eternally untouched.

Not knowing where I was, there was no direction to take. There were no visual clues, no city on the horizon. I limped in a small circle to test my mobility. Every movement, no matter how slight, was a tribute to torture. Strange voices rose out of my throat in reaction to each spike of pain. I was almost relieved when I fell on my face. I was sinking, back into the tar. The death I had so often wished for was ingesting me as slowly as it could, relishing its dismal victory. The end made no impression on me. There was no relief, no regret. No wonder.

+    +    +

Judging by the back of his head, my rescuer was a man in his fifties. He was humming off-key to a pop song on the radio, hitting every bump in the road. I stopped resisting the jostling on the back seat of the jeep and accepted that nothing would ever feel good again. Everything, everywhere, was throbbing. I pretended to be unconscious in the hopes that I could get back into the void.

When buildings began to appear in my periphery, I slept. When I woke, I was being loaded onto a stretcher. I was wheeled into Victoria hospital amid shouts for assistance and the commotion of other emergencies.

The most beautiful woman to have ever been born took my hand and said, *You'll be all right, Darling. Lie still.*

+    +    +

Normal people, people with lives to live, passed in the hallway. Scraps of conversation leaked into my head. I slept as though I had needed to all of my life. A fingertip felt the smoothness of the sheet and I was grateful for it. I tongued the stitches in my mouth and felt intense sadness for all of the butchered softness.

The police came by, but I didn't speak. Words had been

nothing but trouble up to that point, so I decided to stay quiet. My ridiculous plan was to leave in the night, as soon as I was able, and make my way to the airport. My left wrist and right foot were in casts. Two back teeth were missing. There was swelling, spiteful cuts here and there. Cracked ribs. I saw my red eye reflected in the metal bed rail and was glad that I could not see the rest of my face.

There were severed tails of memories, swimming through the shit, trying to weave themselves together: voices and hands, blue uniforms, singing.

I was standing on a small stage, singing at the top of my lungs. I was in the center of the dome that contains existence. A tightening, hungry snake in one out-stretched hand and a tiny supernova in the other, I sang in a language I had never heard before. Anxious birds brushed the smooth dome above with the tips of their wings as they looked for a way out and away from my deafening music. My chest vibrated excitedly with every note and I realized that I could not have stopped the voice, even if I had wanted to. As I sang, the dome expanded. A passing cosmic wave of highest ecstasy burned through, nearly dissolving it. Eyes closed, I threw my arms open to catch as much of it as I could. The snake wound itself so tightly around my arm that it was absorbed, bloodlessly, into my flesh. The supernova shrank to a glowing point of light and etched an unknown symbol into my palm. The passing wave had made me louder and far more powerful. When my song ended, I was pissed that there was no applause; only the anguished birds and my own breath.

I opened my eyes and the most beautiful woman who had ever been born smiled at me. She was holding my good hand, emitting the most pure compassion. I didn't understand, until it was too late, that I was awake. I had been speaking to her, answering questions.

*... give them a ring for you ...*

As she walked away, I realized that I had told her Ann's address. No physical part of me could react, so my mind ignited.

I did not want to see her from that vantage point. Not because it would upset her, I just didn't have the strength to endure her sympathy. My good eye remained locked on the door.

# { 13 }

The pain and the morphine delivered to disguise it caused time to melt. Voices drifted from across the ocean, from across the flat plane of awareness. Some of the thoughts passing through every head, everywhere, were separated out of the silence that our combined blare makes and I heard them, clearly. Chips popped out of acknowledged reality; it flaked away in places and a truer version showed through. This look into actuality exposed what no one should have to know. Seeing how entirely connected, how indistinguishable and interchangeable we are, I wanted to stay under. I knew that we were, all of us, one damaged chain of identical things; attached, irrevocably, evolving out of The Great Nothing for no reason whatsoever.

Not quite asleep, in between worlds, I became aware of a sharp, claw-like bone beginning to protrude from the back of my right hand. The original bones separated for the new addition, new nerves snaked through my arm to my brain. I came to understand, somehow, that this claw was for defense. Injected into the neck of an attacker, it would spurt venom that would make the aggressor see without blinders, without filters. The raw feed would burn through their veins causing every cell wall to contract in stunning agony. In seconds, they would be utterly free.

When I sensed someone approaching, I had to concentrate to make my new claw retract. I knew that if they were to see it, their instinct would have been to put me back in the desert. The venom sack filled slowly, steadily, as the years or days passed. I would be ready. I knew. I was becoming what I would have to be.

One day, one harsh day, my new claw retracted for good and sealed the skin behind it. Standard reality reasserted itself. My real name repeated, on a loop, in my head. I wondered about the man who had brought me to the hospital. He didn't leave a name and, apparently, had no interest in my gratitude.

With no insurance, I knew that my hospital days were numbered. As the pain became less distressing, I realized that I had been sober for twelve days. I had begun learning staff and patient names. I heard more than I wanted about football from the man in the bed across from mine. My head was clear and the extremes in my thoughts seemed to be farther away than they had ever been. I was in the center of it, now, getting an introduction to strange equilibrium. Everything had a quality of newness that was almost hopeful and certainly terrifying.

When Ann and Caz arrived, I tried to make a joke, but they weren't laughing. Ann wept and kissed my bad hand. Caz stroked my hair so gently, I shuddered a little. Their pity was depressing. I wanted to vanish. Ann spoke to a doctor I had never seen before.

*When can we take him home?*

*He can be discharged today, but you understand, it could be a long recovery.*

*We understand*, Caz said, and smiled at me.

As they wheeled me across the lobby, we passed a room with large, bare windows. In it, a man was raving through what sounded like a shredded voice box. I focused with my good eye and was hardly surprised to see who it was contained in the locked observation room. Dave looked as though there was electricity shooting through his body from the floor to the ceiling. He was its infuriated puppet, ripping at his clothes and screaming. The three of us were transfixed, in awe of his chemically induced psychosis.

*That's Dave. One of our resident skaters,* an orderly announced to Caz and Ann.

*What's a skater?* I had to repeat the question several times before anyone understood.

*An ice addict,* the orderly said.

*What's ice?* I asked, unable to take my eye off of Dave.

*Pardon?*

*What's ice?*

*I'm sorry.*

*Ice! What - is - ice?*

*Oh. Crystal methamphetamine. It's a plague. Coming in from China by the ton.*

*Let's go,* I said. No one moved.

*What did you say, Spat?*

*Let's - go.*

We stopped at the hotel on the way and Caz went in to get my suitcase. I could see her talking to the kid at the front desk, explaining more than she had to. They had put my things in storage after my check out date. When she returned to the car, she told me that there were messages to phone Patty.

+   +   +

I took up residence in Mick and Caz's room. She bunked with Ann and I took her futon. I knew that was more than an inconvenience and I resented the guilt I felt. Lying there, stitching myself back together, cell by cell, I decided that I had been life's chew toy long enough. Mick saw my survival as nothing less than miraculous.

*You're so lucky, Spat,* he said. *Do you know how many people go missing in this country every year? And are never found? Heaps. Thousands.*

I did not feel particularly lucky, though part of me was thankful to be back in the house on Arthur Street.

My conversations with Mick were, largely, one-sided. He told me about his childhood, about Dennis and meeting Caz for the first time. I had to listen, closely, as his accent and the uncontrolled movements of his jaw warped his words.

Mick had spent his early years obsessed with flight. He was convinced that if he could only sustain the thought, he would levitate from his bed, go out through the window, and survey the neighbourhood from above. He was so convinced that it could happen that he decided, at age five, to make an attempt. Dennis had found him, unconscious, on the floor. The strange thing was that it was the kitchen floor. How he had gotten that far is still unknown.

*Can you keep a secret, Spat?*

*Of course.*

*I believe that I flew to the kitchen. I believe that the shock of being able to do it broke my concentration and that's why I fell where I did.*

*You're insane*, I told him. He laughed, heartily, and called me a dirty bastard.

*Don't underestimate the power of the mind, Spat.*

*Your mind*, I said.

When Mick was three, Dennis and Ann took him into the bush for a year to collect spiders. They were adamant about Mick having a good education. Though he struggled to even hold a book, he was made to read. He knew the names of every plant and creature he was carried to for an inspection. Pronouncing Latin names became a form of speech therapy.

His parents kept nothing of the world's misery out of Mick's awareness. Dennis and Ann invaded their son's mind with the petrifying facts of global politics; the sacred corruption that protects the rich from the poor. He knew about every war, every brainless act of aggression by every brainless aggressor. No physical hindrance would prevent their son from seeing the world for what it was.

*He never stopped mumbling*, Mick said, one morning. *Right to the end, Dad was always talking.* It was clear that Mick missed Dennis, but was still baffled by his old man's strangeness. The bug man repeated himself, constantly, I was told. Dennis would ask the same question again and again until he heard the answer he'd wanted. He threw fits over details no one else could see. He was, otherwise, solid. When they couldn't hear his low murmur, they knew that he was either out or sleeping.

Dennis had died of a stroke on Caz's birthday, six years before. The family was having a small party in the backyard. Full of wine and unusually jovial, Dennis began to dance like the men at a Greek wedding. Arms wide, nodding his head to imagined music, he moved back and forth, snapping his fingers in time. No one had seen him dance before. Ann took a picture just as his light went out. Mick said that in his last moment, Dennis looked like a scientist doing an impersonation of Jesus on the cross.

*Tell me about your father,* he said. I felt light-headed. I told him that I had to sleep.

+    +    +

Besides his physical limitations, Mick also endured periods of deep depression. About a week after I had invaded his space, he stopped talking. His mother and partner had seen it so many times before that it was simply accepted, like a change in the weather. His silence became maddening, but I gave up trying to break it. I stopped speaking, too, and our noiseless hours became one extended moment. Even when Caz or Ann entered the room, the spell was continuous.

Once, while Mick slept, Caz came in to tidy the room. She sat on the futon and watched him.

*Are you all right?*

*I'm fine,* she said. *I hate these days, when he's down like that. Sometimes I think he just does it to bugger us up.* She looked at me, seriously and whispered, *It's hard to love someone at the best of times.*

*Nothing's perfect,* I said.

*No. Nothing is ... Besides, they just don't sit well together, do they? Love and perfection.*

# { 14 }

The frustration of being stationary began to take its toll. As Mick's outlook gradually brightened, mine became darker. Ann was avoiding me. My curiosity about her and her life with Finn had been replaced by cool apathy. I wanted to be home, in my own place, with my own stuff. Of course, I figured that the landlord had probably put my shit on the street and a padlock on the door when he didn't get the month's rent. I phoned Patty to tell her about what had happened.

*I thought you decided to stay there. Why didn't you call before now?*

I wanted to close the rift between us, but couldn't think of the words that could do it.

*Why didn't you phone Ann?*

*I did*, she said. *That other woman said you went home without saying good-bye.*

*I got beat up.*

*What? Why? What did you do?*

*I'd rather not get into it ... How are you feeling?*

*My feet hurt and I can't stop farting.*

*Are you ... big?*

*I'm showing, if that's what you mean. I told the lawyer you'd phone him about the reading of Hank's will.*

Before I could ask her to see about my place she said, *I have to go.*

Hanging up, I knew that the truce was over. The baby would draw a line between who she was and who she would have to become. I would be relegated to the old world, a bit of history that she would try to forget.

+ + +

There was a blackout. Distant voices cursed dead televisions for a moment and then everyone settled. The darkness was old and authentic, valuable somehow. Mick and I discussed anything, meandering from subject to subject on wobbling ideas. There was still a good deal of physical pain, but I could no longer feel the weight of the dead years. Whiled away and wasted, those cumulative dead years had kept me pinned to the bed more than any beating could. Now with the electricity off we were, however briefly, disembodied in the blackness and free of bones.

*Fear is the problem*, Mick said. *People take it seriously. People nurture it and react to it as though it's important and real.*

*If you're afraid, you're afraid. It's just ... It's automatic.*

*No. It's a choice*, he said. *It's evil to be afraid. It's evil to make people feel fear and it's evil to be afraid.*

*I don't know about the second part.*

*It's evil to be afraid.* He said it with such finality; it was as though he had been sent to deliver this message. I had been motivated and mutated by fear for so long that I told myself I couldn't grasp what he was saying.

*But if you can't help it—*

*Fear is evil and evil is fear*, he said. *No one has the right to be afraid.*

*But in reality, there are all sorts of things to be afraid of.*

*No. In fantasy, there are all sorts of things to be afraid of. In the fantasy of the past and the future, there's not much more than fear. In reality, there's nothing to be afraid of. But reality has been made into the enemy by fearful people. Reality is supposed to be cold and harsh even though it's the opposite of those things.*

*Reality is cold and harsh,* I said. *Look at us.*

*The avoidance of reality makes everything cold and harsh. Resisting reality brings carnage. Trust me, Spat. I've had a lot of time to think and I know two things: Fear is evil and secrets make you lonely.*

*Everybody has a secret,* I said.

*I know. It's a lonely old world.*

*I think it's all just a bunch of pointless accidents.*

*Would having a point make it better ... or just different?*

*It just is what it is.*

*Exactly. It doesn't need to be adjusted. Besides, there is no civilized way to have the illusion of certainty.*

I had to think for a while. I no longer wanted to counter what he was saying. I only wanted to see from his perspective. I considered the hours: the hours as long as days that he had spent in that room. The bed, the walls, the ceiling, the books and the clutter: hard shell for a soft body. Time, in that shell, was far less fluid than it had been in mine. I surmised that he had fewer reasons to be afraid, fewer reasons to be secretive.

*If you're being chased by a bear, you should be afraid,* I said.

*Only if it makes you run faster. And you know that's not the kind of fear we're talking about.*

*I know.*

One of the neighbors, arriving home drunk, was singing and clapping his hands in a sloppy rhythm while his angry wife tried to quiet him. Mick laughed. For an instant, I wondered how he would react to me in that state. If he had seen me and Patty at our worst, what would he think? What would our talks be about, I wondered, if he knew me?

*It's hard to keep fear out of your mind,* I said.

*Not if you put the mind in its place. The mind is just brain by-product ... You know, like shit.*

*The mind is brain shit.*

*Exactly.*

We laughed and I felt lucky. Moments later, the lights came on and the gloom returned.

+    +    +

When I had the casts removed, Ann gave me a walking stick that had been decorated with a dot painting of a snake. I was glad to have it. Sometimes, when I made my way out of Mick's room, I could sense that he resented my returning mobility. When I could put weight on my bad foot, I offered to take him out for some air. He had not been in his wheelchair for weeks. He didn't like being pushed around, aimlessly, the object of odious pity.

*Come on, Mick. We'll just go around the block.*

He gestured, awkwardly, for me to leave him alone.

+    +    +

I did push-ups in the backyard while the others watched television. I could feel my strength returning. With it came all of my old appetites. I would have blown an elephant for a toke. There was wine in the fridge, but I knew it wouldn't be enough. Besides, it was worth holding on to the novelty of my clarity. I sat on the grass and looked up at the moon. Ann came out to join me. It was the first time we had been alone together since my return to her house.

*Don't you think you should talk to the police, Spat?*

*Why?*

*The person who did this can't be allowed to—*

*It was my fault.*

*Well ... How did it happen?*

I sighed, deeply, at the thought of having to explain it. Caz came out to join us after having a brief row with Mick.

*When I was a kid I had a nickname in school that I hated. It followed me for years ...* As I told them about my old name and the events leading up to the bleak morning in that secluded bar, they listened intently. When I told them about hearing the man refer to me as Spat the Dummy and my reaction to it, they looked at each other in amazement. Then the two of them laughed so hard and for so long, it ceased to be confusing and became utterly offensive. They covered their face and wiped away tears as their laughter began to seem unstoppable.

*I'm glad you think it's so funny.*

*No! No, it's not*, Ann said.

*Yes, it is*, Caz added and this set the two of them off again. I waited, giving them my cold stare, until they calmed down.

*It's just an expression*, Ann said.

*Like when a baby gets sooky*, Caz said, *and spits out the dummy.*

*I don't know what you're talking about.*

*The man wasn't talking to you, dear*, Ann said, trying not to smile. *He was just talking about someone who had spat the dummy and you misunderstood.* Caz tried to focus, hoping that I would find it all as amusing as they did once she clarified what had happened. *When a baby is out of sorts and can't be consoled, it often spits out the dummy. The nipple.* She looked at me, nodding quickly, anticipating a gale of laughter.

*A pacifier is called a dummy here*, Ann added.

*So if someone spat the dummy*, Caz said, *he got angry and couldn't be reasoned with. He's like a baby spitting out the dummy. You had a blue for nothing, Darling.* They smiled at me, waiting for me to appreciate the hilarity as they had, but I didn't see anything humorous about it. My stubborn gravity only made them giggle.

*Spat the Dummy*, Caz said. *You big dummy!* Their laughter started again, so I left them. I went to Mick's room where he was watching a documentary about rubber trees. He asked what was so funny outside. I explained it all to him, hoping for a bit of sympathy. He howled with laughter, throwing his head back and arching his body into a taut bow.

*Go fuck yourself*, I said, and went to the kitchen for a sandwich. I eyed the wine next to a bottle of Ian Hewitson's

Kick Arse Barbecue Sauce, but thought better of starting up again on their territory. Besides, wine was for amateurs.

I have often been unintentionally funny. It used to infuriate me, but then, over the years, I began to take comfort in it. If they're always laughing at you, it keeps you on the outside. The Aussie family's reaction to my honest mistake made me sulk a little, though, I have to admit.

I went out walking, feeling stronger than I had in weeks. Of course, I knew that I was really out looking for a nice, dark bar. I was already in the drunken place, mentally, and needed the object of my affection to physicalize it. I started toward the King's Cross, ignoring the life-draining rush of blood to my feet.

+    +    +

The coldness, the wetness of the beer glass, made me giddy. I stroked it with the tips of my fingers, sensing its power, wiping its cold tears of joy at my return. I waited, building up to the moment when beer and I would be reunited. The shitty music took a turn for the glorious as Bob Marley's voice filled the bar. That was the sign for which I had been waiting. Instantly, all was right with the universe. I raised the rim of the glass to my bottom lip and enjoyed its smoothness, moving my head, slightly, from side to side. I poured the golden glee into my throat and down into my gut where it promptly turned around and made its way up and out. With the force of a small explosion, the beer sprayed into the air. I was too amazed to be embarrassed or apologetic. I stepped away from the bar, all but oblivious to the waiter's anger and the disgust of a few patrons.

Outside, I felt toxic and weak. I walked as fast as I could toward Ann's neighbourhood, hoping to stay conscious. The tingly shock quickly turned to bleakness. I cursed the sun, wishing that it would collapse on itself.

The tilt of the new world was making me queasy, so I stood in the shade of a flowering tree and waited for my body to adjust. I thought about going home and how much more I would have to take with me for having been there. I missed Montreal. That made me miss Mick and Caz, even Ann, because I knew that I would be leaving them soon.

A black spider with a red blotch on its ass was dangling near my head. Eventually, I recognized it as the Red Back. One of its dead cousins was under glass, on a wall, on Arthur Street. I wanted to avoid the venomous clump of legs, but I didn't want to be in the punishing sun either. *Fuck you*, I told the poisonous local, willing it to keep its distance. Watching it, I became more and more aware of the permanent change in the world since my big night out with Dave. I wondered if I had been pushed into some parallel universe wherein none of my old objectives would matter to me anymore. For the first time, I considered the impending baby without trepidation. I wanted to go home and start again. I imagined myself without scars, reborn as what I was intended to be.

I saw Finn on Flinders Street. He was on the opposite side, waiting for someone. There was nothing surprising about seeing him there. He noticed me watching him and smiled. He waved and I waved back. He was the Finn I remembered from childhood; always game, always up to something, ready with a joke. A white van arrived and he got in. As it pulled away, I wondered if I had actually seen anyone at all. If there was someone there, I wondered if he only looked like Poppy to me. But he waved and smiled exactly the way Finn would have done. Maybe when we die, we go to Australia for a second chance. Why not? It's no more unlikely than any of the other theories.

Seeing him had little to do with sentimentality and more to do with the unspoken secret that still hovered above me, the heavy black kite kept aloft by my resistance to it. I knew that I would have to have it out with Ann. *Get it over with*, I told myself. I repeated that phrase as I walked, making a primitive rhythm out of it. *Get - it - over with ...*

When I arrived at the house, an ambulance was parked in front of it. My heart began to beat, furiously, as I walked faster.

The thought of losing Mick was too much to bear. I was shaken by the depth of my connection to him. He was vital. Terrified, I wanted to fight. I wanted to annihilate whatever it was that had come to take him from us.

Caz followed the paramedics out. I stopped when I saw Ann on the stretcher. I lost my fight as a primal anxiety invaded. Caz looked at me in amazement. As the ambulance doors closed, she took my hand and said, *You'll stay with Mick, won't you, Spat?* I nodded, holding my breath.

+   +   +

Mick and I watched the muted television and considered the possibilities. He had told me the story as soon as the ambulance left. Ann was in the backyard, just standing there with her arms folded, staring into space. Caz went out to talk to her. She said something Caz didn't comprehend and then blacked out.

His fear made his speech clearer than usual. He was nearly still for long periods and then his body would convulse, briefly, as though to throw off stored tension. I tried to assure him that Ann would be fine, but what did I know? I tried to think of something clever to say. The long silence between my half brother, half cousin and I was strangely comforting. The stillness that used to rattle me was a tonic in the new world. I chose not to think about Ann. I told myself that I was fulfilling the role of older brother, being the strong one.

I thought about Patty and felt a frantic need to be home. Out of the tangled past, I recalled a dinner years before. I looked away from Mick because I could not stop smiling.

Since Patty and I saw Rob and Linda at least once a week, it was inevitable that some relatives or friends unknown to us would sometimes be at the table. Patty was always nervous if we were about to meet someone new.

*Don't say anything,* she'd warn as we approached them. *What do mean, don't say anything?*

*Just make normal conversation, Spat.*

*All Right. Can I show them my nuts?*

One night, Rob's cousin, Patrick, joined us for dinner. He happened to be in town for the night, so he arrived on their doorstep. Hilarious old friends and priests can get away with showing up unannounced. Rob's cousin was not hilarious. I shook his hand, made a bland comment about the weather and used my funeral manners whenever I spoke to him. It seemed expected.

Every time he referred to his much younger cousin, Rob called him Father Patrick. *Get Father Patrick some wine. Tell Father Patrick about the class you're taking, Lin.* Father Patrick's responses to every courteous question were immediate, pleasant and empty. He smiled at us through the light of his secret knowledge, wordlessly reminding us that he had peeked under the veil of The Divine. He glanced at me, occasionally, and I kept my polite grin. I did so not for that lost lamb and not for Patty, but for Rob. He was visibly uncomfortable in his own home, which made me resent little Father Patrick. I resented the apparent ease that the young man felt with the nervous reverence given him: a reverence he would receive, in some circles, for the rest of his life.

The unease left us as we drank and the young visitor's mass was diminished, as all weighty things were, by Linda's drunken cackle. It filled the space and could make even the chaste giddy. I had forgotten about the holy presence when I uttered the room-chilling observation, in relation to the politics of the day, that the hand-job is really just a noncommittal blow-job. Young Father Patrick was not amused, of course, because he had long since transcended the scary pleasures of the flesh. Besides, he knew that it's irreverence and not blood that flows through the veins of the Devil. Linda stared at the table. Rob scowled at me and Patty gave me the look that was our secret code for, *I'll smother you in your sleep.*

I couldn't apologize and move on. I had to proclaim that organized religion was entirely political; little more than organized crime with no girls allowed, so who was that kid fooling with his righteous act? When told to shut-up, I had to bray that pleasure is the only natural reason for existence. There are no holy men. Holy women, maybe, but definitely no holy men. I caught Rob's eye and then tried to soften my stance.

*I'm not trying to offend you,* I said to the snotty little bitch. *It was just a joke, for fuck sake.*

He considered this, tilting his head and furrowing his brow. Finally, nobody's father sighed, looked at the table and said, *We were all reacting with silence because you're extremely vulgar.*

It was sweet, in one way, because I thought that he might have been angry at me for using foul language in front of the women folk. In another way it was cute to see someone so young play at being virtuous, but mostly, it just pissed me off.

*I'm vulgar? Fuck you, ya little cunt!*

Patty's hand grabbed my thigh and she squeezed as hard as she could.

*Jesus, Spat!* Rob had yelled so loudly, his voice rang in the walls. He tried to calm himself, scanning the room for something that could, perhaps, explain my behaviour or offer a quick solution. *Excuse me, Father Patrick,* Rob said. *I'm sorry about all of this.*

*No, I'm sorry,* I said. Patty's grip on my leg tightened. I pried her hand off as I sighted alcohol and my short temper for the spoiled evening.

*I should go,* the sulking cousin said, standing. I wanted to slap him until he shit himself.

*Don't,* I said, rising. *Please. I'll go. I'm very sorry.*

As Patty and I walked home, I launched into my defense. Her head was down; she would not look at me. Her hand brushed her cheek and I was astounded by her overreaction.

*Are you crying? Oh, for fuck sake!* I was indignant. I told myself that I was the last sane person. Patty looked at me through a teary wince and sustained a high pitched squeal. She had been laughing, breathlessly, unable to make a sound until then. Her legs buckled and she held on to me as we scuffed along. Eventually, I carried her on my back and she laughed all the way home. I chuckled, listening to her, making comments about poor Patrick to keep her going. Her warm breath made clouds around my head and ice chips crunched under my boots. I wished that we had lived farther away, so that I could have carried her for a while longer.

I had not thought of that short walk in ages. As the void tempered my fondness of that recollection, I knew that Patty would be starting over without me. I had no reason, maybe no right, to keep her in mind anymore.

After what could have been an hour, Mick said—calmly and with the utmost clarity—*She's your mother, too ... You should go to see her.* I suppose he could sense the tension between Ann and me. I knew that he and Caz had been offended by my abrupt departure weeks before; but after my long recovery under their roof, we had established a shape for whatever we were when the three of us were together. Ann and I were still keeping a safe distance from each other, but the unease had subsided a little.

Secretly, I was planning to convince them that I was the source of Ann's stress so that I could make a clean, if not somewhat altruistic, exit. It was true, so that helped. I was already dreading the hospital smells, the germ war fumes. When it was my turn to go, I thought, I would bring a book so that I could read to her and fill the time that way. I surveyed the books on Mick's shelf. Just then, Caz called. I repeated her report to Mick as she spoke. Ann's heart checked out all right, but her blood pressure was low. The doctor thought it was an anxiety attack.

The moment in our shared history that had dominated Ann's thoughts since my arrival, was taking its toll. The ghost that I had brought with me to Sydney was there, in a corner of the ceiling, as always.

*Finn Ryan will never die*, I thought.

When they arrived home, Ann joked about the incident and reassured us that she felt one hundred percent. She never once looked me in the eye. She took the sedative that the doctor had prescribed and went to bed.

In a loud whisper, Caz told us that Ann had not been sleeping. *I put it down to the heat at first, but it's been going on for weeks.*

*I think my being here is putting pressure on her*, I said. *I mean, it's great being here. But I think I bring back some bad memories, so -*

*Don't be such an arsehole*, Mick said, spitting the word "such". Caz laughed. I resisted.

*Seriously*, I continued, *Maybe I should -*

*Fuck off*, Mick said. I gave up.

+     +     +

In the morning, Caz convinced Mick to go out. He insisted on wearing a jersey from some football team and sunglasses that made him look like Joey Ramone. I wondered if Caz was just giving Ann and me a chance to talk about yesteryear. If that was her plan, it worked.

When Ann woke and made her way to the kitchen, the awkwardness was immediate. I made tea and she sat. Her courteous smile made me uneasy.

*Did you sleep?*

*Yes. Finally. I don't know why I'm ...* She stared at the fridge, either out of words or else feeling no need to finish.

*I'll be going home in a few days*, I told her.

*Oh?*

*Yes.*

I placed a cup in front of her and then stood, leaning on the counter. Neither of us said anything. I decided that we had avoided it long enough and looked for a way to start the dreaded discussion. She spoke first, though. Her tone was one that I had not heard before. She seemed to be dreaming.

*You know, what happened to you ... that beating ... That's what your father used to do to people all the time ... For money.*

I couldn't respond. All at once, I changed my mind. I did not need or want to talk about it.

*He was a violent man*, she said.

*I know*, I said, hoping to end it at that.

She watched me until I felt ashamed of myself. That made me resent her. I was tired of being sorry for having loved the one who had stuck around to raise me.

*Do you remember ... the night I left?*

My heart seemed to stop beating, my bones seemed fused together. Though I could not move, I kept telling myself to pack-up and leave. I could get a flight to anywhere in North America and figure it out from there. I knew that answering her question would change everything. I wanted to stay quiet; but, the word left me because, in the new world, there was nothing to keep it in.

*Yes.*

She considered this for a long time. *I'm sorry*, she said. *Can you tell me what you remember?*

With that, the scene began to play out in my head, only without restraint, without edits or all of the outright lies I had always used to reshape it whenever it invaded my thoughts. I told it to her and she was still, listening closely without wanting to hear any of it.

My feet didn't go near the end of the bed. Even if there had not been a party, the heavy rain would have kept me awake. I was staring at the ceiling, listening. There were two other women's voices, besides my mother's, coming through the wall. There was a record playing, squealing horns and tumbling drums. A man's voice was rising above the others. In retrospect, it must have been Hank. Finn shouted at him to be quiet. They were drunk and so they hollered everything over the music that they kept turning up. The baby woke. His crying made me jealous. Of course, she went to get him, right away. She always did. I heard her shoes in the hall, the door creak. His cry filled the house as she carried him to the kitchen. Finn and Hank were arguing about something I could not comprehend. Ann screamed at Finn to stop whatever he was doing. I was afraid of what might happen to her. I stood, trembling, wondering what

I could do to save her if I had to. I went to the bedroom door and listened for a minute. I turned the handle and knew that it was a mistake.

The fumes of it hit me first. The stabbing light of their insanity was all around them. Their going-out clothes were wrinkled and peeled back. There were glasses everywhere. A third man I had never seen before was asleep in Finn's chair. Curved spikes of black hair lay across his eyes.

I arrived in time to see Finn slap Hank. The crack went through my body, through the walls and out into the pounding rain. I was unable to move.

*You're a fuckin' liar*, Finn said. Hank could not react. Finn turned on Ann. *Shut him up! Shut that fuckin' kid up, now!*

*He's hungry!* She shouted it in his face and I knew that she was in trouble. I was startled by the redness of Finn's complexion. I had only ever glimpsed the seriously drunk version of him once before. The sleeping man woke and slurred something I could not understand. As he stood, he knocked over a lamp. Finn slapped Ann, almost knocking her down. Hank intervened. He was no match for Finn who shoved his brother away and grabbed the baby from Ann. The screaming infant dangled by one arm. The words Finn was yelling drowned in the screams of the women. He threw the baby hard, against the wall.

One of the women fled into the rain, screaming. Polly Beene. Finn had fallen and was still yelling at Ann. Hank was so astonished, so horrified that tears poured down his face. Shaking, Ann cradled the baby. Her voice was low, unable to form words. I ran back to my room.

I didn't cry. I was afraid to make a sound. If I were quiet enough, I thought, I would disappear.

Ann began to look at me with a kind of sympathy that seemed remote and unreal. After I was done, the whole scene played in my head again, only with more detail. It had waited so long to be told that it nearly materialized in front of me.

The image of that baby, twisting in the air, has never left

me. I realized, there in Ann's kitchen, that every moment of my life had been lived in reaction to it.

She told me what followed that night and I struggled to listen.

She had told Hank, in the car, to go back in for me. He said that I would be fine. They went to a hospital where Hank told a doctor that the baby sitter had dropped Mick. Suspicions arose almost immediately given the smell of rum and the young, terrified mother. Hank was sure that the police had been called. He told Ann that they would take the baby from her. While he distracted the nurse, Ann took Mick back to the car and waited.

With the silent baby on her lap, they went to Hank's place in Verdun. In a panic, Ann decided that the only safe place would be with her aunt. Finn had never met the woman and didn't know where she lived. As the sun was rising, they drove ten hours straight to Nova Scotia. Mick did not cry. She was afraid to let him sleep in case he could not wake up again. Red marks, the beginnings of bruises, began to show on his head and legs. The longer he refused to eat, the more desperate she became. Hank wanted to stop in Saint John and take the baby to a hospital there. Ann refused. It was late afternoon when they arrived at her Aunt's house. Mick was unconscious.

*I knew that it was wrong. I knew that we should have left him in the hospital. If I had ... maybe things would have been better for him.*

We said nothing after that. It was shame that held us there, mute. Mine came from love. I loved a man who was capable of the worst imaginable violence. Half of me, from Ann's perspective, was him. Her shame, I thought, came from the choices she had made nearly forty years ago. But there was more than that. Warily, she told me.

*Mick doesn't know any of this ... You can't ever tell him.*

Not only did he not know who his real father was, Mick didn't know how his physical state had come to be.

*What did you tell him ... about the way he is?*

*I told him that he was in an accident.*

She must have known what I was thinking.

*I don't want him to know the truth. No one should have to live with ...*

The differences between us seemed all the more apparent. I didn't have to say what I thought of keeping that secret. I sat because I had a vague feeling of lightheadedness. The chase was over. All that I had been running from was transformed now and floating away from me, however slowly. I was free, but had no desire to leave my enclosure. I had not yet realized that the one-sided walls around me would crumble, regardless.

# { 15 }

My reverence for Finn waned as the exposed truths began to rearrange my interior. While Ann sat in the garden, I stayed in the kitchen and decided that I would tell Mick the truth. Keeping it from him implied that he was weak and I resented that. He was stronger than me, that's for goddamn sure.

Had Finn not existed, Ann and Hank could have lived happily together in Montreal with their able-bodied son. He would have played hockey and married out of high school. Ann would be playing with grandchildren and spending the foulest part of the winter in Key West. Had Finn not existed, I would not have been, either. Ann must have had the thought. After all, I was gone anyway; gone from her life, except for a few scraps of paper and a few pictures. She must have thought about it.

+ + +

My farewell dinner became a discussion about their travel plans to Canada. I assured them that they were always welcome. Ann kept smiling at me, trying to project maternal love, but I knew that she was only trying to mask the horror she felt in reliving that miserable night. While we laughed at the poem Mick recited for me, Ann was still taking the long drive Eastward with her silent baby. We would never be friends because, looking as much like Finn as I do, I would always be a reminder.

I told them stories about my early days and their laughter was comforting. I told them about going to buy cocaine in Lasalle, years ago, and getting cornered by a Doberman. It growled and snarled at me with such ferocity, I was sure that I would be killed. Then, as if to claim ownership, it turned and pissed on my leg. What was more, the coke turned out to be baking soda. I thought Caz would choke she was laughing so hard.

*Stop! Stop, Spat, I'll pee!*

*That dog ruined my acid washed jeans*, I proclaimed. I left out the part about the dealer encouraging me to leave with a shotgun. I then told them about when Patty made me go to the shrink and Caz could not take any more.

Mick said nothing. It was always difficult to imagine what he was thinking. I knew that I had to tell him about his father. I knew that I would have to tell him everything. Catching Ann's gaze, I wondered if she was reading my thoughts.

*How's every little thing?* I asked Mick.

*She's apples, Mate.*

She wouldn't be for long.

+   +   +

On the day before my flight home, the comically archaic queen of England was in town for a visit and this rallied the troops. With a protest to organize, Ann's time was not her own. She had placards to make, countless phone calls, interviews. Though the mainstream papers had no serious interest in Aboriginal people, there were lots of on-line magazines anxious for one of Ann's acerbic quotes. Caz went with her, on the day, of course. That left me and Mick on our own.

As we waited to see if there would be live coverage of the demonstration in Redfern, I considered how to start my talk with Mick. I knew that what I had to say would be devastating for him. I knew that he would need a long time to recover from the shock. If our positions were reversed, though, I would have wanted to know everything.

On one of the morning newscasts, there was a live shot of Ann next to an Aborigine who was making a stirring speech. His delivery was serene; his, like every other truth, did not require passion or defense. He was genuine, not at all modern. Ann was applauding, happy to be in her element. It was obvious that she enjoyed the fight. She was standing on the exact spot where she would be four years later to witness the government's official apology to the Aborigini; an apology for the countless children stolen from their parents, for the misery, for the incalculable loss. Mick and I discussed her devotion to the cause. He alluded to the many sacrifices she had made and the abuse that she received, at times, in the media. When the news was over, I told Mick that I had something very upsetting to tell him.

*What?*

*My uncle Hank was ...* I choked. My resolve waned as I looked at him.

*Was what?*

*Your father.* I looked away. I couldn't stomach the thought of what it did to him.

*I know.*

*You do?*

*The walls are paper thin, Spat. I over-heard them talking about him, years ago ... But he was so far away ... And Dennis was all I knew for a dad.*

*Ann and Caz think you believe that Dennis was your father.*

*He was. It makes the old cheese happy to keep Hank out of the picture, I reckon.*

*And do you know ... what happened to you ... physically.*

*Car accident.*

*That's not true.*

When I told him the story of that night in Montreal, he seemed to have no reaction. I began to say that I was sorry to be the one to tell him, but that I felt he had a right to know.

*Will you leave me alone, Spat?*

I stayed there for a moment. He turned his face away and I went to the living room. As I waited for Ann and Caz to return,

I started to regret what I had done. What difference did it make, after all, if he knew or not? I could no longer think of what good it did to tell him that his physical limitations were the result of brain damage done by a drunk in a blind rage. I had a disturbing thought as my eyes scanned the insects on the walls. What if I had only done it as revenge against Ann for lying, for loving Hank and not Finn, for leaving me? My certainty faded. The truth seemed to matter less than Mick's happiness. My disclosure was about my own sense of outrage, my own idea of what was just. I was, as Patty and many others had so often pointed out, a prick.

When Ann and Caz arrived back, they were energized by the day they'd had. Talking over each other, they were wound up until they saw my face. I stood. Ann knew, instantly, but I said it anyway.

*I told him ... Everything.*

She approached and slapped me, hard.

*Ann!* Caz was amazed.

My long lost mother stood in front of me, studying my face with a potent mixture of anger and disgust.

*He already knew about Hank*, I said.

Caz went to check on Mick. I had not considered what the revelation would do to their relationship. I wondered if he would trust her again now that he knew that she had kept so much from him. The blame, I hoped for their sake, would land, eventually, on Ann.

*Get out*, she said without looking at me.

I had to go to Mick and Caz's room to collect my things. Neither of them would look at me. She was lying next to him, stroking his hair. I packed quickly, deciding that I would go back to the room I had checked into eons ago.

As I walked back to the hotel, a quiet grief inhabited every part of me. The mission was, officially, a failure. Not only did I not find peace on the other side of the world, but I had done some grave damage and for no good reason. I checked in and immediately headed downtown.

I went back to the Maggio Hotel Bar and no one seemed to remember me. I took that as a good sign and ordered a pair of VB's. I drank slowly, making sure that I could hold it down. The next five went much faster and a familiar frame of mind emerged. I almost managed to be what I had not been for a long time—the old Spat, Spat Classic. I moved on to another bar, then another. I found myself shit-faced at the same club where I had met Dave for the second time. I feigned having fun and found myself dancing to a remix of an old Depeche Mode song that I had always pretended to dislike. I flailed around, laughing to myself, oblivious to the new world and its continual slope. It was night, at long last, and I was remembering who I had been before the pointless expedition had begun.

+    +    +

My wake up call came at seven on the nose. Viciously hung-over, I considered changing the ticket again. However, the cost of that change and the thought of another day in Ann's territory got me on my feet. I went downstairs to settle the bill and ordered a taxi. While I waited, someone called looking for me. I shook my head no and mouthed the words *I'm not here* to the woman behind the desk when she said my name.

*I spoke too soon*, she said, to whoever it was. *He just left for the airport.*

*Thanks*, I told her. She didn't seem to expect an explanation for the lie.

In the cab, I immediately wished that I had walked instead. The driver was talking non-stop about some proposed change in the immigration laws and making broad, ridiculous statements about various races. I tried to give him brain cancer by staring at the back of his head and willing it to happen. When the torturous ride was over, I didn't tip him and he glared at me in the rear view.

*Thanks a lot*, he said, sarcastically.

*Go fuck yourself*, I told him and slammed the door way too hard.

In the terminal, I realized that I had misread the time of the flight. I was three hours early. As I roamed a bookstore, I spotted a woman of about thirty-five who seemed to be one of my breed. I approached her and said something about the paperback she was considering. She gave me a long look and told me that she was only killing time and that she had no intention of buying anything. I asked her to have coffee with me and she agreed. We had a few shots with a beer chaser for breakfast.

We found a men's room that was empty. In the stall farthest from the door, we fucked on our feet, trying to be quiet. There was an increasingly potent chemical smell coming from her hair and I twisted my neck trying to avoid it. The fumes could have asphyxiated a small animal. I began to picture what could have been the cause of the fumes and the possibilities were strange. Had she been entirely dipped in something, in some warehouse, as part of some illegal experiment? Was her hair really a wig doused with a type of explosive or did the smell of the explosives permeate her, entirely, as she was strapping them on? It was difficult to concentrate, I was off my game. I couldn't end it. She was done and whispering that if I didn't let her go, she would miss her flight. I pulled out and she put herself together, quickly. She left, muttering, closing the stall door behind her. Finishing alone, legs shaking, a frustrating melancholy took hold of me. It became more apparent that the new world, like the old, was not my place. Even the terrorists had no time for me.

# { **16** }

Miles above the Earth, I was falling and picking up speed. The smoking tail of the jet left my field of vision as it roared in protest of its unplanned descent. I fell through the clouds in a state so far beyond panic that it became something like a trance. My breath was torn from me. Below, through the watering eyes in my fluttering face, the Pacific was impossibly beautiful. It was an ocean of blue liquid gems, accented with streaks of emeralds here and there. Diamonds caught the sunlight as they rolled across the surface in shattering lines.

I began to discern an island directly beneath me. I was almost relieved that I would probably hit land rather than water. Nothing could save me. As the green got closer and the impact that would end my existence came ever nearer, I wanted to laugh in defiance. I twisted my body so that I could face upward and not see the collision coming. The seemingly complex universes revealed themselves as what they had always been—nothing much; a small joke within a joke. But complexity has no intrinsic value and no unifying theory, no matter how awe-inspiring, can erase the pain of loving the one who will never love you.

Entering the jungle canopy at peak velocity, I was slapped by wet palm leaves and then hit the soft ground with an amusing thump. I waited, for a moment, to make sure that there was no pain and then stood and stretched. My thirty thousand foot fall was exactly what I had needed.

Liberated, I strolled through the blooming rain forest. Parting the thick vegetation as I went, I revealed new exotic plants every time. I knew that I was being watched by various hanging snakes and large cats in the trees. It was reassuring. The birds near the canopy harmonized their calls in an attempt to communicate with all of us on the ground. No one understood. Spots of sunlight played over my face. I was perfectly content.

I came to a small pond and knelt in front of it. Looking at my reflection, I realized that the scar on my forehead was gone. I was younger. Grateful, I shut my eyes. I opened them to find myself sitting up in my narrow seat, just a few hours out of Sydney.

I stared at the shitty movie that no one was watching. A visual grab bag of computer effects, it was as though the screen was vomiting up every deleted scene from every bad science fiction movie ever made. My back was already sore. The headache was deep and powerful, conserving itself by discharging purposeful hits of agony at a fixed pace. Digging through the carry-on for something to ease the pain, my thoughts were invaded by Finn.

For the first time, I remembered the hazards of our early years together. I remembered because, for the first time ever, I did nothing to prevent it. There was no one left to keep the secret for anymore.

I remembered how many days I was left on my own, wondering if he would make it back. I tried to estimate the number of hours I had spent in the corner of the library, hiding behind a book, giving him time to pass out before I went home. I could not count how many times I had to escape while he trashed the house in a rage. On most holidays, anniversaries and occasions, he became a free radical that existed only to demolish.

Swallowing pills without water, I reviewed his collection of drunken girlfriends. Each was introduced to me as his "one and only." Each of them saw me as either a hitch in her plan or else a handy prop in the demonstration of her maternal skills. They invaded our house, often taking command for months, until he grew bored with them or when they developed, wisely, a fear of him. They were nameless, but I remembered the faces. I remembered the sting of every betrayal. I still believed, secretly, that my mother would come back one day and find a stranger in her house. She would immediately leave again, I had concluded, so I said nothing to any of those women unless he instructed me to do so.

I loved Finn, I did, but I feared him. He loved me, but he was at the mercy of the old demons bequeathed to him. Until that moment, on the flight home, I had forgotten that I used to pass out when the anxiety from living with him became too much to stomach. It happened frequently, a few times at school. I remembered hitting the kitchen floor, once, with a pot of boiling water in my hand. He was livid about it. The second to last time it happened was after his funeral.

In my psyche, he was human again, almost new. He was still there, maybe, on the ceiling, but it didn't matter anymore. I heard the voice, crying out, but couldn't place it. Only by the worried looks from the couple across the aisle and the wide eyes of the approaching flight attendant did I realize that the sound was coming from me. I put a hand over my mouth and shut my eyes. I faced the window and willed myself to sleep.

The turbulence woke me. The first thing I became aware of was the wetness around my crotch and left thigh. I had pissed myself in order to bring a greater sense of elegance to an already superb situation. Someone had put a thin blanket over me to hide the stain. The plane was shaking so hard that no one was allowed to stand, the food and drink service was halted and the screens were dead. My hangover had intensified. I could feel the idea of vomit forming in my gut. I concentrated on keeping it down as the wings struggled to shake loose from the aircraft. Despite the numerous horrors, I was most concerned about the piss. *You're in trouble*, I told myself, but I grinned like an idiot.

The slope in the new world made it easier to slide through

the boundaries of acceptable behaviour. Anyway, it wasn't hard to convince myself that I deserved to cut loose a little after all I had been through. A little piss was no big deal. The pilot mumbled through the tiny speakers that prolonged turbulence was normal over the equator. I tried to will his voice box to implode.

+   +   +

Changing in the absurdly cramped washroom, I began to notice that my mood had been altered in a way I had never experienced. I had less to carry, but I was now willing to carry it. My only major regret was the trouble I had caused back on Arthur Street. The doubt about my decision to tell Mick the truth was gone, though. It was inevitable that he would find out, I told myself, and he had a right to know.

I recalled Ann's slap, the dramatic end of our association. There would be no more contact, I knew. I would miss Mick and Caz, but it was unlikely that they would ever forgive what I had done. I put them out of my head and focused on the terrible concerto of hisses, clicks and murmuring all around me. The turbulence returned and the seat belt lights were switched on with a low, brain-bruising ding. I was instantly ravenous, realizing that there would be no more food for a while.

+   +   +

With four hours left before landing in Honolulu, the world had become an itchy sweater. I wanted to peel my flesh off. I wanted to go through the cabin punching everyone at least once. The captain was jabbering about nothing and I imagined twisting his head off and kicking it up and down the aisles. For just a second, that image made me remember my beating at the hands and feet of the two Aussie thugs. I refused to be sorry for what I was thinking, though. I shut my eyes and stomped on the folk singer's head. I crushed his fingers under my heel, as always. I did it to prove to some illusory observer that what happened to me on my outing with Dave would not change who I was.

The animated plane on the screen above me that indicated our progress seemed to be stopped. Time was slowing down, I thought. It would reverse and I would have to live my days Down Under again, but backwards. It occurred to me that it would all end the same way. More or less. I slept for a while and was woken by a wary flight attendant for the landing in Hawaii.

We were marched through the dank Honolulu airport to be sent through American security. The line-up was long and the aggression in the air was exacerbated by the general grime and minimal staff. Most of the other passengers and I had been sufficiently broken, however, so no one made a fuss. We were put in a small ugly room to wait for an hour.

The flight to Vancouver was two more bad movies and even a fucking newspaper. I had a drink every hour or so to stay afloat, but it was work. The man seated next to me since Hawaii had moved to an empty row in the back because I was muttering to myself, complaining nonsensically. I was anxious to be home, but I decided to stay the night in Vancouver and sleep. Insanity was becoming an issue.

+ + +

The bed in the hotel near the Vancouver airport was nearly enough to cancel out the worst of the journey home. I slept for about nine hours. When I woke, it was evening, but I wasn't sure what day. I remembered phoning to change the flight before crashing. I read the note by the phone and determined that it was the evening of the same day I had arrived. Glad, I ordered room service for the third time in my life.

When the food came, the man delivering the tray was a Rastafarian with a perpetually arched eye brow and a skeptical grin. I looked at him for a few moments deciding whether or not I should ask. As he lifted the lid on my pepper steak, I told him about my trek back to Canada and asked if he had any weed he could sell. He smiled and chuckled.

*You're lucky, my friend. This is my last day in this fuckin' place.*

His accent was comforting. He had to go to the kitchen, but he said he would be back with a joint. I devoured the dinner he had left while I awaited for his return.

+   +   +

On the roof of the hotel, I realized that summer had followed me home. I thought that I was missing a chunk of the year, but it didn't seem to matter. I was glad to have evaded much of the winter. I was even gladder to have a stinky, fat joint in my hand. My new friend, Caesar, had long since acclimated to the B.C. weed, but to me it was almost overwhelming. I listened to his story about leaving Jamaica for Canada sixteen years ago. With a wife and twin girls to support, he took the job at the hotel and gave up on becoming an engineer. Now, he was preparing to take his family to Barbados where he would work construction and escape the West Coast "weirdness" he had never gotten used to.

He said that the water around Barbados is like a mirror because it's so calm. A reef breaks the waves before they can reach the shore. He was rapt by the idea of returning to island life. He asked why I had gone to Sydney and I told him. He wondered if I would ever go back there to live with my foreign family. I told him that I didn't expect to see them again and by my tone, he knew that there was bad blood. He thought about this, solemnly.

*You have to spend time with your mother. To know who you are.*

*I don't think so,* I said, immediately.

He shook his head, becoming serious and preoccupied. That would have been distressing had I not been so blisteringly high on the most magnificent bud on the planet.

*You'll regret it,* he insisted, *if you don't.*

I said nothing, hoping that he would let it go. I resented the air of truth in his vague statement, but I didn't really feel that resentment. There was only the warmth, the familiarity, the pulse of the heart beating outside the body. We watched the planes in the distance, taking off and landing. I thought about Caesar's sacrifice for his family. I reflected on the power a child has over a parent. A normal parent. I began to question my willingness to sacrifice anything for anyone. Once the novelty of the baby's arrival had worn off, would I drift? Would Patty even let me see our kid or would I have to sue her for the right?

I thanked Caesar for the toke and he shook my hand with a tight grip. He looked me in the eye and stated, firmly, *You don't know who you are yet, my friend.*

As we parted company, I wondered if everyone in the new world was going to be so frank and cruelly perceptive. I went to the room to phone Patty. I gave up dialing the number when I realized that the physical distance between us had been drastically reduced. Our proximity always dictated the level of hostility between us and five thousand kilometers was close enough for trouble.

I ate cashews and baked in front of the television. The unblinking Cyclops whore had many channels, all screeching that Doubt wasn't in anymore. Compliance was in. Stupid was in, but had it ever really gone out of style? There was a litany of pretend issues to rock us, gently, to sleep. Everything was under control.

# { 17 }

Waking up in my own bed, my gratitude was obscured, instantly, by a dense cloud of regret. I had arrived at the furthermost point of Misery and that inevitable destination—the one that most people will see only once or twice in their lifetime—had become familiar. I felt a small pang of guilt when I realized that I was thankful to have Hank's death as a valid reason for phoning Patty.

In the shower, I planned what I would say. I would bait her into asking just the right questions so that I could mumble sad answers to rouse her pity. I wondered what she looked like now, if she were much bigger.

Mostly dry, I went to the kitchen to make coffee. The window pane that I had repaired with duct tape, months before, had been replaced while I was away. Or else, in this world, that strange accident had never happened. I made a note to call my landlord to ask him about it and to ask why he hadn't phoned looking for the rent. Then I had to sing "Dear Landlord" by Bob Dylan, up to the word "control". It happened every time I thought or said or heard the word "landlord".

I rolled one for the road and walked to the Main. Small details had changed, here and there. It was all beautiful, even where it was ugly. I walked to Chinatown and had ginger chicken and wonton soup. After that late lunch, I stepped into the rusted frame of a gutted building next door. There where two junkies there, arguing, burning out their scant remaining brain cells. When they wandered off together, I smoked the joint and felt half-way normal. By the time I had started back up to the Plateau, it was nearly four and I wanted a drink. I was sweating by the time I made it to Gilda's.

The bartender I knew didn't seem to recognize me. The stereo puked shitty blues rock from the seventies, the kind that doubles as a last resort laxative for music lovers. I ordered a shot of gin. A woman sat next to me and I got a chill.

*I thought I recognized that ass*, Linda brayed. She laughed her huge laugh as she threw her arms around me. I was as happy as I was horrified. *Hey*, I said, but nothing else would follow it. She was plastered. At least I wouldn't have to listen to the sober version of my new travel agent.

*How was Australia? Was it awesome?*

*It was fantastic*, I told her.

*I'm here with Rob's cousin, Barb. We're celebrating her new job.*

*Oh. Well, don't let me take you from -*

*Come over and say hi!*

She dragged me to her table where Barb, a woman of about fifty, was working undercover as a woman of thirty-five. Her plastic surgeon was as greedy as he was overconfident. She was incoherent, but her instinct to flirt kicked in when she saw me. Linda introduced me to the less than life-like mannequin who tilted her head and grinned.

*I'm Barb.* She put her hand out and I gave it a squeeze. Winking at me nearly caused her to fall into a coma. Linda pulled me down into the seat next to hers and almost crushed one of my fingers pulling her chair up against mine. I began to form an escape plan.

*So how was Australia?*

*It was—*

*Spat went to Australia to visit his mother*, Linda told her all but cataleptic friend.

Barb managed to say, *Oh!*

*Poor Spat*, Linda said, rubbing my arm. She kissed my cheek and told me that she hadn't seen me since the cave men were in diapers.

Mumbling to herself, and suddenly angry about something, Barb stood and started out. Linda followed her, wooden heels farting as they were dragged across the stone floor. I decided to slip out past the sloppy duo. Just as I stood, Linda was back.

*Fuck her. Spoiled sport*, she said.

She was happy to be rid of her friend and told me that Barb was born with a hole in her heart and that no one had expected her to live past twenty-five. Linda hollered, laughing, *She's way past twenty-five now!* I couldn't help but grin even though I wanted to be anyplace else.

*So how was Australia? Tell me all about it.*

*I had a really good time.*

*Good. And how's your mother?*

*Fine. She's fine.*

*Doesn't Patty look great?*

*Well -*

*She looks great. She'll be a great mother.*

*Yeah.*

Suddenly maudlin, Linda shook her head and eyed the floor. I wanted to kick myself, hard, for not having gone to Debris.

*Rob didn't want kids ... but I did.*

*Well ... I had nothing.*

*You ever see him, Spat?*

*No.*

*He lives with a prostitute*, she told me with hilarious gravity. *At least I think that's what she does. Anyway. He ruined his life and there's nothing I can do about it.*

The rest of her monologue was equally fascinating, but as much I hated being with anyone more intoxicated than me, it was nice to hear that laugh again. I felt sorry for her and decided to be a pal.

We did shots of Tequila and cackled about nothing. After a while, it seemed like old times. I missed Rob, for a minute. I longed for my old life and my old problems. I wanted to be me again.

In the cab with Linda, I was relieved to not have to walk. I was drunk enough to ask her if she knew about Rob's secret oral fixation. She didn't blink.

*I often thought he might swing a little ... on the inside.* As we stopped at my intersection, she asked if I wanted to see her new place. I tried to consider the consequences, but they no longer existed. We were, both of us, piteously free.

+  +  +

Hung-over again, I began to discern a pattern. Linda's bed smelled like a battlefield where rival flowers had been beating the shit out each other for a few hundred years. There were so many colours in the room, it was unsettling. There were pictures of beautiful vistas, each with a platitude in calligraphy across the bottom. There were small assemblies of stuffed animals, some of which were positioned to be peaking around lamps and books. All that was missing was a demonic voice telling me to *Get out*.

Linda snored away, still contentedly detached from the physical plane. I had to think like a rat about where I had been and what I had done. I had to then learn it all backwards, as the rats do, so that I would know the way out next time.

I slid out of the over-stuffed bed and dressed as quickly as I could. *You need a job*, I told myself, silently. Just as the second shoe was tied, Linda blew past me like a transfer truck on a summer highway and slammed the bathroom door behind her. *Fuck*, I said aloud, as she puked her guts out. She was flushing the toilet in a vain attempt to cover the sound. I sat on the bed and waited, unable to take the disgusted curl out of my upper lip. When she emerged from the bathroom, she seemed far less wretched than I had expected her to be.

*What's a girl to do, eh, Ducky?*

*Are you OK, Lin?* We both flinched, visibly. Rob had always abbreviated her name that way.

*I have to get ready*, she said. *I'm going to a meeting.*

*Oh.*

*Do you want to come with me? It's right in the neighbour-hood.*

Realizing, by her tone, what kind of meeting she was referring to, I declined but told her that I would walk her there.

On our way to the church, down the block, I tried to make a few jokes, but Linda wasn't biting. She looked so despondent that I just stopped talking and matched her gate, respectfully. I could tell that she was embarrassed. I was, too, but didn't know why. I didn't have the strength to resent her insinuation that I was some kind of a drunk like her. I was up to my chin in my own despair, desperate to be home.

Once, while Mick was down, I tried to cheer him up by singing stupid radio songs off key and out of time. I did it for what could have been an hour, relentlessly, without a breath. He had no means of escape. I imagined having to suffer that performance in the state he was in and felt such profound shame that I broke a sweat.

*Well ... I'll see you, Spat.*

*Take care, Linda.*

*Bye.*

She went to the side door. I pretended not to notice that she couldn't open it and I kept walking. For blocks, I could still hear her knocking. I wondered what was in there that she needed so badly. I wondered why she had arrived so early to get it.

+    +    +

When I woke, it was late afternoon. Enthusiastic sex with Linda played back in my head until the memory of the morning ruined it. I hoped that she wouldn't call. I hoped that there had been a condom. I was missing large portions of the night's festivities.

Later, Linda told my machine that she was sorry about asking me to come to the meeting with her. She explained that she had behaved the way she did with me because she was drunk. She had only started to drink again a few days before and was going to try to get sober again.

*One day at a time,* she said. There was a pause before the line went dead, as though she were going to say something more but had thought better of it.

+     +     +

I deleted three days with a bag of bud and slept as much as possible. The landlord explained that he had replaced the kitchen window at Hank's request, while I was away. My dead uncle had come by to pay my rent for the next year as a way to commemorate his impending conclusion. In our exchange, the Dear Landlord said that he had replaced another window on the same side of the building after the night of the meth lab explosion. It was only a block away, but I saw nothing of it until my head ornament arrived through the glass. In the gale that was blowing, the blast had been all but absorbed, I guessed. When he said "meth lab", I thought of poor Dave, of course. It was hard to imagine him in a church basement, coming clean and getting humble.

+     +     +

Patty didn't call. I broke down on a Saturday morning and phoned her. A man answered and I held my breath for a moment.

*Who's this?*

*This is Brian. Who's this?*

I hung up the phone. My new archenemy was Brian. That fucking asshole would get his, one way or another. Who was he to ask who I was? That little prick. Moments later, the phone rang.

*Hello.*

*Hello,* Patty said and sighed. *I think we should meet.*

I said nothing.

*I have some information for you,* she deadpanned. *About the keys to Hank's.*

I wanted to spew every unused insult, every quieted barb, at her. My voice, delivering them through the phone line, would turn her neighbourhood to dust and vaporize Hitler where she stood.

I mumbled, sulking, *Where do you want to meet?*

+ + +

I waited for her in the café on Fairmont that we used to go to on Sunday mornings. I was high enough to stomach a heavy emotional scene, if it went that way, but not so high that I wouldn't care about it. With Patty, things could go in any direction.

There was music playing, somewhere. Seeing myself in a mirror behind the counter, I couldn't help but to notice that I was made entirely of scar tissue. Outside the mirror, I probably looked the same as always. More or less. Both, probably. In that glass, however, there was poetic truth—a truth that had advanced far beyond quaint reason. With another glance, it gave me the distinct sensation that everything was inside-out and backwards, but that our species had evolved to be oblivious to that fact. Our senses were really only defenses against our truth, a by-product of living in, and as, an illusion. While I knew that the Inside-out Hypothesis probably wasn't valid in any literal way, I thought it was nonetheless convincing. The hopelessly insane were, I further theorized, the rare few among us who could perceive our real state. Becoming one of them, I had already begun to romanticize the condition.

Next to the mirror, a picture of a man with his hand over his eyes reminded me of what Caesar had told me on the roof of the hotel. I tried to convince myself that he had not really been talking to me when he offered his advice. I decided that he had been projecting his own longing to know himself and that it had been filtered through homesickness and undeclared doubt. I wondered how island life was treating him.

In the new world, everyone seemed to know me, or at least something about me. The waiter smirked a bit as he delivered the coffee. I wanted to give him a smack. I wanted to complain about the music, but I still wasn't sure where it was coming from or if it was, more disturbingly, internal.

I shuddered at the thought that I might still be lying in the Australian desert, dreaming as I slowly bled to death. If I were making up my life, though, I could have done a much better job of it.

I tried not to, but I thought of Mick. I thought of him as a child, floating to the kitchen and then falling to the floor in amazement. He had probably never really hated anyone until I came along. I drove him from my head by repeatedly counting the eleven postcards that were clustered around a picture of Albert Einstein with his tongue out.

Brushing my cheek with finger tips, I realized that I had never stopped feeling the slap. I wondered if Ann regretted it or if it were the only memory of me that gave her any contentment.

It seemed that I had become a universal antagonist. I could show up anywhere, I thought, and spoil everything. I was more a device than a man, randomly bringing unwanted change to happy people.

Seeing Patty coming, her large belly leading the way, I almost laughed. Then, instantly, I felt the presence of something sacred and mysterious. She was abundant and fundamental. She needed someone to take care of her. That was why she had this Brian guy hanging around, I decided. He was subbing for me until I got my shit together.

*God, you look terrible*, she said.

*Who's Brian?*

She eyed me for a moment, sharpening up her words before firing them at me.

*He's my partner, Spat. He's the baby's father.*

*I thought you weren't sure who -*

*Well, it's most likely him.*

*So then why did you tell me that it could be mine?*

*I was trying to do the right thing. I didn't come here to fight with you.*

*So why are you here?*

She dug through her purse for an index card. She tossed it in front of me and folded her arms.

*Is there any point in talking to you?*

I didn't answer. I only looked at her and wished that I could be normal.

*I slept with Linda.* There was no telling why I said that.

She raised her eyebrows and grinned a little. *Really?*

*I just thought you should know.*

*Why? ... I don't care who you sleep -*

*Tell me about Brian.*

She sighed. *I don't want to fight with you, Spat.*

*I'm making conversation.*

*No, you're not. You're looking for a weakness to exploit. You're trying to see if there's any hope for me and you, but there isn't. We're done ... We were done before we even got started.*

There had definitely been a change in her. There was no conceit in her tone to bait me into retaliating. She didn't need or want to fight. She had moved on, just as I knew she would.

*I love you,* I said and wondered if it were true.

She scoffed, quietly. She shook her head, looking at me as though I were a dog who had just been playing with her underwear.

*Oh, Spat,* she said. *Shut the fuck up.*

*What if I'm the father?*

*Then we'll work something out.*

*Do you hate me?*

*Of course, I don't hate you. Grow up.*

That she didn't hate me seemed like enough, all of a sudden. She asked about Australia. I told her that it would take a while to get it all out. I expected her to make an excuse to leave. Instead, she sat, took a sip of my water and said, *Go.*

She was actually interested and that gave me hope. Subconsciously, I suppose I knew that I didn't really want her back. I just wanted to forget everything I had learned.

Telling her about Ann and Caz and Mick, I realized how much space they had come to occupy. When I got to the beating, I told it with as much detail as I could. I wanted to stress how close I had come to dying. She was trying not to react and I was glad to have some effect, however small. Of course, I didn't tell her why it had happened. I didn't need to listen to her laughing about that. When I told her about how the last day with my foreign family had ended, a rogue tear escaped and I was embarrassed. I was still not sorry for telling Mick the truth, but I was sorry about the result.

*I wish I had kept my mouth shut.*

*You did what you thought was right.* She put her hand over mine and I had to fight to hold myself together. I wanted her to touch my face. I wanted her to forgive me. I wanted forgiveness from her for things about which she knew nothing.

*It's going to take a while to figure it all out, Spat. Give it time.*

Having it, I began to no longer want her sympathy. I picked up the index card and read it.

*It's Hank's lawyer's number,* she said. *He has the keys to the house.*

I smirked. *Fucking Hank,* I thought. *What a dick. I should go,* I said. *Sorry for being an ass.* She would not let go of my hand until I looked her in the eye. When I did, she tried to convey something to me, but it was far too understated for me to comprehend. She left me there to speculate.

Walking home, I willed everyone I saw to die in a messy and spectacular way. The bodies in the street behind me did little to erase Patty's words. *He's my partner, Spat. He's the baby's father.* Imagining her new partner's head so that I could hack it off with a dull ax did nothing for me. Brian had to die. I knew that his name meant "strength", but I was sure that he would not live up to it. Even if he did, taking another thrashing would not change anything in the vomiting pool swim that I had come to know as life. I was sweating hatred; fumes rose from me, blurring the background above my head. Windows rattled as I passed and animals cowered. Beams in roofs creaked, asphalt buckled. Cars within my field of vision exploded into colourful dust. Carving a chaotic path of destruction across Parc. I stopped, briefly, caught in the bog of my own disgust. I stared at the sidewalk and counted silently. I wanted to explode and explode and explode. I wanted to leave a crater so huge that it would have made this planet look like a crescent moon.

+     +     +

Hank had left enough booze to supply a good sized funeral or a couple of weddings. I went from room to room, inspecting each one like a prowler with no fear of being caught. I was being watched, though. There were two of them now, up there on the ceiling. Finn and Hank, reunited in death, were haunting me out of boredom. Soon, with no one willing to remember them, they would be gone.

Hank had obviously scoured the place before his departure. Dry cleaned clothes hung in the sparse bedroom closet. There were boxes on the shelf above them. I didn't want to be, but I was curious.

Sitting in the middle of the floor, I went through the hundreds of photographs quickly, disallowing sentiment. There were many of Ann, a fewer number of Ann and Finn together. There was only one of Hank with the woman he had loved. It was a party and they were seated together, singing. Seeing their youth, captured in a black and white slice, gave me a moment of boundless empathy. But mostly, looking back at a history I had spent years trying to revise and forget left me cold.

I found a stash of "girlie magazines" from the seventies under a box of bank statements and wondered why they were hidden. I flipped through them until it occurred to me that all of those women would be old now. Or dead. There were cameras, ancient and complicated. There were two old travel books about Australia. He had planned a trip, I surmised, until she told him about Dennis. Or maybe he had once planned to go there to kick some scientist ass.

When I found the picture of me holding Mick when he was a baby, all of the possibilities that were long ago forbidden by ego and alcohol, showed themselves in a jumble of bright images. Nonetheless, I didn't waste any time mourning things that never were. Instead, I accepted what had become of us because there was no way to undo it.

I knew that there were other facts that I needed to face, so I poured some gin into a beer mug and listened to "Chet Baker Sings" on Hank's prehistoric stereo. That voice made me higher than I had been in years. It warmed the house and cleared the ceiling of eavesdroppers.

Chet Baker was beaten, badly, in the summer of 1966 by five men. It happened in San Francisco and was possibly drug-related. People always said that the assault cost him his teeth, but the heroin took those. He deteriorated after that beating until he had become his opposite. I liked that Hank was a fan.

My uncle had managed to lose most of what he didn't want, which, for some of us, is as good as getting. I had no reason to judge him. I had no reason to hate him. I knew that he would have left me something in the will, despite the vast distance between us. Mick would get the most, I imagined, because he was closer.

I woke on the stairs where I had been sitting. It was dark outside. I had to get a look at the mysterious Brian. I had to know if he were bigger than me or younger. I finished what was left in the beer mug at my feet. I knew I couldn't walk very far, so I searched the house for a phone and a number for a cab.

+   +   +

Sometimes we do things that get us into trouble in order to resolve long-standing issues in a memorable or flashy way. Waking up on Patty's couch to the aroma of fresh puke, I held my breath in a vain attempt to induce a fatal heart attack. I knew that if I could stand, I could probably run out of there and never look back.

*Oh, for fuck sake!*

*I'll clean it up*, I said, weeping with pain.

*Just get the hell out of here!*

*I'm sorry.* I wanted to sit up, but I couldn't.

*Just go!* She screamed so loudly, a vein burst in my right temple. No matter how hard I tried, I could not will myself to move. *Now!* She kicked my foot and I felt nothing.

*I can't move.* I was sobbing, now, like a he-man or superhero. *I can't move!*

*You fucking asshole. I hope you have alcohol poisoning!*

As distraught as I was, it was nice to have the old Patty back.

*This is why I can't have you around when the baby's born. You're way too out of control to be near a newborn. Or any kid. You're fucking disgusting. Look at yourself. Look!*

I managed to drop my left foot to the floor, but I still had no capacity to move the rest of the body. From my point of view, the room got darker for a moment and I felt my stomach turn again. There was buzzing in my ears and I seemed to be losing consciousness. A gutful of hot acid made its way upward. I swallowed to stop it, but I was too late. It spewed from me in short blasts like water coming from a pipe full of air pockets.

+   +   +

I woke-up in the middle of the night, unsure of the date or time or location. There was a rat on my chest, curled up, sleeping. I knew that if I moved, he would wake up and I would be bitten by one of my own kind. It was a city rat with city rat ideas. He ate high quality garbage and drank from backyard pools. He had padded through the night like a spy, fearless and determined, until he found me. As my eyes adjusted the sewer king became a cat. I touched its head and it looked at me with its pupils flashing gold and green. It began to purr and kneed my chest. I realized that I was at home. I blinked hard, a few times, but the cat was real.

When I got up, it followed me to the kitchen. The apartment door was open. My pants were hanging out of the sink. There was a broken glass on the table. My visitor stood in the doorway and surveyed what it had evidently claimed as its territory. I tried to shoo it out, but it raised its tail, walking in figure eights and meowing. I winced as my perpetual headache reasserted itself. I closed the door and went back to bed. The cat curled up at my feet and sighed through a low rumble.

As soon as I had shut my eyes, the phone began to ring. I knew, immediately, who it was. When the out-going message finished playing, there was a brief pause before the dial tone. I wondered what time it was there and if they were all right.

# { **18** }

Under self-imposed house arrest, I hardly had a toke for days. I didn't drink. I did squats and push-ups, crunches. I ate nothing but vegetables and fish. I needed a clear head to develop an effective redemption scam. There had to be a way to get back into Patty's good graces. I knew she was right about me. I was a stinking, disgusting fucking mess. Secretly, I had no intention of changing anything, permanently, but she would see an entirely new man when I was done. All I had to do was stop drinking and stop showing up at her door at five in the morning, intending to pick a fight with her boyfriend.

I found Linda's number and left a message. I apologized for not calling sooner and asked if I could go to a meeting with her. My new roommate stared at me, seemingly judging my performance. His fur was a tapestry of mismatched patches, his nose and ears had been scarred by many expert claws. His tail was too short. He was a wretched exile who looked as though he had been hastily assembled out of spare parts, but his gratitude had already given way to a smug sense of entitlement. I named him Adrian, not that he cared. He squinted at me when I finished my message to Linda. Even he could tell how full of shit I had sounded.

Linda called back within the hour.

+ + +

The church basement smelled as though it had once experienced a fire that had been beaten out with wet wool blankets. I steeled myself against any remorse I might have felt for being there on pretense. Looking at that serious assemblage of people, it was hard to imagine what they could have had in common. Besides the apparent desire to share dreary stories and smoke cigarettes, they could have been invited randomly. After a prayer and some other chatter that I ignored, Linda talked about how she had gone to work drunk and had told her boss to suck an egg. It didn't seem like a big deal since she didn't get fired, but she cried over it.

I kept quiet. The important thing was that I was there. I knew that Linda would tell Patty about it. I could keep my distance and lay the foundation for long term deceit—the old fashioned kind, the all-weather deceit that stands up to shit like reason and integrity. It was an acting job, I decided. I had only to learn what to say and how to be. I had always thought that I would be a good actor, but that it would be hard to keep from laughing.

Near the end of the meeting, I became acutely aware of a man sitting a few seats from me. He was about sixty, maybe older. He had white hair, the ghost of a crew cut. He had a hooked prosthetic for a left hand. I avoided his X-ray gaze by scanning the walls. He saw through me the way we all see through everyone, if we look, but he had an intention. I knew, immediately, that he had something to say to me that I wouldn't like. I knew. He smirked at me as I was leaving and I shivered. I had not felt anything like it for years. I was deeply afraid. There was no malice driving him, I could tell, but that made him all the more disturbing. He was a different kind of trouble maker: a truth teller, a peeler of lies.

Walking home, I wondered if Finn might have been responsible for the loss of that stranger's left hand. Being a dead ringer, I knew that there was always the prospect of having to pay some old debt to some old man with a bad memory. I saw him pulling my heart out with his hook and I almost chuckled.

+ + +

I went back to the creepy church basement, hoping to get some information about Patty. Sadly, Linda was a no-show. I was pissed off, staring at a spot on the floor, waiting for the right moment to leave. It was that day when the odd stranger first introduced himself. There were lots of empty chairs, but he sat next to me. I kept stealing glimpses of his prosthesis and he kept catching me and grinning. When the meeting finally ended, he invited me to join him for coffee. So persuasive was everything about his character, that he easily extinguished any possibility of my saying no. He was a messenger and there was no stopping him.

We walked in silence for a while and I wondered if he would turn on me with his hook in my face and tell me to stay away from his church.

*I'm Gil.*

*Spat.*

*Spat?*

*Yeah.*

*Like the shoe?*

*Yeah.*

*Do you have a sponsor, Spat?*

*No,* I said, not knowing what he was talking about, but assuming that it was group related.

*Are you high?*

*No. Of course not.*

*Of course not.*

Out of terror, I ignored his mildly sarcastic tone. My character was becoming, under his friendly scrutiny, more evident. There was no safe subject.

In the café, I dreaded sitting and having to face him. To avoid an interrogation, I told him about my trip. His face was in a state of constant surprise, tempered by easy compassion. He had tattoos on his forearm, symbols and letters from foreign alphabets. It was a fractured and scattered equation that had probably added up to something, once. I speculated that a piece of it, if not the solution, had been on the back of the lost hand. My fear of him waned, as I spoke, but I still anticipated a shock.

He told me that he owned a used bookstore. He married and divorced three women in forty years. He had two sons, both musicians, who he had not spoken to in more than twenty years. He had drunk himself into a hole and attempted to take everyone around him down into it. He had been an unrepentant serial drunk, but he had now been sober for eighteen years.

*What made you come to the meeting, Spat?*

I knew that there was no use in making up a sad story, especially since he already had me pegged as a liar. I told him that it was all about scoring normalcy points with my ex.

*I knew Linda would tell Patty that I was getting sober and then I could give her time to cool off and then, you know, start over.*

He laughed, gleefully and regarded me as though I were some quaint, comic relic from the past. *Linda won't tell her anything Spat. We're anonymous. Besides, your ex will know you're still drinking. She's seen it all by now.*

*I don't drink that much,* I said.

*Hardly at all, probably,* Gil said, smiling.

*Yes, I drink. But not like you guys. Not like you.*

*I'm only teasing,* he said. *Why don't you keep coming to the meetings, anyway?*

Again, something about him made it impossible to decline.

*Sure,* I said. *I should get going.* I left him there, and tried to feel suspicious of him. He had no defense and that was his strength. He didn't need a cover anymore.

+    +    +

The calls kept coming and I kept ignoring them. If there were something urgent, she would have left messages. Then, I wondered, if it had been Mick and not Ann dialing my number.

I had never seen him use a phone. I didn't think that he could manage it on his own. It had to be Ann. I didn't want or require her apology, if that was why she was calling. If she only wanted to hurl more of her disgust at me, I didn't need that, either. I didn't imagine that it was Caz phoning. I had hurt the man she adored and there was no forgiving that.

The days got warmer and longer. I started running on the mountain every morning. The dog walkers and joggers were all but invisible to me. In the new world, things unobserved did not exist. I was getting stronger, almost back to the way I was before Aussie.

I went back once more for a meeting. I can't say why. Someone I didn't know took me aside before it had started and told me that I smelled like weed. Apparently the reformed drunks didn't like people getting high either. I left without saying a word. A week or so later, out of curiosity and maybe a little guilt, I found Gil's store. He seemed to have been expecting me. I wasn't there for ten minutes when he offered me the "job."

I spent three days a week "working" in Gil's cramped, chaotic "bookstore". It was a literary compost heap in a box. There was no order, even as far as Gil could tell. Regulars came in to browse for hours and piss me off with stupid questions, most of which I couldn't answer. Gil came in and out all day, checking up on me, getting on my nerves.

Our arguments were frequent and satisfying. I had a feeling that Gil was on a mission to save me. For that, I felt obliged to him and my resentment of that obligation grew, steadily.

*Have you talked to Patty yet?*

*No. Mind your own business, ya old bastard.*

*You're afraid. You know you can't face her until you can do it sober.*

*Wow, you're really insightful.*

*You know it, Jack.*

If I'd had a nickel for every time he called me Jack I would have at least three dollars by then, which was just slightly less than what he was paying me per hour.

I had thought about trying to reconcile with Hitler, but I was still focused on the approaching battle. I had a clear picture of the evil Brian in my head and had devised innumerable ways for that oily fucker to die.

Though I wouldn't admit it to Gil, I had not had a drink since the last time I had left the church basement. I felt better than I had since doing push-ups in Ann's backyard. The tilt in the new world seemed less obvious. I was adapting.

# { 19 }

I was rolling a joint at the kitchen table when a sickening feeling of dread nearly turned my stomach. There was a knock at the door and the feeling intensified. I chose to ignore it and continued my work. The knocking persisted and I sensed that the potent malevolence outside would not quit until I faced it.

When I opened the door, I revealed a vision so horrible that my first thought was to gouge out my eyes and fill the holes with putty. Patty's scabrous mother, Constance, stared at me with her arms folded. She was ready to brawl.

*May I speak with you?*

I considered her question for a good minute while she waited, staring. Finally, my curiosity made me step aside and gesture for her to come in.

She entered and inspected the room, wincing at the broad-spectrum grime. I smiled at her, happy that I still repulsed her so. I pulled a chair out from the table and made a big show of brushing the seat clean for her. Knowing how much she hated having her ugly name abbreviated, I said, *Have a seat, Connie.* She cringed and sat as though she were landing ass-first into a bucket of warm innards. I offered her tea.

*I know what you think of me*, she said.

*I think you're a peach*, I told her and finished rolling. She watched me, waiting for me to be done so that she would have my complete attention. There was almost something sentimental about her scorn for me. When I was done, I put the spliff in my mouth and gave her a much practiced look of total apathy.

*Please don't light that*, she said. I put the joint down and smirked at her. Just then, as though sensing her hatred for all noble creatures, Adrian jumped into her lap. He sniffed at her chin. Constance recoiled, raising her hands.

*Get it off me!*

*He won't bite*, I said.

She stood to force him to jump. He hung on for a moment, his claws hooked in her white slacks, and then let go. I made a mental note to bathe him. I didn't want the atrocious stench of her perfume on my buddy.

Constance turned away from me, getting a look at the long forgotten dishes in the sink. She sighed, heavily and shook her head. When she faced me, I thought that she might cry.

*I came here to make a proposal.*

*Well. As flattered as I am, Connie, I'm not looking to get married again.*

*Listen to me, you ...* She calmed herself and contemplated the shit in her head for a long time. *When you have a child*, she said, *you realize that who they'll be depends on who you are. Even when they're adopted, like Patricia was, you—*

*What's this about, Con?*

She gave me such a defeated look that her humanoid form seemed almost real for a second. Adrian meowed at her, demanding her attention. She stepped away from him and asked if I would put him out.

*He's agoraphobic.*

*All right*, she said, approaching me. *This is my proposal.*

I put my elbows on the table and rested my tilted head in my hands, smiling at her.

*I will pay you to stay away from Patricia and the baby when he's born.*

Her offer didn't surprise me. It was almost funny, but her referral to the baby as a male bothered me.

*How do you know it's a he?*

*I know. The point is ... we think that, for the child's sake, you should stay away.*

*Who's "we"?*

*All of us! You ruined enough of my daughter's life. Let her raise her son without your ... God, look at this place. Look at how you live!*

Finally, I knew for sure that the baby was mine. I wanted to celebrate. I lit the joint. Constance tightened her puckered lips making her mouth look like a lipstick smeared anus, more so. I blew a cloud of smoke in her direction and all of the abhorrence she had ever inspired in me renewed itself and then dissipated in an instant. I was having a son and the surprising delight I felt gave me an even greater distance from her disdain. Not even the shadow of the other man could spoil it.

*Are the drugs your escape*, she asked, quietly, *from being what you are?*

*You want some of this, Connie?*

*This isn't a joke, you stupid ...* Again, she reigned in her fury while avoiding Adrian. I began to see how much she had aged. I imagined her funeral and the many ways in which I could add to the merriment of that occasion.

*Ten thousand dollars*, she said, and I cackled until I coughed up a piece of lung. I went to the sink and discharged a gob onto a crud-encrusted plate. I began to giggle at her revulsion and danced a little to infuriate her. She watched me with the determination of a predator and I thought that I would burst with joy. I danced with more gusto, shaking my ass at her and laughing.

*Ten thousand dollars*, she repeated. *That should buy all the dope you'll need until you finally manage to kill yourself.*

I picked up Adrian and cuddled him against my face. He purred and cleaned my cheek with his sandpaper tongue as we swayed together. Finally, having adequately angered Constance, I stopped dancing and leaned against the stove. I smiled at her and wondered what her gourd of a head would look like on a stick.

*Do you care, at all, about the baby, Spat?*

It was the first time she had ever said my name in my presence. She was showing me how serious she was about her duty.

*How can I explain this to you, Constance?* I put Adrian down and matched my enemy's posture. *Your opinion of me has no relevance anywhere, with anyone. My relationship with my son is none of your business. And you and that slack-jawed cadaver you're married to can go fuck your revolting selves back to hell.*

*Twenty thousand*, she said, unfazed by my poetry. I was only half aware of her. I was euphoric and rattled, too, from speaking the phrase "my son". I knew that I had to see Patty soon. I was sure that she had nothing to do with her hideous mother's plan.

*Twenty thousand*, she repeated. *You could go to live in Australia. They have dope down there, don't they?*

I smiled and told her that the Aussies had some awesome weed. It troubled me that Patty had told her reptilian mother anything about my trip. I had to wonder if she were finally becoming one of them.

*I don't want your money, Con. I don't want anything from you.*

*Don't you care about the baby? Don't you want him to have a better role model?*

*Like who, Brian?*

*Brian? My nephew, Brian?*

A light went on. Suddenly, I remembered him. Young Brian was a boring and exceedingly likable kid who was studying at Concordia the last time I had seen him. There was no boyfriend. There never was any other contender. Patty had gambled that I would not remember him when she referred to Brian as her partner. I smiled so broadly and so genuinely at Constance that it confused her.

*Your nephew, Brian.*

*Take my offer, Spat. Please. If you care anything about that child, you'll stay away.*

*Is Brian living with Patty?*

*He's been helping her out since she's on her own, now. Mind you, she always was.*

*Listen, Constance, I love you the way flies love pig shit, but you can shove all of your money all the way up your bony old ass. Now get the fuck out before I sic the cat on you.*

With that, she went to the door. She stopped, as I knew she would, to make one more plea. I farted, a brief trumpet solo. She left. I tossed the roach into the ashtray and picked up the phone.

I began to leave a message for Patty. *Hey, Sweetheart. It's me, Spat. Listen, your mother was just here and I had to call to let you know that I -*

She picked up. I could feel her apprehension already.

*She went to your apartment?*

*Yeah. It was really nice to see it again. It offered me money to stay away from our son.*

Silence. I waited. It seemed as though the phone had gone dead until I heard a man's voice in the background.

*Is that Brian I hear?*

*Yes*, she said, quietly.

*Your cousin, Brian?*

*What do you want?*

*I want you to show me some respect! I want you to stop lying to me!*

*You first*, she said and the line went dead. I re-dialed and Brian answered.

*Hey, Brian, it's Spat calling.*

*Oh ... Hey, Spat ... Um ... I'll get Patty.*

Her voice was different now. It was a tone I had never heard before. There was a sobering sadness and finality in it.

*I lied to you because I don't want you around the baby.*

*I don't give a fuck about what you want, you lying fucking bitch.*

*It wasn't my idea to try and buy you off. That was her idea.*

*You knew ... Fuck! You knew that he was mine. You knew that we were having a boy and you didn't tell me.*

*We aren't having anything*, she said, coldly. *I'm having a baby. You're having a party that never fucking ends.*

*I don't drink anymore. I don't get high. I don't deserve to be treated like a—*

*Oh, shut the fuck up, Spat! I've had enough of the stupid, stupid, stupid fucking lies you tell.*

*You're the liar! You were going to pretend that someone else was the father of my kid, for fuck sake!*

*And why would I do that?*

*Cuz you're a giant-sized bitch, that's why.*

*Tell me this, Spat. If you were a kid, would you want Spat Ryan for a father?*

I had no rebuttal. I stood there, squeezing the phone, my heart pounding. Her question was pain itself because I knew the answer. I would not want Spat Ryan for a father, maybe not even for a friend. I dropped the phone and stared into space. Adrian was sitting on the table with a bud in his mouth. He eyed me, startled by the sound of the phone hitting the floor. The last part of my resistance had crumbled, quietly, revealing vast fields of regret.

Walking to the bookstore, I replayed my conversation with Patty's mother and reversed our positions. Seeing through her eyes, having even a little sympathy for her, was stomach-churning and bordered on the obscene; but, I had no protection from the increasing awareness that had begun dogging me. Her offer of money, as hilarious as it was, came from love—or at least, Con's attempt at love. Her family was closing ranks against the return of the all-purpose villain: the one whose name is also the name for baby oysters. At least, the weird sisters say that it is. I have never checked. The sad Virgil's were set to drive me into the sea where I could join the other spats and die, out of sight and mind.

*Looks whose here*, Gil mumbled when I arrived at the store. I said nothing and went to the window. I watched the traffic and was lulled by the drone of the speeding thoughts that had silenced me. I saw the faint reflection of Gil in the glass, turning a page as he looked my way.

*What's up?*

I could hear him, but I could not respond. Somewhere in the drone, I was sorry for having gone to the store where he could see yet another view of his friend's decline. I was sorry that I had told Patty that I didn't get high anymore. I was nothing but sorry.

*Ya all right? ... Spat?*

The light drained and I was blind. Before I could react to that loss, gravity pushed on me until I collapsed.

+    +    +

When I returned to the waking world Gil was crouching, watching me as though I were appearing before him out of nothing. I was sitting up in a chair that had been covered with stacks of Stone Age encyclopedias when I came in. My eyes focused and he smiled.

*Ya all right?*

My voice had not made it back with me. I opened my mouth, coaxing a sound, but there was nothing. I stood, a little unsteadily. Gil held onto my arm.

*Maybe you should stay in the chair.*

I took deep breaths, trying not to panic. I forced air out, hoping to engage my voice but it was gone. I looked at Gil and he knew that something was wrong. I went to the register and found a pen. I tore a page from his Daily Inspiration calendar and scrawled across it, "I can't speak." We stood there, the two of us, baffled.

*This ever happen before?*

I shook my head no.

*Well ...* He seemed to be considering the possibilities as they speeded past him. *Did you hit your head?*

I shrugged. He approached and went into his obnoxious military mode, taking over.

*We're going to the hospital.*

I indicated the negative by sneering at him and wandering back to the chair.

*Come on. This could be serious, Jack ... Listen, to me.*

I shook my head and sat. I picked up a tattered magazine and flipped through it, looking at the pictures while I tried to fathom what was happening to me. I told myself that I should never have let Patty go. I should never have left Montreal. I should have followed the prints in the dirt ahead of me, instead of going my own way. I had taken so many wrong turns and for so many ridiculous reasons, it was becoming clearer that the second half of this ride would be a lot worse than the first. There was no happy end in store, I knew. I was too old to start over. I knew that "too old" couldn't have been more relative, but I wanted it to be true. I wanted to be excused from everything. I wondered if I was willing myself to shut down, a bit at a time, in a sort of prolonged suicide by thought. I dreamed, then, that the Virgil family had, by combined will, made me mute. And why not? I had nothing to say, anyway. Something sharp poked my arm hard enough for me to yell, *Ow!*

*There's your voice*, Gil said, folding his pocket knife shut.

*What the fuck?!*

*I figured that you just needed a little jolt to kick it into gear*, he said, sauntering back to the register.

*You're a fuckin' medical mastermind, Gilrod.*

*It worked, didn't it?*

Relieved and almost grateful, I scowled at him and went back to the window. He stayed quiet for a few minutes, but I knew there would be a million questions.

*What made you faint?*

*I don't know.*

*Low blood sugar, maybe.*

*I don't know.*

*That could be serious, Jack. You should see a doctor.*

A college kid came in and Gil, as usual, greeted her as though she were a regular. She smiled at him and nodded, adjusting her knapsack. She began to dig through the bins, feeding the anarchy. I was focused on the street again, watching people and wondering how they manage to make it through the day without kicking someone's head off.

*Excuse me*, the kid said. She was next to me, smiling like someone who had never been out in the world. She was cute, but that wasn't the worst of it. She had clearly been loved enough and probably hadn't seen past the surface of anything yet.

*Yeah?*

*Do you have a copy of* Animal Farm?

*No*, I said.

*Are you sure?*

I sighed and almost sneered at her. I told her, *No, I'm not sure. Look at this place.*

*Lose your voice again*, Gil said, approaching. *We have a whole herd of* Animal Farm*s in here, somewhere.*

*Thanks, anyway*, our sole customer said, grinning at me. She followed Gil to a box of ravaged paperbacks. He decided to fill her in on recent events.

*He just fainted a minute ago.*

*Really?*

*Yeah. Then he couldn't talk.*

*Shouldn't you take him to a doctor?*

*He's as stubborn as a jackass.*

*My Dad's like that*, she said.

As annoying as they were, all I could think about was Patty's question about who would want me for a father. The thought of never seeing the baby and not protecting him from the Virgil's and all of the other vermin in the world was unbearable. He needed me and would eventually set out to find me, anyway. Why put him through all of that? But then, why put him through the misery of having a giant asshole for a parent? Change was looming, a giant bank vault suspended above my head with fishing line.

*Found one*, the kid said. She flipped through the tattered *Animal Farm* as she scuffed to the register. *How much?*

*Is it for school?*

*Yeah.*

*Nothing.*

*Really?*

*Sure*, Gil said, shrugging. *It's not that good.*

*Thanks!* She started out and called to me as she went, *Bye, Fainty!*

I knew that the restored silence wouldn't last. I thought of a good excuse to leave and considered telling him that I was going to a hospital.

*What's going on, Jack?*

*I don't want to talk about it.*

*Why? What did you do?*

*It isn't what I did*, I said. *It's ...*

*What?*

I told him about the offer from Constance and about Patty's question. He thought for while. To me, his silence implied that the Virgil women had a case. He was looking for just the right way to call me a dick.

*Come to a meeting, Jack.*

*Will you let that go, please?*

*You won't stay sober on your own for long. And it's not just about abstinence, anyway.*

*Look. I don't like your church.*

He insisted that the program wasn't a religion and that the higher power could be anything I wanted it to be. I told him that the whole god concept was only a way to divide people, the means to feign moral superiority.

*If you don't believe that there's anything greater than you, I feel sorry for you*, he said.

*No, you don't. You feel insulted and threatened because I won't play along with what you're pretending.*

*I have beliefs, Jack. I have faith. I'm not pretending anything.*

*Believing is pretending. I have enough fiction.*

He shook his head and walked away.

*Poor Spat*, he mumbled.

*Fuck off*, I answered, quietly.

Later, after he had time to mull it over, he said, *But you have to admit that there seems to be some intelligence in the universe. Why else would it all be so -*

I barked, *I don't know! I don't know and you don't know! That's what we have in common with everyone else on Earth ... and with everyone who has ever existed. We don't know.*

That shut him up, but I knew that he would not concede anything. I was a nut to crack and my would-be savior was up to the challenge. He was muttering to himself, sweeping the floor as though he were gathering up the shards of our dispute to make some new assertion from the pieces. Of course, there was nothing new to be said on the subject. I had long since chosen to ignore opinion, popular or otherwise. Besides, knowing how much blood would be spilled in its name, a truly benevolent deity would never allow itself to exist.

*If you have no faith*, Gil said, *what do you have?*

*Nothing*, I told him. *You're right and I'm wrong. You're good and I'm bad.*

He shook his head and exhaled through his teeth rather than telling me to go to hell. There was a long silence, interrupted only by his snide grumbling. I didn't need him distracting me as I was beginning to formulate a plan to smarten the fuck up.

*Sooner or later*, the guru mumbled, *you'll give up the fight.*

*What fight?*

*The fight ... You don't have to fight, you know—with everything and everybody.*

*Maybe I should let go and get God.*

*Maybe you should ... at least let go.*

I headed for the door.

*Where are you goin'?*

*Drinkin'*, I said, slamming the door behind me.

# { 20 }

Walking east on Saint Catherine's, a revolving wreath of gin martinis encircled my head like cartoon concussion birds. Each was frosty and wet, spinning and tempting. I counted vertical lines to distract myself, to avoid the allure of the generalized resentment that always leads to trouble.

*You don't know who you are yet, my friend.* Caesar's words were as clear in memory as they were the night he made that accusation. It was obvious that I had always been little more than a collection of reckless adaptations and lies. The man I was supposed to have been would never be retrieved, but I had no inclination to mourn the loss.

Two and a half crack heads were begging outside a fast food shit shop. I noticed that one was wearing what looked like the winter coat I had lost, months before. His eyes widened when he saw me and I knew for sure. He pointed at me, nudging the smirking corpse next to him. I pretended not to see him there, beaming toothlessly, teetering above his death. Though I had no recollection of having met him, there was something familiar in his voice as he yelled, *You're that guy!* I chuckled. When I was nearly a block away, he hollered, *God bless you!*

When I arrived home, there was a letter from Hank's lawyer. It was to inform me, officially, that I was now the owner of my uncle's house and all of its contents. His extravagant and unexpected gift felt, immediately, like a burden; a mess he left for me to clean. I did not want to live there, in the skin of the life he had shed. Nor did I want to be a landlord. My first thought was to sell it and get stinking rich. I smoked a joint and began to discern the thunderous progress of the past, rolling like a juggernaut behind me. For the first time, that sound was getting further away. Either I had moved forward or it was giving up the chase.

*Fuck you, Hank.* I phoned Patty. Brian told me that she had gone to see her doctor.

*Is she all right?*

*Yeah, but she had a false labour last night and it scared her a bit.*

*Well, is she all right?*

*Yeah.*

I had run out of words and waited for him to offer some details.

*How are you doing, Spat?*

*I'm ... Is she eating enough and everything?*

*Yeah. She went out with her mother then they're going to The House for supper.*

"The House" was the Virgil family home. Though I found it strange that Patty wanted to breathe the same air as her sinister family, I knew that Con was right—her daughter was alone. She was going through the trauma of reproducing without anyone on hand who knew her. I ached to be close to her. Staying away was impossible. I told Brian to tell Patty that I would call back. I needed to run.

On the mountain, drenched with sweat, I sat on the wooden stairs that led up to the chalet. I wondered if my heart might explode. A dog with three legs hobbled over to me and sniffed my hand. I patted his head and he seemed to be relieved that he had found me. He had no collar and I wondered if the little tripod belonged to anyone. I knew, already, that I would take him home if no one came by to claim him. Adrian would adjust. The dog began to whimper and I tried to imagine who he was missing. Slowly, I began to realize that he was reacting to what he saw in me. He was offering me pity and the idea of that was so heart-grinding in its implication that I wanted to atomize and scatter myself across the world. *Enough*, I said aloud. I withdrew my hand, but he stayed.

Seeing a woman in a garish track suit approaching, the mutt ran to her. She smiled at me and said something in French that I didn't understand. I smiled and waved, anyway. Her dog looked back at me and barked twice. I mumbled, *No, you fuck off.* Watching them go, I was amazed at how envious I was of their bond.

+  +  +

Between sleep and waking sleep, I curled on the bed, willing myself to stop: the breathing, the storm of thoughts eroding the inside of my skull and the curiosity that had sustained me for this senseless marathon. I didn't know what day it was. I didn't care. I heard knocking and hoped that I had locked the door.

*Spat?*

The sound of Patty's voice pulled me from the inward into the outward lunacy. As much as I wanted to see her, I didn't move. She knocked again and called my name. She was crying. I sat up.

She slouched on the couch, stroking Adrian's ears. I assumed that her inability to stop crying was related to the impending birth. Days could have passed. I sat beside her, but I knew that if I'd tried to comfort her, there would have been a fight. Anger was always the closest exit from her grief. When she spoke, the pain in her voice nearly obscured her words.

*I want this to end.*

I had a chill because I knew that she wasn't referring to her entanglement with me.

*You want what to end?*

*Everything ... I keep having dreams that there's something wrong with the baby. That he's deformed or—*

She sighed and let her head hang forward for a moment. *My*

*mother is going to kill me ... I'm just a husk, to her ... She'd cut me in half to get to this baby.*

*You don't have to let her -*

*I have no choice!*

*Of course, you do.*

*No, I don't. I'm broke, Spat. When I went back to school, I spent everything. I either let them help me or I'm on my own.*

*I have money.*

She shook her head, wearily.

*We can't go back, Spat.*

*I know ... I don't want to go back ... But he's my baby, too. He's my responsibility.*

*I know you want to do the right thing ... I know who you are, Spat ... But you're just not ready for this ... I've had months to get used to it and I'm still terrified.*

*I know you don't believe me, but I don't drink anymore.*

*So, you just get high now.*

*Listen to me.* I wondered what I would say. My heartbeat accelerated. *I know my word isn't worth much anymore ... but I promise you—I will do anything for this baby.*

She laughed and wept, simultaneously. She touched my face. *I know you want to,* she said. *But I have to be realistic, now.*

*Hank left me his house. I don't want to live there, but you can.*

*Spat.*

*Please ... Please, let me help you.*

In the roots of my insanity, I wanted her to reject me so that I would be off the hook. Then something changed. I put my hand on her swollen belly and the future son was more real than he had ever been. We said nothing after that.

+    +    +

The move into Hank's house was peppered with many dramatic phone calls and ambushes by the rabid Virgils. Constance and one of the weird sisters would arrive, demanding to see my captive. Their well rehearsed argument got sharper and more noxious every time. There were threats of lawsuits and peace bonds to keep me away, lots of comic hysteria. I must have had Patty hypnotized or drugged. Why else would she live with "the biggest mistake ever made". Even Ronald, Patty's carcass of a father, made an appeal. The man who rarely spoke at all repeated bits of the speech Constance had drilled into his head the way a shy kid at a recital would mutter a poem. He had aged in dog years, but no longer seemed to feel the acid burn of his regret. I knew that he didn't hate me. Even as he repeated his wife's threats, he seemed relieved to be in the company of another man and away from the shrieking chimp he had been saddled with for the past million years. Patty stayed upstairs whenever her family would make an attempt to lure her back to the burrow in Westmount.

I had replaced the bed in Hank's room and painted the walls and ceiling the colour of robin's eggs, Patty's favorite blue. I was grateful to be busy. I stopped going to the bookstore and focused on collecting anything a baby might need. I was grateful to Hank for having given us neutral ground on which to build the nest. The house was neither hers nor mine; it was a temporary shelter that belonged to our son. Even Adrian did not seem to claim the space as his own. He took a spot on a window ledge in the kitchen to stand guard.

Miraculously, Patty and I did not have a single fight. This was mainly because we avoided speaking. We lived every moment in preparation, reading and considering every possibility. I massaged her feet, I washed her hair, I cooked; all of it in silence. Taking care of her took me out of my head and gave me a sense of purpose. I usually stayed with her at night, sleeping in a guest room that had probably never been used before.

+     +     +

Collecting the mail at my apartment, I was surprised to see a letter with Australian postage:

*Dear Spat,*

*I have been dictating this letter to Caz for days, starting and starting over. I want you to understand that none of us, Mum included, harbour any ill will toward you whatsoever. Once the shock had worn off, I realized that you told me the truth because you felt that it was the right thing to do. It was. Mum is relieved, I think, to have everything out in the open.*

*Lately, I'm curious about Hank. If you have pictures of him, I would love to see them. He left a huge amount of money to me that I hope to spend on as many electronic toys as I can find.*

*I have so many things I want to tell you. The past is dead and we can't change it. Life is happening now and it has an infinite number of forms to take. It doesn't require people, so we should be thankful for the time we have. Life's experiment with us could come to an end at any time, so let's not let the past pollute the present. (Sorry about the alliteration.)*

*In a sense, we're born falling, backwards, into the abyss of the unknown. But if life happens in this predicament, that is part of the character of life and I, for one, embrace the uncertainty. Not knowing the how and why of our existence is a gift. It invites us to be aware and to choose our own path. Since all darkness begins in the mind, all light can come from the same infinite source. Let's be in the light, together. I hope I don't sound like a giant arsehole. These are just the things that come to mind when I think of you and I think of you often. I love you.*

*Your brother, Mick*

+    +    +

While Patty slept, I gathered photographs from the albums Hank had left. I took the best pictures of my uncle and ordered them from oldest to newest. I punched a hole in the upper right hand corner of each one and made a flip book of his life. I found unsent letters to Ann, but chose not to include them.

I spent the day working on a response to Mick's letter. Nothing sounded smart enough or true enough, so I simply listed the facts of my current situation. I told him about living with Patty again and that Hank had left his house to me. I said a hello to Caz and Ann and wondered if they had, in fact, forgiven me or if Mick was playing the mediator.

# { 21 }

As the delivery date approached, Patty decided to reduce her stress level by ending the feud with her idiot parents. I went to the bookstore so that they could screech at each other in peace. Once they understood that Patty and I were together only for the baby's sake, they would call a truce. At least, that was what we were expecting.

I found Gil trying to steady a wobbling stack of bloated boxes by gently nudging them toward the wall.

*Hey, stranger.*

*Sorry, I haven't shown up for work, lately.*

*How've you been?*

*Sober, if that's what you mean.*

*It wasn't, but that's good.*

He smiled at me and walked away from the stack of boxes as they collapsed behind him. He growled his disgust and I chuckled.

*Fuckin' books,* he said and scanned the mess around him. *Paper graveyard.*

*I'm going to be a dad,* I said. *Any day now.*

He grinned. *It's a privilege, you know, raising kids. You gotta be on your game, Jack.*

*I am.*

He gave me a long stare. I knew what was coming and I was ready for him.

*The baby won't keep you sober, though.*

I concentrated on keeping my anger reigned in. I smiled and approached him.

*Does it really matter why I don't drink?*

*Yes.*

*You're in a cult*, I said. *You have to spout their bullshit.*

He laughed loudly and for as long as it took to piss me off.

*You have to be right*, I said. *I don't.*

*Poor Spat.*

*Blow me.*

We both became aware that we were being watched. The kid who had come to find *Animal Farm* was back.

*Hi. Do you guys have a 1984 lying around?*

*Probably*, Gil said. *Let's have a look.*

The kid smiled at me and looked as though she might laugh. *How you doin', Fainty?*

*Just great*, I told her. *Thanks for asking.*

While the two of them dug through the clutter, I began to sense that my molten core was cooling. There was calmness in me that had never been there before.

*Is 1984 any good?* the kid asked Gil.

*Yeah, it's all right.*

*How did you lose your hand?* She asked the question without even a trace of apprehension. Gil grinned and told her that he had lost it in a card game.

*My Aunt has a glass eye*, she said. *She lost it in an accident. Hit by a drunk driver.*

*Well, to her, things probably only look half as bad*, Gil said.

The kid laughed so loudly that Gil and I exchanged a look of disbelief. Our non-paying customer was embarrassed by her inability to rein it in. I could see her silently scolding her real self for forgetting that not laughing too loudly was part of the superior self she was building. She rallied her restraint, getting back into character. Watching her, I had a common, but no less dismal, moment of clarity. We are, all of us, pretending to be distinctive. Without the armour of adopted belief, we could never muster the conflict we need to create the emotional surge required to sustain the dream—the infantile alternative to dirty old realism. Everyone is wearing something borrowed and far too small; so small that it constricts the breath. Only a society of addicts would adapt to something so perverse.

*There you go,* Gil said, handing her a yellowed paperback of Orwell's classic. *Free of charge.*

*Really?* She tilted her head as he grinned at her. *Thank you! I'm going to keep coming back here, I can tell you that.*

*Thanks for the warning,* I said.

She stuck her tongue out at me and then smiled at Gil as she left. Catching his eye, I wished that she had stayed long enough for him to forget our inane argument.

*Even if you're sober, after a while, you won't really be there. The kid'll be talking to you and you'll be acting the way you think you're supposed to, hiding it. The stress will build and as soon as you get mad enough—*

*I'm doomed.*

*I'm only saying—*

*We're all doomed.*

*Without something bigger than yourself, without the higher power—*

*I'm doomed,* I mumbled. *You stay sober because you have a place to go where people will listen to your shit.*

*And what's wrong with that?*

*Nothing. Whatever blows your skirt up. But I don't want to join your club.*

*I'm not trying to sell you on anything. Forget the program, I'm just asking you—seriously—don't you think there's some power at the center of all of this?*

*I don't think the question matters enough to warrant a response.*

He shook his head. *Arrogant asshole. You're full of shit.*

*Agreed.*

He seemed to have given up and I wasn't set to feel so disappointed. He went into the back room and pretended to be looking for something. I wondered how Patty was doing with the peacemaking.

+   +   +

As soon as I opened the door, I knew that she was gone. Adrian was standing on the back of the couch, watching me. He knew what had happened. He knew there would be trouble. Patty's clothes were gone. There was an apologetic note on the kitchen table. She had written it quickly, as though she might have been caught in the act. I knew that if I called The House, they wouldn't let her take the phone. On my way to the metro, I made a plan for every possible scenario.

I remembered the first time I had met the Virgils. It was a Sunday dinner, but they were dressed for a coronation. I thought it was a joke. I was baked and had to work to contain myself. Constance began a casual interrogation as soon as her maid delivered the minuscule dessert. She wanted to know who my people were and where I came from, my ambitions. Patty answered most of the questions, leaving out anything that might make me appear mortal. Her father only watched me, saying as little as he could without seeming too obviously contemptuous. The weird sisters wore a permanent smirk, sizing me up, waiting for Patty to drop the ball.

My euphoria was an affront to Constance. She saw through me because I did nothing to shield myself. That was Patty's job. I wasn't fucking her whole family, so I didn't give the smallest of shits about their opinion of me. They had the same impact and relevance as characters in a Hollywood movie; representations of people, one dimensional and weightless. I knew that they had decided who I was long before I had arrived. Since I had been judged inadequate and incapable of improvement, the pressure was off.

When I got to The House, I wondered what I could say to make Patty leave the safety of her old prison. I was sweating and sporting big half-moon pit stains. Everything looked exactly as it did the last time I had been there, years before. Constance was ready for me. She opened the front door and announced that the police would be summoned if I did not leave her property immediately. I said nothing, staring into her all but empty eyes. What remained in them was primal and simple, little more than a willingness to fight. *Go*, she said. I stared.

One of the weird sisters came out, sneering. She had a crystal globe in her hand which, I assumed, she intended to use as a weapon.

*Patty doesn't want to see you*, she croaked.

*What happened to you? You look like shit*, I told her.

The weird sister seemed startled by this observation and was, apparently, struck dumb. She looked at me as though I had more pertinent information for her. How much worse did she look? What kind of shit? Time had taken the much admired glow out of her and I almost regretted my appraisal of her facade.

*I'm phoning the police*, Constance said and walked, too purposefully, into the house. I could see her, standing just inside the foyer, waiting. I knew that she would not want the neighbours to see the cops on her doorstep. Her reputation was all she had. A pregnant daughter was the fat promise of something more and she would not give it up easily. A grandson would be a great accessory and would soften her, the way candle light or a few inches of powder could. The weird sister was still gaping at me, wondering how badly her exterior had deteriorated. Even though the insult had come from me, I was a man. Any male's opinion of her looks mattered more than oxygen. I thought that she might cry.

Constance returned to tell me that the police were on the way. Ronald blew out of the house behind her, screaming so loudly that I got chills. His face was red and his grey hair was hanging in his petrified face. His words were all but lost in the spitting fury that burst out of him. I knew, without wanting to, that his long subdued anger had little to do with me.

Unexpected empathy and sadness, heavy and ineffable, left me unable to react. Constance was so shaken by his outburst that she stood perfectly still with her eyes locked on her senior hostage. The weird sister tried to lead Old Virgil back into the house and he threw her hand from his arm so violently that I felt the urge to stand between them.

*I just want to talk to Patty*, I said.

*Get the hell out of here*, the sister said, pointing.

*Just get Patty*, I said. *I'm not going anywhere.*

Spent, Ronald mumbled to himself and scuffed back inside. Constance followed him, cautiously, still in shock. She looked back at me and there was authentic helplessness in her face. When they were gone, the weird sister approached me.

*Come back on Sunday. Before noon. I'll have her things packed.*

*What?*

*My parents will be out all morning.*

*Why are you helping me?*

*Patty's your problem*, she said. *Not mine. I have enough to deal with.*

*You're a sweet kid.*

*You're an asshole. I'll tell her you're coming. You better be here.*

With that, she went in and shut the door.

Walking home, I tried to imagine what Constance could have said to convince Patty to go back to the Virgil lair. I resented Patty's disloyalty, her weakness. Of course, I knew that Constance had always given her adopted baby just enough to make her want for more. Patty was continually in need, always outside. She could see it, clearly, but could not resist the learned reaction. She had always been a willing servant, tethered to her mother. Then she found me. When she stumbled into her lunatic saviour, Patty thought that she was free. She thought that everything would finally start. Everything was going to be, at least by comparison, great.

# { 22 }

The phone rang as I was napping with Adrian. There was no information in Caz's message, only the time and date and that she hoped I was well. She said that she would try to reach me at Hank's number. It was nice to have been removed from another shit list. The flip book of Hank photos must have helped my case. I considered calling, but couldn't imagine what I would say if Ann were to answer. I wanted a drink. The part of me that lived to obliterate, the free radical, was quietly creating scenarios in which there could be an exception to the No Alcohol rule. It offered them up to my conscious mind like ornaments made to impress a tyrannical king. It was strangely comforting. I knew that it wouldn't always be so, but the future was no longer worth fretting about. Just as the past retreated, the future had moved further forward until it was too far away to be considered. Life had become immediate, as thoughtless nature intended.

I cleaned Hank's house in anticipation of Patty's return. I remembered the weird sister's words and began to see that my ex and I had more in common than either of us ever wanted to admit. After all, she had chosen me. Her civility might only have been visible against my crudeness.

+ + +

I woke at five on Sunday morning and ran on the mountain to burn off some of the anxiety that had been building. When I returned home, there was a message from Patty telling me not to go to her parent's house. She had fought with the weird sister who wanted her out and was on her way to Hank's. It seemed too easy. I showered and then ate, steadily, for about an hour.

By the time I got to Hank's house, she was there. *I made you some breakfast*, she said. Calm and content, she sang along to some would-be song on the radio and scratched behind Adrian's ears. He was on the fridge, dipping his head toward her, squinting with pleasure.

To keep the peace, I forced three of her lethal pancakes and a few strips of bacon into my bloated stomach.

*Aren't you going to eat?*

*I did*, she said and grinned at me as though we didn't know each other. *I'm sorry*, she added.

*For what?*

*For letting my mother roll over me. I'm a bit too old for that.*

I nodded, but said nothing. Her new found serenity was almost unnerving. It was not as though she had made peace with something, but with everything.

*You look good*, she said.

*Thanks.*

I might have blushed. There was definitely something different about her. As I chewed the last bit of bacon, I realized that there was another aroma mingling with the breakfast fumes. She had never been interested in marijuana while we were married, but it was certainly in the air.

*Do you know what my sister said to me before I left?*
*What?*
*She said that she hoped I would die giving birth.*
*Fuck her. She's a puddle of vomit.*
*I think that's my mother's fantasy, too. That I'll die and she can swoop in and steal our baby.*
*You're not going to die. And no one is going to take our baby anywhere.*

The way she smiled at me, it seemed as though she wanted me to see that she was high. I looked at the clock. It was not even ten, yet. She giggled about something, lifting Adrian down into her arms. I watched her, trying to think of a way to initiate a discussion about weed and pregnancy. I was nervous about ending the tenuous truce between us. I was paralyzed, briefly, by the thought that I might have been becoming the sensible one. The pressure to act was huge and instant, but I had no authority over her, no cards to play.

*Patty?*

Yeah?

*Are sure it's a good idea ...*

*Is what a good idea?*

She seemed to be waiting for the punch line of a joke I was telling. I decided to wait a few hours before raising the issue.

*Nothing. Thanks for the pancakes.*

She grinned and kissed Adrian. For the first time, I felt older than her. The pregnancy seemed all the more accidental, as haphazard as everything else we had ever done together. We weren't ready for what was coming. Neither of us would ever be ready.

*We should go to the Biodome,* she said. *See if the big, lonely rat's still there.*

*Today?*

*Whenever.*

She wandered away, singing to herself. I tried to muster some anger about what she had done, but it was immediately squelched under the weight of my history. I had no right to tell her anything, but there were three of us now. Life was not about our laughable marriage or any of our trivial conflicts. We were rapidly shrinking in importance.

I thought about Patty's confrontation with the weird sister. She would never admit to feeling crushed by it, but I knew. Any illogical or unwarranted assault did not compute and so she would simply deny its impact. The empathy I felt for my ex competed with my renewed hatred for the weird sister.

MACDONALD { 209 }

I went to the living room where I found Patty swaying a little to remembered music. I embraced her and she laughed. She pressed her head into my chest and gripped the back of my shirt in her fists. For a long time, we stood there, locked together.

*What's wrong with me, Spat?*

*Nothing*, I said. *Nothing at all.*

+     +     +

That afternoon, I told Patty that I had to go to the bookstore. I went to the Wyre internet café to research the effects of THC on an unborn baby. After reading for a while, I was convinced that the kid would not be born with a tail. On the way back to Hank's house, I went to the health food store and bought anything that looked familiar. During her spelt bread and pomegranate juice days, Patty would often come home with organic cubes of beige compost that she would persuade me to eat. Even though none of it tasted bad, I would always spit it out and pretend to have been poisoned. I only did it to motivate the insults that she would toss at me. I was a toxic meat puppet, a walking landfill, a less discerning vulture.

Of course, Constance was pounding on the front door when I got back. By the shrillness of her yelps, I knew that she had been there for a while.

*You won't get away with this*, she rasped at me, while repeatedly pressing the doorbell. The weird sisters waited in the car, staring forward, clearly resenting their mother's campaign. I opened the door and shut it behind me as she tried to enter the house. Patty had taken one of the chairs from the kitchen and was seated near the porch, facing me.

*I got some organic stuff*, I said.

*Thanks*, she said.

*Why are you sitting there?*

*I'm just listening. It's nice that she thinks she cares so much.*

*You want me to get rid of her?*

*No.*

Patty followed me to the kitchen where Adrian was licking drops of water from the faucet. Constance kept up banging on the door.

*I can't listen to that much longer*, I said.

*She's desperate*, Patty said to herself. She went to the living room. Big Band music began to blare. She returned, laughing.

*I don't know what's more obnoxious*, she said. *Look how fat I am!*

*You're beautiful*, I told her.

*My belly's as hard as a rock.*

She inspected the over-priced groceries and helped me put them away. The phone rang. She answered.

*Hello? ... Oh! Hi. How are you?*

Instinctively, I caught her eye and mouthed the words, *I'm not here.*

*We're both doing really well*, she told the caller. *Great ... Yeah, any day now ... Spat just went out to get some groceries. He shouldn't be long. I'll tell him to phone you as soon as he gets in. OK. I will. Bye.*

Hanging up the phone, she gave me a suspicious look.

*What? Who was it?*

*Your mother ... You haven't spoken to her since you got back ... Have you?*

*I'll call her later*, I lied. Some residual bit of Spat Classic told me that I was about to be re-domesticated. Familial duties were gathering. Soon, there would be slacks.

*You should call her.*

*I know.*

Between songs, we realized that Constance was gone. I looked out at the street to make sure.

*She won't give up that easily*, Patty muttered, staring into the pit of her dread.

+ + +

Sleeping in the spare room, a question began to dig at me. Why hadn't Patty ever tried to find her birth mother? She had never even expressed curiosity about the woman who surrendered her to the heinous Constance. I wondered if she knew where she had come from, but had been keeping it secret. I concluded that discussion of the issue had probably been disallowed in the Virgil household and that I knew Patty about as well as she knew herself. I worried that everything unresolved in her internal life would be, unwittingly, passed down to our son. We could play normal for him, but like anyone who looks, he would see through us. Sooner or later, we would be blamed for all of his troubles.

The bedroom door opened. Finn was there, in the overcoat he wore for dates and funerals. He approached the bed.

*Are you asleep?*

I thought that if I didn't answer, he would leave. I could smell gin and that repulsive cologne I had given him hundreds of years before.

*Spat?*

I sat up and looked at him. He was younger than he had been at the end. Adrian rushed to the foot of the bed, his eyes flashing as he looked back at our visitor. Finn tilted his head into the window's rectangle of moonlight, squinting at my buddy.

*Cats smother babies,* Finn said. *You should get rid of it.*

*What do you want?* He didn't answer. He kept staring at Adrian. I stood and faced him with the bed between us. I wanted to tell him that I wasn't afraid of him. I wanted to go back to sleep and ignore the intrusion, but my heart was pounding. Common sense and a sickening adrenaline rush urged me to get out of the room.

*What do you want, Finn?*

*Call me Poppy.*

*What do you want, Finn?*

By the look he gave me, I knew there was real danger. He walked around the bed, leisurely, as though he were strolling on a beach. When we were face to face, he grinned. *Spat*, he said. *My Spat.* He pushed the hair out of my eyes and studied my expression as though he were reading directions in a foreign language.

*You can't be here*, I said.

*I can be anywhere.*

Adrian hissed as beams in the ceiling strained to break free of each other. I tried to think of a plan.

*My Spat*, Finn said. *What happened to your hand?*

I was afraid to take my eyes off of him, but I had to see. My left hand was gone, replaced by a sharp, jagged hook.

*You're mine*, Finn said. *Death is only a disguise. It's not the end. You keep wishing, but there's no end.*

He could not be reasoned with, I knew. *I'm sorry*, I said and swung my amended arm toward his throat. He did not flinch as the pointed hook caught his jugular. I pulled hard and his blood sprayed outward in a fan. His head rolled back and he became the center of a red fountain, soaking the room. When he brought his head forward, the steady shower of blood kept falling until every part of the room was drenched. I was warmed by the soaking and felt strangely reassured that I had done the right thing.

Finn looked tired, now. A wide stream still poured from the gash in his neck. He winced at me.

*I'm sorry*, I said.

*No you're not.* His voice was deeper, less familiar.

*You have to go.*

He didn't move. Before I was aware of it, the hook slashed at him again. When the wet metal struck him, he blew apart in fragments of burnt paper. The black flakes floated to the floor and were absorbed by the red pool.

Looking down at the blackening mud, I felt no remorse, no fear. I got back into the bed. The rain was stopping. I counted the last drops of blood as they landed on me. At twenty-one, I drifted back into sleep, back into the comfortable Nothing.

## { 23 }

*How'd you sleep?*

*Great*, I told her. Patty looked happy and I had to wonder if she had already begun to wake and bake, habitually. I sniffed the air in the kitchen, but there was only the smell of coffee.

*This house is haunted*, she said, smiling.

*What makes you say that?*

*I don't know.* She shrugged. *I hear things.*

We grinned at each other. I knew that I was about to risk our new found amity, but curiosity made me ask.

*How come you never tried to find your birth mother?*

She didn't seem surprised by the question. She considered me the way a parent would a child who had asked about something beyond his years. She leaned back in her chair and said, *I did.*

*When?*

*Long ago.*

*Where is she?*

*Dead, now. She lived in Toronto. Crazy.*

*What kind of crazy?*

*The kind you're born with*, she said. *I never mentioned her because ... I don't know why. Constance is my mother. Whether I like it or not.*

We laughed. Smiling at each other, we might have looked like newlyweds or guests on a talk show.

*Thank you*, she said.

*For what?*

*I'm going to take a bath*, she mumbled.

I listened to her climbing the stairs. I waited to hear the bathtub filling and then went to check my stash in the cupboard above the fridge. I had three large buds and a few papers in an old tea tin. One of the buds had been picked at, pulled apart instead of being cut. I could not tell exactly how much she had been smoking. By my standards, though, it wasn't enough to make a cricket high. I decided that her indulgence in weed might have been a one time trial. Still, I whispered to the unborn above me, *Hurry up.*

+  +  +

Walking to the bookstore, I thought about the rain of blood and Finn's second demise. It wasn't any more disturbing in memory than it had been the night before. Of course, I knew that the dream was, at least in part, about Gil. I regretted not spending more time with my only friend.

*Spat Ryan returns*, he said, when I arrived at the store.

*What's up, Gillard?*

*I'm ...* He stopped as though he had to consider whether or not what he was about to say was actually true.

*I'm going to Winnipeg. I got a call last week from my oldest.*

*That's great*, I said.

*Well ... We'll see.*

It occurred to me that he was afraid. Eyes down, he pretended to be working at something in the mess of papers in front of him.

*What's wrong with that?*

*Nothing*, he said. *It's just ... I don't know what to expect.*

*Doesn't matter what you expec*t, I said. *He wants to see you. That's all that matters.*

He shook his head. I had never seen him look so unsure of himself.

*I don't know why he wants to see me ... And I'm afraid ... that I'll drink. Haven't been on a plane in ...*

The least qualified person on Earth to offer advice on maintaining sobriety, I told him that it would be fine. I assured him that if his son wanted to see him, there was nothing to fear.

*You don't understand*, he said.

That was true. Gil was no less mysterious to me than he was when we first met. The power alcohol had over him was clearly different from my slow dance with it.

*I don't trust myself*, he said.

*But you haven't had a drink in eighteen years.*

*I haven't left this town in eighteen years.*

I watched him and felt our roles reverse. I had to say something to cut through the bullshit, but it was hard to do the exact opposite of the thing for which I was constructed.

*You're not afraid of getting drunk*, I theorized, aloud. *You're afraid of facing him.*

*I'm afraid of facing him sober.*

Out of words, we stood there looking at the books. The mess seemed necessary and beautiful.

*I'll take care of the store. You go and have a good time.*

Arms folded, he shook his head and gave me a look of total uncertainty. I felt no shame in staring at his prosthetic. I was curious. He watched me for a moment.

*You know where my hand is?*

I shrugged.

*Me neither ... The only person who knows is my youngest.*

I realized that he had never called them by name. Oldest and Youngest were the designations he used to keep the memories of his children at a safe distance. From the way he spoke about them, I always knew that there was a lot of regret attached to the youngest of his sons. I was not ready to know why the baby of Gil's family was the only person who knew the location of the missing hand.

*This is a secret*, he said. *You can't tell anyone.*

I nodded. As he spoke, it was hard to imagine that the Gil I knew was the same one in his story. As he told it, I wished that he had opted to keep it to himself.

It was at Christmas, the traditional time for family horror and a heavy snow was falling. Gil was as drunk as he could be without being unconscious. Weeks before, his wife had asked him to build shelves for their bedroom. He was busy drinking and the construction didn't happen. As their fight about it intensified, she followed him to his workshop in the garage.

*You want shelves*, he said. *I'll make your fuckin' shelves.*

Afraid that he would hurt himself, she struggled to get a circular saw out of his hand. He pulled her hair, forcing her face away from him. The Youngest, who was ten years old at the time, came to his mother's rescue. When he jumped on his father's back, Gil pushed his wife away. All of the screams blended under the louder shriek of the circular saw. Gil's hand was off and the saw was at his feet before anything could have been done to stop it. However, that was not all that made it a Yuletide to remember. As Gil cried out in agony and his wife screamed, the Youngest grabbed the severed hand and ran outside. In his pajamas and rubber boots, the boy ran into the woods behind the house. Wherever he had buried the hand, he would not say.

The falling snow covered the trail of blood drops and foot prints. By morning, it was impossible to tell which direction he had taken. His mother begged him to tell her, but the boy said nothing. No threat from the Oldest, no bribe, no therapist, no injection of guilt could break the boy's silence.

*He thought he was saving his mother's life ... Maybe he was. He never told you ... what he did with it?*

*No ... He didn't speak at all for a long time after that ... Maybe he told her ... after I was gone.*

*It's a heart-warming story*, I said.

*Isn't it? ... I have a nice collection of those ... I don't blame him, you know. I never did.*

I shook my head, trying to look thoughtful and grave. I was imagining a small altar in the woods, made from a shoebox.

The youngest, I suspected, had found an anthill in the spring and left the decaying hand on it to be cleaned. When the bones were bare, he polished them up. He made them into jewelry and arrowheads. Slices of the skeletal trophy might have found their way into Mother's Day presents and Halloween rituals. I concluded that the Youngest had stolen the left hand as proof that he was not helpless, but I kept that theory to myself.

Like anyone's secret, Gil's hidden coil of worthless information might have also served as a delay tactic. I had nothing to offer for advice.

*I'll take care of the store for you,* I said. *Go.*

He shook his head and mumbled to himself. He stacked a bunch of random papers and set them aside.

*I'm afraid,* he said, *that the Oldest will tell me things I don't want to know ... My youngest could be in an institution somewhere. I mean ... How does anyone recover from something like that?*

*If you don't go,* I said, *you'll regret it.*

He nodded. My gut told me that nothing good would come of his trip westward. Gil looked smaller to me, vulnerable. I wished that he would get mad and hack away at his doubt with sarcasm and wit. I wanted him to be tough, even if he couldn't be strong.

# { 24 }

The baby must have known that we weren't prepared. He bided his time, keeping mum as the due date passed. Patty's impatience manifested itself in fits of rage, crying and cleaning. Sweating, strands of hair sticking to her face, she would scrub the bathroom floor or wash and then re-wash pots as though doing so could make time move faster. Anything I said resulted in a fight, so I kept my mouth shut. The post-divorce honeymoon was over. Though I was afraid to leave her alone, she insisted that I give her some breathing room. I would run on the mountain, come home to check on her, get told to fuck off and then go to the bookstore to wait.

There were no more debates with Gil. His anxiety had all but silenced him. Finally, on a Tuesday morning, he had made peace with a decision.

*I'm going to Winnipeg next Friday*, he said.

*That's good.*

*I don't know about that. I'm going anyway.*

*I'll take care of the store*, I told him. *You stay out there as long as you want.*

No matter how much I tried not to, every time I looked at him, I thought about the boy running away with the severed hand. As disturbing as it was, I wanted to know more about that night, more about the boy who made the cut. Something in me sympathized with the Youngest and what he had done.

Of course, I didn't tell Gil that. I didn't insult him or make jokes about him anymore, either. The fun was over.

Gil was staring at the cover of a ravaged copy of *Macbeth*. I could almost see into his head. He was playing out scene after terrible scene.

*What are you so nervous about?*

*It's been too long! There's ... The boys don't have any happy memories of me, Jack ... I was a terrible father.*

*We love our parents no matter what, Gil. It's one of nature's ways of fucking with us.*

*I left my parents' house when I was sixteen*, he said. *I can hardly remember them ... I never looked back. Not once.*

He told me about how trapped he had felt when the first of his sons arrived. He resented the newborn, shamelessly, suggesting that they name him Last Call. The child was, as far as his drunken, selfish father could tell, the end of Gil's youth. He resented his wife for having wanted the baby so much and for her easy devotion to motherhood. He openly resented her adoration of the infant. Gil did not hold the baby until there were enough relatives with cameras around to coax him into it.

*You must have loved the kids, though, Gil ... In your own way.*

*I didn't love anybody. I loved being drunk.*

I felt a twinge for the stranger in Winnipeg. I knew why he needed to see Gil. He needed to be told that his birth was not the cause of all of the misery that followed it. He had to be absolved of uncommitted sins and imagined transgressions that normal people would have considered trivial and forgettable. He had to know for sure that the guilt he had always felt had been unwarranted. More than that, Gil's son in Manitoba wanted a chance to meet the sober version of his old man.

The phone rang and I leapt for it, expecting to hear Patty breathing too fast and telling me that it was time. The caller hung up when I said hello. I imagined him on the other end, tapping the bone of an index finger against his cheek and wondering who had answered.

As Gil told me about all of the birthdays he had ruined over the years, I began to imagine something that wanted to be a realization: What if his sons were only setting a trap? What if the reunion in the West was only about revenge? It seemed unlikely, but then everything did at some point.

Though I had no valid reason to, I longed to tell Gil to reconsider his trip. As I searched for the words to say it, I had to consider where I stood in the Insanity Spectrum. He didn't seem to think that I was crazy, but he couldn't see what went on in the head jar. The sense of dread kept rising, until I had no choice but to declare my concern about the meeting with the Oldest.

*Gil?*

*Yeah?*

The words wouldn't come. In the uncomfortable silence, I concluded that my apprehension was really only fondness for my friend. *Of course he should go*, I thought. *Of course.*

*Nothing*, I said and went to the back room to clear a path to the fire door.

+  +  +

White people with dreadlocks had always been a source of amusement, but the kid in Laura's apartment didn't seem at all absurd. I tried not to be, but I was a bit revolted by the blond rat on his shoulder. The perpetually curious, sniffing thing matched his keeper's mock dreads perfectly. In the wild, a blond rat was probably less likely to survive than its more mundane cousins, so the young Rasta wannabe had probably saved its life.

*If you take care of them, they're basically immortal*, the kid told me as he scratched under his pal's chin. I nodded and looked away, not wanting to hear any more of his theory on extending the lifespan of vermin. I realized that the shame I was feeling had less to do with not being at home with Patty than it did with my age. I had nearly twenty years on everyone in the room. I felt like a predator, creeping up on a henhouse.

*You a friend of Laura's?*

*Yeah*, I told him.

He was sizing me up, smirking a little. I looked him in the eye and that was the end of his gentle smugness.

*She's great*, he said.

*Yeah.*

Until he said it, I had forgotten her name. I wondered if I was after something besides sex.

After walking Gil home and assuring him that his trip would be a great success, I met Laura on Sherbrooke.

*Hi, Fainty*, she said, smiling.

*Hey*, I said.

*I haven't been to the bookstore in a while.*

*I hadn't noticed.*

She giggled then pushed her tongue into her cheek, enjoying some illicit thought. She seemed to be considering what to say next and, being a dick, I was flattered that she was making an effort.

*Where are you off to?*

*Nowhere*, I told her.

*I'm having a party*, she said, *before the Arcade Fire show.*

*Oh.*

*You should come. It's just a primer before we go out.*

*I don't know*, I said.

Of course I knew what she had in mind. It was flattering, but strange, too. Young people always assume that they're an exception and not just a minor variation on an old theme. For them, there's still potential in the ruins.

*I should probably head home*, I said, without much conviction.

*My name's Laura*, she said and offered her hand.

*I'm Spat.*

*Spat?*

*Yeah.*

*Like a little fight?*

*That's right.*

She smiled and then bit her bottom lip. *Come on, Spat.*

She began walking toward the Plateau and after pretending to think about what to do, I followed.

*I like your friend,* she said. *At the store.*

*Gil.*

*Yeah. And not just because he doesn't make me pay. He's nice.*

I agreed and asked what she was studying in school. We discussed her contempt for world politics and her theory about how impotent old men start wars because of the jealousy they feel for their younger, virile rivals.

*It's all about sex,* she said. *Nine eleven was all about sex.*

*Was it?*

*Ultimately. People who feel contempt for their biology are bound to be violent.*

*I think violence is about belief,* I said. *You can't have violence without belief.*

*And belief is about fear. Nine eleven was just one backward, primitive theocracy smashing its face on the shins of another.*

*It's not about specific countries,* I said. *Countries come and go. It's about the believers. They'll kill us all.*

*Nature will beat them to it,* she said. *Biology.* She laughed, tickled by the notion of nature's revenge. I felt a pang of nostalgia and wondered how long it had been since I felt passionate about anything as frivolous as politics. Laura's naive certainty was endearing, almost desirable. I decided that we would be friends, somehow.

When we arrived at her small apartment on Bordeaux, I began to feel conspicuous. *What are you doing here?* I almost said the words aloud when I saw the place. An alarmingly thin girl was slumped on an inflatable red chair in a cluttered corner and barely looked up when we entered. She seemed trapped by the over-sized headphones she was wearing. She had trouble holding her head erect.

*That's my roommate,* Laura said. *Ignore her.*

For a moment, I could not take my eyes off of the sullen stick figure and noticed a flash of jealousy in my new friend. I almost expected her to whine, *I said ignore her!*

I was considering good excuses for making a fast exit. The place was actually dirtier than my apartment. There were books and clothes scattered all over, plastic cups with white rings of dried milk inside, cigarette butts crushed into an empty sardine tin. A lone, tiny fish looked up at me from under a crooked filter.

While I rolled a joint for us at her filthy kitchen table, other friends of Laura's began to arrive. Within a few minutes, the place had the atmosphere of an after hours club. Each of Laura's acquaintances came over to meet me and I tried to look unperturbed. Young, they were beautiful regardless of their looks. I rolled a few more "party favours" as Laura called them and declined several offers of beer and wine. I wondered what Patty was up to. I considered phoning her, but couldn't get a moment alone. Once I was stoned, my attention shifted inward.

Laura had changed for the concert and looked as innocently sluttish as anyone could. I hoped that her intentions were pure and that we'd do some fucking before she went out for the night. Playing hostess, she reminded everyone not to try to engage her roommate in conversation and to jiggle the handle of the toilet to keep it from running.

*This could be your last chance to get some,* I told myself when the stink of guilt began to invade. I saw myself, stuck at home, finally and irreparably tamed. I repeated the phrase in my head to stay focused on the goal. *Last chance ... Last chance ...*

*Are you coming to the show?*

I handed the joint back to the rat boy and wondered what he was talking about.

*The Arcade Fire,* he said.

*Oh. No. I have to get home.*

*You should come,* he said and gave me a look that made it clear that Laura had some competition. I grinned, grateful to still have some kind of impact on anyone, anywhere.

Laura seemed to have become instantly drunk. Louder than the others, she barked orders at her eccentric friends and told everyone to be ready to go in an hour. I approached her, hoping that I would not have to initiate everything.

*Oh, shit. You don't have a ticket, do you?*

*For what?*

*For the show. It's sold out, too.*

*That's all right.*

*Maybe you can get a ticket from a scalper.*

I began to see that she had no interest in sex with the old man from the bookstore. She was just being nice or else showing her friends how diverse her group of contacts had become.

As they made their way down the spiral staircase, a few of her friends were singing, *"Every time you close your eyes. Lies, lies …"*

*Well, I should get going,* I said to Laura as she struggled to get an arm into her tight, Gothic coat. A ring of black feathers encircled her head when she finally managed to get the thing on and buttoned.

*I don't know why you won't come with us. There's bound to be scalpers.*

*No, I have things to—*

*All right. Well, see ya, Splat.*

She was gone. I listened as she joined the chorus of voices below. I looked to where her roommate had been slumped. The emaciated girl was gone. I waited by the door for the gang on the street to leave so that there would be no more interaction with them. As I was about to make my way out, I heard retching.

Though I knew that I should have gone when the hostess left, I followed the sound to the bathroom. Just as I was about to knock on the door and ask if she needed help, the roommate appeared. She was a bit unsteady, sweating.

*Are you all right?*

She considered my face for a moment, as though she were trying to remember where we had met.

*Who are you?*

*I'm Spat. I'm a friend of Laura's.*

That seemed to change my standing. She sneered and brushed past me.

*What are you still doing here?*

*I heard you ... I just wanted to see if you needed some help.*

*Why?*

I shrugged. She looked me up and down.

*You don't seem like one of her friends*, she said. *How old are you?*

*Forty.*

*Oh ... OK.*

*You and Laura don't get along?*

*Me and everybody*, she mumbled.

Slumping back into her inflatable chair, she sighed and stared at the floor.

*You want to go out for a drink, man?*

*No, thank you*, I said.

*Come on. Have a drink with me.*

*No. I shouldn't.*

*Why not?*

+    +    +

In a dark corner of the sad pub, we could have been old buddies who were feeling a bit sentimental. Nearly everything she said seemed to come with a shrug and a tone of accepted futility. I actually listened without thinking about what I would say next. I doubt that there are more than a few people in the world with whom I have ever felt so immediately comfortable. Her appearance and attitude no longer seemed so severe. I had forgotten it, but felt no embarrassment in asking, *What's your name again?*

*For fuck sake! Carla!*

We laughed. I told her that at my age, the memory goes. She chuckled and then squinted at me.

*I'm not as young as you think*, she said. *Just childish.*

*How old are you?*
*Twenty-eight.*
*That's young*, I said.
*I know. But I'm not a kid.*
*I know.*

We chuckled at nothing and clinked glasses. Her body seemed alluring now, her movements slow and sensual. I was getting hard.

*How do you know my roommate?*

*She comes into the bookstore where I work sometimes.* Carla nodded and then moved her head, slowly, from side to side. She inhaled, deeply, and then exhaled with a sigh.

*She's such a liar. She told me you only had one hand.*

*That's my buddy, Gil.*

Saying his name, I was almost ashamed to be so drunk. The image of the young boy running into the woods with the bloody hand flashed in my head. His pajamas were tucked into his rubber boots; large flakes of snow were melting on his face and gathering on his hair. His heart beating hard, his breaths short and shallow, the panic he felt made it hard to decide what to do with his prize.

*Give me your hand*, Carla said.

The way she examined my palm, it seemed as though she were going to read the lines in it. I was trying to think of the most polite way to tell her that I did not go in for that sort of bullshit. She raised my hand to her mouth and moved the tip of her tongue in a small circle on my palm. I shifted, feeling the pressure in my pants. She watched me for a second and then moved my hand under the table. Pressing my fingers into her, her eyes locked on mine, she was giving me the all clear. I was hoping that she was one of those hard women with a predatory instinct who would see me as something to conquer and forget. I wanted to be used up and mercilessly drained by her.

*You want to come to my place?*

*What for?* She asked without irony, enjoying my fingers.

*I wanna fuck you.*

*We don't have to go anywhere.*

She began grinding herself against my hand, moaning a little.

*We really should go*, I said, noticing a few of the sad patrons watching.

*Tell me you want to fuck me.*

*I wanna fuck you*, I muttered.

Eyes closed, almost growling, she squeezed my fingers between her thighs. Though I had no problem with public demonstrations of affection, I knew that lonely people were angered by them. I hoped that it would not take her forever to finish and that it was a warm-up to the real show.

*You wanna fuck me*, she whispered, squeezing her eyes shut.

*Yeah.*

*You're a stranger.*

*Yeah ... Everybody's watching you*, I said.

That was fuel. Stabbing at herself with my sore hand, she began to rock forward and back. Everyone, including a sour bartender was watching us, now. He approached, slowly, giving me time to tell Carla to calm down. There was no reasoning with her, though. It would have been easier to reason with a cat or me. Shaking, she threw her head back and cried out. There was no mistaking the sound. By the time the bartender arrived, Carla's eyes were opened. She returned my wet hand and smiled at the stern, embarrassed man.

*We'll have two more*, she said.

Any objection he might have had was gone. He said, *Coming up*, and sauntered back to the bar.

Carla squeezed the base of my cock, through my pants. Her strength surprised me.

*You're an excitable boy*, she said. Still gripping me, she told me that she had not been "penetrated" by a man since high school. He was a geography teacher who had been doing at least three of her friends. His approach to romance demanded a lot of restraint for the object of his desire.

*The smell of twine still makes me sick*, she said. *Anyway, I don't like getting fucked. Let's drink.*

She let go of my personality and finished off what was left of her cocktail. I tried not to seem too pissy about it, but she could tell.

*I'm sorry*, she said, not looking at me.

*That's OK*, I said.

*I shouldn't have made you think I was looking for ...* She searched for the word, but couldn't find it. I downed the drink in front of me and wished that the hard-on would subside.

*I'm sorry.*

*Don't be*, I said.

During the long silence, we both tried, albeit half-heartedly, to get back to our comfortable rapport. Canceled sex changes everything, though. I wished that the dimwitted stick insect would leave so that I could at least drink in peace. Of course, she was neither dim nor insect-like, but I was as hard as granite and no longer interested in having a new friend.

*I should go*, she said.

*So soon?* I offered no encouragement for her to stay.

She stood and adjusted her clothes, glancing at the others in the room.

*I'm the only girl here*, she said to herself and started out. She stopped near the exit. Head down, she folded her arms. A troll at the bar was looking at her and then glancing at me. Over and over, he seemed to be telling me to do something. Of course, he was probably only looking to make sure I was no longer interested in her before making his move. Minutes passed. She had not budged.

*Fuck*, I whispered.

I reached into my pants and pointed my shrinking hero downward before going to see what was wrong with her. She turned to face me just as I was about to stand. I was relieved to see that she was not crying. She came back to the table.

*What's the matter?*

She shook her head, ashamed. *I'm sorry, Spat. I shouldn't drink.*

*It's all right*, I said, trying to sound relaxed.

*It isn't. Walk me home and maybe we can come up with something.*

The phrase "come up with something" reignited my pitiable lust and I reminded her that we had drinks on the way. When they arrived, I paid and we downed the doubles like pros.

By the time we got to her place, I was no longer interested in what the substitute for sex might have been. I was drunk and slowly imploding. Carla was telling the story of when she and her sister had come home from school to find her father with his head in the oven. It was not a gas stove, so his drunken suicide attempt became just another comical story to tell.

*After that, we called the oven Dad's tanning booth.* She was laughing, which led to some startling coughing. It was as though she were coughing for the first time, getting nearly three decades worth of gunk out of her system.

*You OK, Carla?*

She was not. She lurched forward and vomited with tremendous force, hitting me, squarely, in the crotch. It was as though she had not made her disdain for the male appendage clear enough and felt that a more straightforward display was in order.

I stepped back and gave her a minute to empty. When she was done, she stumbled backwards a little. Seeing my pants, she began to cry.

*It's all right,* I said.

*I'm so sorry.*

*I know. Forget about it.*

I turned and walked toward my neighbourhood. She was saying something to me, but I wasn't interested in hearing it. Her feet pounded the metal stairs as she climbed to the apartment. Laura's voice barked something at her from above. After a few moments, there was loud slap. I stopped and looked back.

Carla and Laura were on the balcony, hitting each other as hard as and as often as they could. Though I probably should have done something to break it up, I was too tired to make the effort. Each of them had managed to grab two fistfuls of hair and, for a moment, it seemed as though they had come to an impasse. Inspired, Laura stomped Carla's foot and the skeletal girl went down like an armful of kindling. Wearing only black boots, the rat lover burst out of the apartment and dragged Laura inside. She was yelling incomprehensible threats and then screamed so loudly and with such unrestrained fury that it gave me a chill.

Carla cried, *You still love me! You still fucking love me! Bitch!*

I turned and walked with a slight sway. People passing gave me the usual look of disdain, the specialized local version. We love to pretend to be liberal and open and free, but we police each other like Nazis here. I contemplated the religious residue, self-loathing and shame; all of the unintentional low comedy. I said hello to everyone, being a friendly neighbour.

By the time I made it to my apartment, I had grown accustomed to the stench of Carla's vomit. It had cooled, considerably, and my pants were sticking to me. At my door, I emptied my pockets and nearly fell over the stairs as I stepped out of the jeans and underwear. I left the whole mess outside and went in to shower.

Just as the water reached the ideal temperature, there was a hard knocking at the door. My first thought was that one or both of the mad girls had followed me home. I put a towel around my waist and stumbled to the door. When I opened it, it took a moment for me to recognize Brian. He was staring at the soiled clothes near his feet. His look of disgust changed to one of fearful pity when he saw me.

*Spat. Where have you been?*

*What do you mean?* I sounded drunk, even to me.

*I've been calling you all night*, he said. *Patty's in the hospital.*

*What?*

*I had a bad feeling so I dropped in to see her and she went into labour. The baby's OK.*

*What about Patty?*

*I'll be in the car*, he said and started down the stairs.

# { 25 }

Constance and Ronald were seated in the sparse waiting area, holding hands. The weird sisters stood next to them, fuming. None of the Virgils sneered at me, so I knew that the situation was dire. A young nurse approached me and asked if I was the father. I nodded. She took my arm and told me that I could not enter the delivery room. She was explaining what had gone wrong, but the words jumbled in my head and all I knew for sure was that Patty was in trouble. When I made it clear that I would not be kept away from her, the nurse squeezed my hand. *Brace yourself*, she said.

There was a lot of blood, but that wasn't what struck me hardest. Patty looked so utterly spent, so pale and lifeless, that my eyes filled. Doctors and nurses milled around her, speaking quietly and in code. Death was nearby. I could feel the stolen beats of its heart moving the air around me.

*The baby is fine*, the nurse said, holding my arm. *Eight pounds, two ounces. He's perfect.*

*What's wrong with Patty?*

I could feel the compassionate stranger choosing the right words. There weren't any. *She lost a lot of blood ...* She explained that the hemorrhaging was from the umbilical cord. A blood vessel, a tear. I tried, but I couldn't listen.

As I went to the bed, hands tugged at me, sympathetic voices coaxed me to leave and let the doctors work. Patty's eyes were closed, but it didn't matter. I knew that she could see me. I put my hand on her forehead and told her, silently, not to worry. We had never needed words for anything but combat, anyway.

*Come with me*, the nurse said. *See the baby.*

I couldn't move. The baby was still in the future. I was back in time, with Patty, trying to catch up. She opened her eyes a little. She smirked and tried to motion with her hand. She whispered, *Go.*

I had to wonder if she was telling me to leave because she knew that she would be all right or if she didn't want me to see life rejecting her, pushing her out of the stream.

When I emerged from the room, Constance gave me such a sympathetic look that I got angry. Only an impending death, premature and wholly unfair, could have tempered her hatred for me. I wanted to spit at her. I wanted the reassurance of her revulsion. Ronald looked as though he had been hollowed out and painted to be as life-like as possible. By his empty gaze, he had no idea where he was. The weird sisters, upstaged yet again, stared at the floor and dreamed.

*Fucking Virgils*, I muttered.

*What?*

The young nurse was still there, holding on to me, ready for anything.

*Patty won't die*, I told her.

*I know*, she said, but there was only doubt in her face. She had already seen too much injustice and knew too well the fragility of our biology.

*She won't*, I reassured her.

*I know.*

+ + +

The nameless stranger's impact was so profound, so life-altering, that words could not contain him: Beautiful, mysterious, frightening, perfect. I could go on, but language is a long way down from where we were. The lack of sleep, the wonder of it all, made every moment singular and relevant. Time no longer flowed. It stopped and started again according to what the boy needed. Much of me had died to make room for him. It was a relief to be rid of some of Spat for a while. The energy of the folk singer head stomp became an imagined dome of protection over the infant.

Once, while Mick and I shared a room, we talked about why he and Caz wanted, so desperately, to have a baby. He said it was so that they could keep living. I told him that it was unfair, if not dangerous, to think of a child as a mere continuation of his parents.

*A baby isn't a device*, I said. *It exists regardless of the meaning you apply to it.*

*But we don't want the little bugger to just relive our lives*, he said. *Of course, the baby can be whoever she is, but the raw material will have come from us.*

*So?*

*So it's a miracle. Fuck off.*

*You fuck off.*

I called Australia on the day I brought the baby home. Ann answered. She was so elated that I wondered if I was capable of feeling the full impact of my son's arrival the way a normal person would. Caz was in the background, yelling to Mick, *It's a boy!* There was joyous pandemonium down under. Ann had so much to impart that she began to stammer. I made an excuse to hang up, but I was glad.

Whenever he could, Brian came by to do dishes and laundry. I was grateful to have him around. He sat with Patty, reassuring her that everything was under control. Sobbing, Patty could not communicate what was happening to her. Her depression seemed to have doubled the gravity around her. The sight of the baby left her inconsolable. Her pain and the shock of what she had suffered had taken all but her physical life. I would attach the breast pump and almost pray for it to work. Whenever she wept, the milk let go and it was rain on parched land. Brian suggested formula, but my gut told me to keep going to the source. Every failed attempt to attach the baby to her breast would send Patty deeper into the tar of her gloom. The baby, in those first days, was merely a reminder of the bomb that had gone off inside her. She wished that the delivery had killed her. She told me, nearly every day that she wanted to die, but my sympathy for her was eclipsed by the immense love that I felt for our child and by the colossal responsibility of keeping him alive. I doubt if I had ever really loved anyone before him.

The battle with Constance was over, for the time being. Though we did not speak during her visits, there was no malice left in either of us. Once, while she was sitting with Patty, I heard a shriek. Running to the room, I had images of blood, of a self-inflicted gash. I got there in time to see all of Patty's stored anger, years of saved-up fury, being hurled at Constance. With a long, horrifying scream, it severed the ties between them.

*Get her out of here!*

*What's going on?*

*Get her out!*

Stunned by her daughter's rage, Constance could not react. I led her from the room, becoming far too aware of her regret. *Close the door*, Patty said, nearly passing out. I wanted to detest Constance for upsetting Patty, but my hatred would not budge.

In the kitchen, I asked Constance what had happened, but she said nothing. When she looked at me, I noticed that she had tried to cover a black eye with make-up. For some reason, that seemed like a place to start.

*What happened to your eye?*

She smirked and looked away. I waited, noticing clues of her impending debility.

*Ronald hit me.*

*What?*

*Yesterday. I was trying to button his shirt and he hit me.*

*What's ... Why?*

*He has Alzheimer's*, she said.

*Oh ... I'm sorry.*

She sighed, too exhausted to dismiss my sympathy. I had nothing else to offer.

*I don't know what he'll do*, she said. *Some days ...* As she wept, I was at a loss as to what I could do to make her stop. I wanted to know what had made Patty scream at her.

*Is that what Patty was ... reacting to?*

Constance laughed, bitterly. She folded her arms, tightly, but I could still see her hands shaking.

*No. She just hates me.*

I had no means to reassure her and no real desire to do so. Whatever she had said to Patty must have been a directive to straighten up and fly right, to get out of bed.

*They all hate me*, Constance said, as though she had just noticed it. I said nothing. I suppose that I could have been more sympathetic, but even as she talked, I was listening for the baby's cry. I had things to do, lunch to make, milk to pump. Besides, Constance had spent years sowing that misery and it was hers alone.

*Can I hold the baby before I go?*

*Of course*, I said.

She whispered, *Thank you.*

When the local grandmother finally went home, I went to the bedroom to check on Patty. For the first time since she left the hospital, she seemed to have improved a little.

*What was that all about?*

*I don't know*, Patty said, looking almost content. *She was telling me what I had to do—You know the way she goes on— and I just ... snapped.*

*Just like that?*

*Just like that.*

*Are you all right?*

She scoffed. Obviously she was not all right. She was still bleeding, still healing, still in shock.

*He didn't wake up when I screamed*, she said. *Did you notice that?*

*He's designed to sleep through ... noise.*

*He doesn't even know I exist.*

*He doesn't even know that he exists yet,* I told her, but there was certainly a gap between them. I wanted her to hold him, to try to breast feed, but it was clear that she would have to be ready. Having been opened from the inside, there was bound to be stores of anguish punctured during the ordeal.

*I'll change your pad after I get lunch,* I said.

*Thank you.*

Closing the door, I realized that I had moved on. Patty was still in the past, waiting for the strength to join us. Adrian was sitting at the top of the stairs, watching me. I picked him up and realized that I had forgotten to feed him. I apologized to him on the way to the kitchen and he purred his forgiveness.

Gil dropped in on the morning of the day that he was leaving for Winnipeg. He was still so reticent about the trip that I had him give me his son's number and a promise to call when he landed.

*So, show me this baby,* he said.

Seeing his veil of regret as he stared at the baby, I made a promise to myself to take nothing for granted. It was possible that he had never held an infant more than a few times.

*He's beautiful,* Gil said. I wanted to make a joke about shitty diapers and exhaustion, but my sense of humour was gone. Wonder reigned.

*I'm proud of you, Spat.*

I managed to say thank you before my vision blurred and my throat closed. I didn't want to sound emotional, so I took a deep breath and tried to lighten the mood.

*Yeah, whatever,* I said. *Call me when you get there.*

*I will. I better go.*

He didn't move for a few minutes. Silenced by the baby, we watched him sleep for a while.

His prosthetic brushed my shoulder when we embraced at the door. I tried not to see the Youngest, running through the snow, but the image was there. I had a deep feeling of dread as I told Gil that everything would work out the way it should.

*You'll call me*, I reminded him.

*I will*, he said.

Watching him walk away, I felt profound gratitude.

# { 26 }

To stop relying on Brian, I began putting the crib next to Patty's bed while I went out for provisions. She would stroke his cheek with the back of her fingers and coo at him. She never objected, though, when I moved him back to the guest room.

I had come home from a run to the drugstore when I discovered a couple of suitcases, packed and waiting at the bottom of the stairs. It was the first of many moments that reminded me that because we were divorced, I had no say in where she lived or where she took my son. Immediately, I chose to be a calm and logical adversary. I would stay composed as I reasoned with Constance. I would make her see that there was no longer any question as to who was in charge.

Climbing the stairs, a distilled rage began to surface. Focused and necessary, it was different from the old, recreational rage.

Ann stood when I pushed open the bedroom door. She embraced me as though a gust of wind might have made her airborne. There was an undeniable sense of relief in seeing her again. Patty was beaming. It was the first time her unrelenting misery seemed to have subsided, however briefly. Ann took my face in her hands.

*You must be exhausted*, I said.

*Not as much as you two. Caz made a bunny rug for the baby. It's beautiful. And I have a letter from Mick, too.*

She spoke so excitedly, it was as though she were on

something. I realized that telling Mick about what had happened to him had freed her.

*You should get your mother something to eat,* Patty said. *I'm going to sleep for a bit.*

Ann went to her and kissed Patty's forehead. She squeezed her hand, looking her in the eye. Though I couldn't say why, their immediate friendship made sense to me. Patty thanked her for something that I decided was none of my business.

My fatigue minimized the awkwardness there would have been in seeing her again. I felt sorry for Ann, knowing how punishing the trek from Sydney must have been, but she seemed perfectly content. After sitting in the kitchen for a few minutes, we became acutely aware of Hank's absence.

*The house is so big,* she said. *I never would have imagined Hank in a place so huge.*

*I can't believe he left it to me.*

*You deserve it.*

She grinned at me as she stirred a curl of milk into her coffee. *It's strange to have money,* she said. *Hank saved us.* I nodded and hoped that we would not have to discuss her old flame. She seemed younger, somehow. I wanted to apologize for not having called her after our last meeting.

*The baby is so beautiful, Spat.*

*Isn't he?*

More than beautiful, he was the eye of the storm. As long as I was with him, everything was calm. He did more than give me purpose, he untied me from myself. When I held him, the tilt in the world was gone.

*It must be hard for you, doing everything yourself,* Ann said.

*Not really,* I lied. *A nurse at the hospital gave me a crash course in diapers and bottles and all that. I have a few books.*

*It may be a while before Patty's herself again.*

*I know.*

*I have a room at a hotel on Sherbrooke. I'll come back as soon as I'm checked in.*

*You can stay here. I have an apartment, too. If you'd prefer that.*

*It's not up to me*, she said. *I'll be wherever you want me to be.*

*We can put a bed in Hank's office. I'd be grateful to have you here.*

I meant it and she could tell. There was no longer pressure to make peace with her and I needed the help. I had so little rest that my Nirvana had become a night of uninterrupted sleep. I was afraid of passing out with the baby in my arms.

*Patty is lucky to have you.*

*Well ... We haven't made any long term arrangement. There could be a fight down the road for custody.*

Ann looked confused and surprised. There were still details about which she knew nothing.

*She loves you*, Ann said.

I thought about the content of their conversation. In her weakened state, Patty might have said anything.

*It's weird*, I said, *with me and Patty.*

*How so?*

*Well. We're not married. She got pregnant after the divorce.*

*Oh.*

I wondered why Hank had never told her that. He must have omitted anything from his reports about me that she would not have wanted to hear.

*Me and Patty are ...* There was no sensible explanation. I searched for the words, but it was difficult to describe the situation. I loved Patty, but that was neither here nor there.

After an almost full night's sleep, Ann convinced me to take a day for myself.

*What will I do?*

*Whatever you want. I have everything under control.*

I had to think about how I could fill a day. Ordinarily, I would have spent it high and drunk, fucking around. Those days were gone.

*I'll go for a walk*, I said.

*Good. Clear your head.*

Wandering past the bookstore, I wondered how Gil was

getting along with the Oldest. He had not called as he had promised, but I knew that he would when he was ready. As strange as my family reunion had been, his had to have been far more daunting. I thought about what he had said about how the baby could not keep me sober. It seemed impossible to imagine going back into the shit. I could not imagine that the novelty of being Dad could fade over time.

Without any consideration, I stopped at a shop and bought a bicycle. I don't know why. The kid behind the counter gestured to a wall of helmets behind him.

*Vous aimez un casque aussi?*

The thought of wearing one made me smirk, but the realization that I could no longer take any physical risks was sobering. My life mattered because there was someone helpless who needed me. I chose a black helmet that made me look like an idiot and wore it as I walked the bike up Saint Catherine's. I stopped at a pay phone.

*Hi. How's everything there?*

*Everything's fine*, Ann said. *The baby's sleeping and Patty's having soup. What are you doing?*

*I bought a bike.*

*A motorcycle?*

*No, a bicycle. A mountain bike.*

*Good for you. You won't get fat.*

The third time I called, Ann told me to stop worrying. I didn't realize that I had been, but I agreed to stop checking up on her. Even though I knew that she was more than capable of caring for him, being away from the baby started a timer in my head, counting down to when I would see him again.

Peddling up the mountain, sweating under the stupid helmet, I felt a foreign bliss invading every molecule. I stopped near the stone water trough, sat on the bench and laughed and wept.

*Spat?*

For a second, I didn't recognize him. He had grown some facial hair that looked too young for him. His shades were the kind Bono was always wearing. He was sweating after a long run.

*Oh. Hey, Rob.*

*What's up?*

*I was just ... We had a baby.*

*What?*

*Me and Patty. A boy.*

*That's great,* he said, smiling stupidly. *You and Patty are back together?*

*Well. No.*

*Oh.* He gave me a quizzical look. *Are you OK?*

*What? Yeah. I've never been happy. Happier,* I corrected, but the truth was out.

*Were you crying?*

*Yeah.* I smiled at him. *I was.*

*You look good, Spat.*

*Thanks, Rob. You too ... You ever see Linda?*

*Yeah. I've seen her. She seems to be doing OK.*

*You should come by and see the kid,* I said. I gave him the address of Hank's house and told him that Patty would love to see him. As he jogged away, I hoped that he would never turn up at our place. I felt no malice toward him. I had always liked Rob, but the past was done.

When I arrived home, the baby was crying. Ann was pacing in the kitchen, patting his back and telling him, *I know, I know ...*

*I'll take him,* I said.

He stopped crying when I held him and this pleased me more than just about anything else could have done.

*How's Patty?*

*She's fine ... I suppose.*

*What do you mean?*

*She's ... She's in a serious depression, Spat.*

*Yeah, it's that postpartum thing.*

*That's part of it ...*

She stared at the table. A look of concern creased her forehead. Ann didn't know Patty like I did, so I didn't take her concern to heart. I took the baby up to his crib and found the paper on which I had written Gil's son's number. When he finally picked up the phone, I mistook the Oldest for his father because they sounded so much alike.

*Hey, Numb Nuts.*

*Excuse me?*

*Oh. Hi. Is Gil there?*

*Who's this?*

*Spat Ryan. I'm a friend of your Dad's ... In Montreal.*

*He's not here.*

*Oh. Do you know when he'll be back?*

The Oldest sighed, heavily. I could feel that he was trying to repress his anger.

*He never showed up here.*

*What?*

*It's not exactly a big surprise, Mr. Ryan.*

He hung up. In my gut, I knew that something was wrong. Either Gil had never left town or else he had taken a detour en route. I phoned his place. There was no answer.

# { 27 }

The baby sleeping on my chest, Ann and Patty deep in conversation on the other side of the wall, I read Mick's letter.

> *Dear Spat,*
>
> *You arsey bastard. Congratulations. I'm green with envy and it looks good on me. I can't stop thinking about the universe, which is ridiculous since the thing thinking about the universe is made of universe. It's impossible. The water can't feel its wetness. A tangle of ideas couldn't hold it all, anyway. It's such a strange soup of light. Wet light, like. I've been thinking about life a lot and change. I hope that the changes the baby brings make you feel abundantly alive. Please send pictures and come to see us when you can.*
>
> *Love, Mick*

Out of nowhere I had an overwhelming feeling of what I could only describe as homesickness. Being with Mick and Caz again began to seem vital, not only for me, but for the baby.

I fell asleep to the sound of Ann's muffled voice as she tried to reassure Patty. Nearly everything was as it should have been.

Constance returned on a Thursday afternoon. She had a bag of gifts for the baby and for Patty. She had obviously rehearsed what she would say and how she would say it. Ann embraced Constance when I introduced them. The stunned Mrs. Virgil looked as though someone had covered her with bees. I remembered that Patty had told me, years before, that her mother didn't like to be touched.

Knowing nothing about the bad blood between me and Patty's family, Ann invited Constance to stay for dinner. Her refusal was met with more invitations that seemed to strike our visitor like embers blown from a bonfire.

*Your daughter is lovely*, Ann said. I tried not to chuckle, remembering the last time Constance had invaded.

*Thank you. Is she awake?*

*I'll check*, I said.

Patty was sitting up, staring at the window. Her hair was matted, her skin was pale. I sighed, regretting the news I had for her.

*It's here*, I said.

*Fuck.*

*You might as well try to make peace with her.*

*Yeah, right.*

*I can say you're not up to it.*

*She'll only come back later.*

I waited for her to tell me that Constance could come up to the room. She looked as though she had forgotten what we had been talking about. She was healing, physically, but the gloom that had shrouded her since the delivery seemed to have gotten heavier.

This is a secret: a part of me was glad that Patty felt a distance from our son and from motherhood. The baby was mine, no one else's. I pictured a future when all concerned had accepted that I was his sole parent. I imagined that Patty could start over with someone else, far away from us. Her imbalance was a serious liability.

*Shall I bring Dame Virgil up here?*

Patty sighed. *That would be great.*

Ann and I went for a walk. I was uneasy about leaving the house, but I kept that to myself. Despite her intention to make peace, Patty's visitor brought the usual misery. Once again, she was ejected from the bedroom where Patty was beginning to take root.

+     +     +

On our way back to Hank's with flowers and chocolate Ann said, *The baby needs a name.*
*Yeah. I've been thinking about that.*
*You don't like your name?*
*Spat?*
*No, your real name.*
I pretended to consider it, but there was no chance of that happening. The only thing I intended to pass down to my son was a healthy suspicion and the will to live his life his way. I would teach him to look misery in the eye and spit, to ignore all of the expectations, to be free.

Constance was waiting downstairs for us to return. While I went to get the baby, Ann sat with the wretched scarecrow and asked about what was upsetting her.

Changing the baby's diaper, I kept thinking about Gil. Darker possibilities were surfacing. I resisted my default cynicism, but it was possible that facing up to what had happened to his family was too much for him to take.

I could hear Patty sobbing in the other room. I considered, not very seriously, getting a prescription for an anti-depressant and feeding it to her without her knowing. I figured that I could grind the pills into powder and stir them into orange juice. Of course, anything she consumed would be consumed by the baby, too, so it was out of the question. At that point, the hours she had spent with him would have added up to less than a day. I didn't want to pressure her because I didn't know how she would react. Given the state that she was in, there was always the chance that she would go back to The House with the moldering Virgils. It was plausible despite or because of her struggle with Constance.

Linda's laugh, that had been hilarity itself, had become an affected irritant. She was parked at the end of Patty's bed, her wine glass precariously tilted, reminiscing about nothing. She was digging for something genuinely funny, but she was well into the bottle of wine she had brought for us. It was a relief to know that Patty was, at least, capable of shaking off the gloom, but her sudden mood swing was pissing me off. I kept busy, staying in the kitchen, waiting for an appropriate time to start moving our guest out. I estimated that saying good-night to Linda would take about a half-hour. Any remorse I would have felt for wanting to be rid of her was only the memory of remorse. I didn't envy her drunkenness, either. It was embarrassing. Ann had gone to a movie with a cousin she had not seen for forty years. I was glad that she was missing the show upstairs.

Before putting her in the cab, I asked Linda if she had seen Gil. She had not been to a meeting, though, since before he left town. I decided to phone the Oldest again to see if Gil had made contact with him.

As I dialed the number, the baby started crying. Patty called for me to get him. She made an attempt at breastfeeding, but he squirmed and wailed until she gave up. She backhanded my chest when I tried to help her with the pump. Her physical strength was returning, but she still showed only the most obligatory interest in the baby. I expected her to come around when her hormones had levelled off, but it was becoming clear that her issues were not the result of any chemical imbalance. To think that she could have been reborn through her pregnancy now seemed preposterous. The burgeoning maturity I had seen in her months before was likely little more than depression. She was who she had always been. So was I.

By the time the baby had gone to sleep, my will to call the Oldest was gone. I thought of Mick and the phone rang. It was Caz.

*Hey, Big Daddy!*

*Hey, Caz.*

*Auntie Caz, you mean. Where are the pictures you promised us?*

*Oh. I haven't gotten around to -*

*That was a joke, Darling. Here's Mick.*

I could hear her rings clicking against the phone as she held it for him. I suggested that he invest in a headset, but he said holding the phone gave Caz something to do. She had a comment, of course, for that and just about everything else he had to say. We talked about the baby which led to a discussion of procreation in various other species. Our lengthy talk ended with his attempt to explain something about Heisenberg's Uncertainty Principle to me. By then, Caz said that she had work to do. They squabbled the way newlyweds would as we were saying good-bye. They must have been enjoying having the house to themselves.

When Ann came back, she scooped up Adrian on the way to the kitchen and told me about her evening. Her cousin had brought her up to speed on everything that Ann had missed in the last four decades and they had enjoyed their reunion. As they were walking to her cousin's car, Ann spotted an old friend of Finn's driving a cab. He had been dying his hair and it still fell in black icicles over his eyes as it did when he was twenty. He looked almost the same, she said, except softened with regret. She had pretended to not recognize him even though he had lit up when he spotted her.

*I don't want to look back anymore*, she said. She put Adrian on the fridge and sighed and smiled. *What does that get you?*

*Nothing*, I said. *Less than nothing.*

# { 28 }

Ann convinced me to go out one muggy morning, so I went biking on the mountain. Peddling hard past a homeless man sleeping on a bench, I replayed the conversation that I had, the night before, with the Oldest. He was just as curt as he had been during our first talk. I tried to convince him that there had to be something wrong, that Gil would have told me if he had decided not to go, but nothing I said could penetrate his anger. He probably resented that some far away stranger with an odd name knew so much about his delinquent father. I had details and insights that the man in Winnipeg was too wounded to learn.

*I know it's difficult, from your perspective,* I said, *but I know that Gil wanted to make amends.* I thought that using language from the Program might remind the Oldest that his father had been sober for nearly two decades.

*I called him,* he said, *because I wanted to tell him, in person, how much trouble he ...*

He sighed and I felt sick to my stomach. I was twisting the knife, I knew, but I had to convince him that his father might have been in serious trouble.

*My father ruined my brother's life,* he said. *Do you know what it's like, Mr. Ryan, to watch a kid grow into a fucking monster because of ...*

In the pause that followed, I could hear him trying to delay a torrent of grief. I wanted him to phone the police and report his father missing, but it occurred to me that the Oldest would not have been able to give them an accurate description. I was missing a friend, but Gil's son was missing a parent, an explanation, an apology, countless shared experiences, love.

*I'm going to contact the police,* I told him. *I'll find him ... I promise.*

When he had settled himself, the Oldest said, *He doesn't want to be found, Mr. Ryan. You don't know anything about him.* I listened to the dial tone for a few seconds after he had hung up. I realized that throughout our discussion I had been clenching my left fist so tightly that it had begun to throb.

Flying over the front of the bike, I was glad to have bought the helmet. I landed on my back and slid a little. I lay there, looking up at the scraps of sky through the leaves. The pain was minimal. I was glad to be lying down. My exhaustion had become part of me. I fantasized about the time when the baby would sleep through the night. A somber haze had surrounded me and the lack of sleep had left me unable to get angry the way I had in the past. It stole my sarcasm, my will to offend. I lived on a schedule for the first time since elementary school. It already seemed like years since I had to think about what to do with my time. For a moment, squinting up at the light in the trees, there was an undeniable feeling of being eternal, of being more than I had been before.

When I came home, from the mountain, Ann was sitting at the kitchen table with scissors, papers and a small bud from the tea tin. Her reading glasses at the end of her nose, she struggled to keep the bits of weed in the paper as she rolled it.

*Hey. What are you doing?*

*I'm making a joint for Patty.*

I sighed and folded my arms.

*There's enough milk in the fridge for the baby,* she said. *I couldn't say no.*

I went upstairs to the bedroom where I found Patty flipping through a magazine. The baby was next to her, sleeping. I had no doubt that it was my mother's idea to put him there. It was, to my mind, as though Patty were going to be rewarded with a toke for spending time with him.

*I don't want Ann to leave*, she whispered.

*I can't ask her to stay. She has a life back home.*

*Why are you all sweaty?*

*Why are you smoking weed?*

She cackled, briefly. My question didn't deserve a response, as far as she could see. She focused on a page and then turned it with a flick. I decided to take a more subtle approach.

*How are you feeling?*

*Shredded*, she said, without looking at me. I watched her for a moment and then went back to the kitchen.

Ann was on her second attempt to roll a joint. She was aware of the tension but had, apparently, chosen to ignore it. I knew that she wouldn't want for us to part company with another confrontation.

*I'll do that*, I said.

While I rolled, Ann fed Adrian and tried to make small talk. I wanted to yell some of my thoughts regarding Patty's weed consumption, but having lived the way I had for so long, it was unlikely that I would be taken seriously. Wordlessly, I handed the finished joint to Ann and she took it upstairs.

*Bring the baby down with you when you're coming, will ya?*

*OK*, she said.

+ + +

The baby shower was Ann's idea. Luckily, Brian volunteered to help, so I didn't have to do much. His boyfriend, Sam, had worked in a bakery and the two of them spent the day making sweets and sandwiches. They were of that generation that seemed perpetually amused by the quaintness of everything that had come before them. At one point, they started a sing-along with Ann. It sounded as though someone were squeezing the shit out of a trio of wolves. They had made a run to SAQ and Ann was enjoying the local beer.

Patty spent nearly two hours getting ready. I assured her, until she told me to shut the fuck up, that we could cancel at any point. Watching her applying mascara, I thought about how women are always expected to simply know what to do and how to do it when a baby happens. No one ever expects that motherhood might be a bad fit for any of them, but Patty was decidedly undecided.

The weird sisters showed up an hour early and brought with them the happy news that Constance would not be in attendance. By then, it was understood that Ronald would no longer be socializing. Patty's siblings placed themselves near the fireplace in the living room, where they could make note of any misconduct. The combined stench of their rival perfumes made me want to put them in the yard and hose them down. Brian and Sam tried to thaw the area around the icy bitches with compliments and wine, but to no avail. Ann offered bits of small talk, but the sinister duo gave her the same nod and wince they reserved for anyone who seemed unashamed of being alive. In their dead, lizard eyes, my mother was the brazen vessel from which I was loosed into the world.

Rob made a loud and overly enthusiastic entrance. He had brought us a car seat and launched into a litany of reasons as to why I should become a driver. I liked it because it looked comfortable. The way Rob hugged me it was as though I had just been recovered from the wreckage of a plane. He became subdued when he held the baby and looked as though he might cry. I put the car seat on the coffee table and Rob put the baby in it to see whether or not he approved.

*He'll grow into it*, Rob said. *Where's Patty?*
*Getting dressed.*

I was surprised to learn that Patty had friends that I had never met. It was as though the two cheerful academics had been sent to neutralize the stinking evil of the weird sisters. The obviously bookish women threatened us with games that we could play, but Sam was the only one interested in learning the rules. The baby shifted, pulling his tiny fists into his cheeks and everyone was silenced by the only authentic person in the room. He was all potential, with no agenda, no biases and no lies. We watched him, all of us, subconsciously wondering if there was a way back to that state. The peaceful melancholy he created in the room didn't last, though. Patty was ready.

She seemed far too giddy about the gathering. After receiving the requisite adulation for her appearance, she was getting laughs by describing the torment that she had been through. I was the butt of nearly all of her jokes, which was fine, although most of what she was telling them was fiction. Her account of the delivery was nearly bloodless and quirky.

*Tell them where you were,* she said.

*What?*

*While I was giving birth, tell them where you were.*

*I was out,* I said.

*Yeah. Out drinkin'!*

Rob slapped my back and laughed. The weird sisters smirked and exchanged a look. Brian giggled but watched me, waiting for some retaliation. The others thought that it was all in fun.

*I was celebrating,* I said.

To change the subject, Brian announced that Ann had come all the way from Australia. This led to a discussion about the weather and wildlife down under, the fires and floods that had been in the news. Ann's solemn speech about the plight of the Aborigines was interrupted by Linda's entrance. Well primed for the party, she threw her arms open and hollered, *Fun's over, People!* I put a finger to my lips to tell her to reduce her volume, but she didn't notice.

Out of habit, Rob scanned the room for reactions to her apparent inebriation. Patty whooped and applauded as though we were all going to do shots until the cab arrived to take us to a club. Linda made the rounds, introducing herself to each guest. When she got to Rob, she muttered, *Hey, cocksucker.* It was subtle enough for Rob to ignore, but loud enough to be heard by Ann and the academics. With the pleasantries out of the way, Linda knelt in front of the car seat and held the baby's feet. In a scratchy falsetto, she said, *Hello, baby. Hello, little baby.*

The weird sisters were clearly pleased to have an opening for the story they would tell Constance. Patty offered Linda a drink and sneered at me, briefly, as I glared. Rob stewed until I asked him for help in the kitchen. Linda made a comment as we left the room, but I couldn't make it out.

*Fuck, I wish she'd get struck by lightning,* Rob said, leaning against the counter.

*She's a handful,* I said, not wanting to get into it.

*You know, she calls me. At least once a month. At all hours. Shit-faced.*

*I don't now what to tell you, Rob.* He looked like an awkward teenage boy who had been grounded for something he hadn't done. I suggested that he stop answering when she phoned, to change his number or to get an unlisted one. He was still attached to her, though. I theorized that he had to take her calls or else risk pissing her off and having all of his personal eccentricities revealed to every bar fly in the city. It was the first time that I had begun to think seriously about the inherent peril in every concealed truth.

Sam and Brian appeared, looking as though they were trying not to laugh. They began taking trays of food out of the fridge.

*You seem different, Spat,* Rob said, picking up Adrian.

*How so?*

*I don't know. Calm, I guess.*

*It's fatigue,* I said.

*Well. It suits you. You look great.*

Brian and Sam exchanged a glance and smirked. Rob released the cat who had been squirming to get down. He reached into the open fridge and asked me if I wanted a beer.

*No, thanks,* I said.

*I'll have yours, then.*

He cracked the bottle and downed half of it. I was glad that there was now one less beer. As soon as the alcohol was gone, Linda would leave. Ann arrived as the other room erupted in laughter. *Linda knows how to have a good time*, she said, quietly.

*Yeah, she's a real pistol*, Rob said. *I used to be married to her.*

*She told me that.*

Rob flinched and finished off his pint. Ann watched him, smiling sympathetically. She asked what she could do to help and I told her that she could put a gag on Linda.

*She's just having fun*, Ann said. Rob rolled his eyes and put his near empty bottle on the counter.

The academics came to the kitchen to make their apologies for having to leave early. Ann insisted that they take a plate of sandwiches and went about collecting them.

*Come and hear this*, Patty yelled.

Knowing, instinctively, that she was referring to us, Rob and I went to the living room. Brian and Sam followed us. Linda was telling what she thought was a story. It was a disjointed tirade about her boss. A glass of red wine in her hand, she made broad gestures to enhance the incoherent anecdote and cackled to remind us of how funny it was. The weird sisters sneered and seemed physically sickened by the display. Patty and Brian laughed when Linda laughed, trying to make the sad performance seem light.

Nearing the punch line of her long-winded joke, Linda threw her arms open. The red wine in her glass arced slightly as it left her glass and splashed across the baby's face. Her stammering apology was lost in the din as the baby screamed and everyone stood. I picked him up and carried him upstairs. Ann trailed behind, telling me not to panic. I could feel the sting of the alcohol in his eyes and my hands began to shake. Ann held him as I ran warm water over his face. When the wine was gone, I held him against my chest. Patty came into the bathroom, looking more ashamed than angry. She looked as though she were about to make some excuse for Linda, but thought better of it. She watched us for a moment and then went to the bedroom and shut the door.

# { 29 }

Whenever I remember it, I'm still astounded that the two of us had managed to hold it together, under the same roof, for as long as we did. Though not by blood, Patty was every bit a Virgil. There were many moments in those days when she seemed to be doing a disturbingly accurate impression of her adoptive mother.

At Ronald's funeral, Patty and the weird sisters clung to each other as though they had always been inseparable. Constance did not speak to anyone. She remained stoic, waiting patiently for the dreary ritual to end. After that, we rarely saw her.

In Patty's mind, or what was left of it, I became a surrogate for her parents. Though I had not even the slightest curiosity about her anymore, I was constantly accused of trying to control her. She had made it clear, repeatedly, that she was not going to stop living simply because she had given birth. She went back to school and emerged, two years later, with a master's degree in Fuckogy. She dated a lot—Virgo's and Libra's, mostly. She loved the baby, to be sure, but she had learned love from people who might have been all but untouched by it.

As he grew, our baby looked to me for everything. We both learned to expect his mother's absence. It was miserable to watch him pine for her and almost worse when he didn't. I was always relieved when she stayed away because it made everything easier. I looked forward to her ski trips and spa dates with Linda. They had become inseparable drinking buddies, haunting places that even I would call dismal. The loudest regulars at the Mojo Lounge, they were going to hold on to the wriggling eel of their youth no matter how much toil and how many Margaritas it took to make them believe it.

I started living off of the settlement money and focused on creating the illusion of normalcy. I tried to get out and meet people, but I could never find a babysitter I trusted. Brian had moved to Toronto and the thought of leaving the baby at The House made me nauseous. If I had simply left him at home with his mother for the night, I would have had to endure her standard rant about how I would not be allowed to start "easing out" of my responsibility. Her fear of being left alone with him never waned with time.

Patty and Linda's friendship came to an abrupt end a little over two years after the baby shower. During a night out, Linda had taken a run at some coked-up goon that Patty had been pursuing. Their drunken squabble over him degenerated into slapping, kicking and hair-pulling. A reporter and cameraman had been stalking an American actor who was in town shooting a movie, but stopped the hunt long enough to capture the spectacle. The whole scene was played out on the news. Patty wasn't embarrassed by the exposure, but felt that she looked fat in the footage. She blamed the kid for her weight gain rather than her continuous intake of pastries and rum.

For a while, she drank at home, baking in front of the television and complaining about anything that came to mind. With a few drinks in, she would always remind me that I had ruined her life. Everything would have been a lot better, she told me, if I had never seduced her all those years ago.

+ + +

Sure that they would give him a good home, I gave Adrian to Rob and his new wife. I delivered him to them the day before I left. Rob was on crutches, following a mishap at work. His new wife, a yoga instructor with an unnameable accent, chuckled when I handed the cat to her. As she offered me coffee, Adrian sniffed and then began to chew her hair. I explained that Patty had developed an allergy to cats and that was why Adrian had to move. Rob accepted the lie without question but gave me a dejected look. It was as though he knew that we would never see each other again. I wished that I could have stayed and talked for a while, but my head was teeming and there were still things that had to be handled. I said a quick good-bye and then walked back to Hank's.

On the verge of doing the worst and best thing that I have ever done, I tried not to consider the fallout. Apart from the anxiety of keeping my plan secret, I was still shaken by my most recent conversation with the Oldest. I had phoned him, as I did every six months or so. He had not heard from Gil and had long since given up on ever seeing him again. It got harder to picture my absent friend's face, to remember his voice. I told myself that he had remarried one of his former wives and had settled in a small, western town. He had a new name and a new life. The more likely scenarios were too miserable to consider. The last time I went by the bookstore, the windows had been boarded up. More than half of the block was set for demolition.

+     +     +

By the time we arrived at the Vancouver airport, Michael Ronald Ryan had decided that going on a plane was not nearly as exciting as he had thought it would be. His head on my shoulder, his hands around my neck, I carried him to a window where he could see a row of jets waiting for take-off.

*See the airplanes?*

He didn't look, but he gave me a sad, obligatory *Yeah.*

*You want to have a nap before we go, Buddy?*

*No.*

I started calling Michael "Buddy" when he began walking. I was cognisant enough, though, to resist actually becoming his buddy. I was not his friend. I was his guide and his protector. That much, I understood.

The main reason I had opted for kidnapping him was intense fear. Like me, he had been born into the Age of Idiocy; the time of smug superstition and proud regression. The odds were against him from the outset, so I wanted him to be with sane people. I needed for him to have more than his ludicrous parents, to have a stable family.

We sat across from a monitor where a lacquered meat puppet was reading the news. Watching the earnest liar do his part in the corporate make-over of reality, I saw myself unscrewing the top of his head. I wanted to release the toxic smoke within the anchorman's skull and fill the empty space with an egg.

While I indulged my disgust, part of me was busily listing the reasons why I was doing the right thing. I had a litany of crimes of which Patty was, undeniably, guilty. I kept reminding myself of her nights out that had so often ended in chaos, her fits of rage and her brief romance with the volatile drug dealer. I told an imaginary judge about how she had left for two weeks, once, when the baby was teething and how she had missed his second birthday in order to spend a week in Cuba. I dug for every ugly memory, reassuring myself that I was justified in moving our son to another country.

I did it because it had to be done. I had to make the choice for Buddy: Would he have a mother who secretly resented him or one so far away that she could be remade into anyone? I chose the latter because I knew the terrain. I did it behind her back because if I had gotten her consent to take him from her, it would have been too awful a secret to keep. I knew that I would have to tell him everything, someday, so I cast myself as the villain. His mother's version of events might have been entirely different from mine. I can still only guess as to what motivated anything she has ever done. I suspect that it's the same for her.

Restless, Buddy squirmed so I put him down. He tuned in to his internal rhythm and began to dance. Bobbing his head and stomping his foot, he put his hands up and lost the world to his music.

On the television, the anchor told a story about a deeply religious man who had driven a truckload of explosives into a school. The un-dead disciple had slaughtered the enemy children for some imaginary spot of perfection hiding out behind the cosmos; for martyrdom, for the love of a wholly ridiculous, but unshakable, conviction. If love and perfection don't sit well together, belief and morality are mutually exclusive.

I watched Buddy to quell the intense anger inspired by the news, but it was hard to look away from the screen and its insistence that we should all be afraid. Ever since Buddy's arrival, I had begun to take them more seriously—all of the fascist christers, spreading like red ants on a fallen fledgling. In a few years, when he's ready to know, Ann will explain to Buddy that the politicos and other social climbers need for the people on whom they ascend to be rigid with fear. Otherwise, they fall. Buddy will learn to subvert, to stay aware in a time of requisite amnesia. He'll learn to be who he is, wholly and abundantly.

Watching him dance in the airport, I thought about how greatly out-numbered we were and hoped that we were headed toward a safe corner; safe from the rising water and the worshipers of death. I was glad that we were going to another country with enough wild places in which to be lost. I used to catch myself begging the universe to protect him and to keep me alive long enough to watch over him as everything shifts.

I always changed them according to our proximity to the encroaching mayhem, but as we boarded the flight to Hawaii, I made three wishes for Buddy. The first was for Patty to come to the end of her adolescence and join us. The second was for Mick to hang on long enough for Buddy to know him. The third was for all of those people willing to die for their beliefs to do so without delay.

+     +     +

As we flew over the Pacific, getting closer to our new home, Buddy was peeling the pages out of his colouring book. He stopped when he got to a picture of a king.

*He's a king*, Buddy said, *Cuz he sits on a frone.*

*Yeah, he's on a throne*, I said, hoping that he would discern the difference in our pronunciations.

*No, frone. I don't like dat king*, he said, slowly ripping the page from the spine.

My resolve to never return to Canada was waning. I would miss the Plateau and the mountain, even the winter. I suppose I knew that Patty would never emigrate. She had been a visitor in our home, a distant relative who worked to maintain that distance. I tried, but could not muster any grief over the end of our time together. I packed a single picture of her for Buddy. I had taken it during the ice storm. She was laughing at something Rob had said and looked like someone who had never peered into the darkness and found herself drawn to it.

I quizzed him on what was happening outside his dream. I asked him who we were going to see and he answered, *Grandma.* I asked who else and he said, *Uncle Mick.*

*And who else?*

*Aunt Caz.*

*Aunt Caz. That's right.*

*And how old will you be when we get there?*

*Free.*

*Yeah, three.*

*No. Free.*

+     +     +

I walked through the humid jungle with Buddy on my back. We stopped singing when we heard the birds. We looked up to see that they had begun flying, with impossible slowness, in a circle. Buddy called to them, imitating their language. The birds called back and he laughed, pleased to have been understood. I considered trying to communicate with them, but, mercifully, I had no voice. Rain dripped from the canopy, but the sun remained, illuminating each ample drop. The tiny spheres of water and light landed all around us, filling the shadows and showing us a clear path through a tangle of fallen vines.

 **Ed Macdonald** is one of Canada's most accomplished screenwriters. He has written for CBC's top rated comedy series *This Hour Has 22 Minutes* and also numerous episodes of the series *Made In Canada*. Ed has won two Gemini Awards for excellence in television writing and has been nominated numerous times. He has also won the prestigious Writers' Guild of Canada Award and The Golden Sheaf Award. Ed is a respected playwright as well. He lives in Montreal.